W9-CFN-044

A Fatal Fiction

A FATAL FICTION

KAITLYN DUNNETT

THORNDIKE PRESS
A part of Gale, a Cengage Company

Copyright © 2020 by Kathy Lynn Emerson.
A Deadly Edits Mystery
Thorndike Press, a part of Gale, a Cengage Company.

ALL RIGHTS RESERVED
This book is a work of fiction. Names, characters, and incidents either are products of the author's imagination or are used fictitiously. Any resemblance to actual persons living or dead, or events, is entirely coincidental.
Thorndike Press® Large Print Mystery.
The text of this Large Print edition is unabridged.
Other aspects of the book may vary from the original edition.
Set in 16 pt. Plantin.

LIBRARY OF CONGRESS CIP DATA ON FILE.
CATALOGUING IN PUBLICATION FOR THIS BOOK
IS AVAILABLE FROM THE LIBRARY OF CONGRESS.

ISBN-13: 978-1-4328-8518-2 (hardcover alk. paper)

Published in 2021 by arrangement with Kensington Books, an imprint of Kensington Publishing Corp.

Printed in Mexico
Print Number: 01   Print Year: 2021

A Fatal Fiction

CHAPTER 1

Most people wouldn't consider successfully filling the gas tank in their own car an accomplishment, but I'm not most people. For the bulk of the last half century I lived in Maine, where "full service" still means someone else will handle the pumping and clean your windshield while they're at it. Only since moving back to New York State have I had to deal with this task on my own. The fact that paying for the gas generally involves inserting a credit card into the slot by the pump just complicates matters. Those machines hate me.

For more than a year after my return to Lenape Hollow, I took advantage of the friendly staff at Joe Ramirez's gas station, waiting patiently in my Ford Taurus at one of the self-service pumps until someone noticed me and came out to give me a hand. On one nippy morning in mid-April, however, when dark clouds hung low over the town and a snowflake or two had been mixed in with a scattering of raindrops earlier in the day, the combination gas station and convenience store was busier than usual. I may be getting older, and I'm not above letting others do the dirty work whenever possible, but neither am I helpless. After a brief hesitation, I decided to give waiting on myself a try.

I knew the routine, of course. I'd watched other people do it often enough and had fumbled through the process myself on a few occasions. Unscrew the gas cap. Stick the nozzle in. Try not to inhale the stinky fumes. The only tricky part is persuading the electronic brain behind the machine to do what it's supposed to do. Even the simplest computers have high opinions of themselves. They think they're smarter than the seventy-year-old woman pushing their buttons. Hah! I inserted my credit card the right way up on the first try *and* got the gasoline flowing without staining my gloves.

Three other drivers were doing the same thing I was, and two more cars were waiting their turn. I recognized several of my fellow gas customers. The village of Lenape Hollow is a relatively small place with a population of under 4,500. Add in the hamlets that make up the *town* of Lenape Hollow and there are still under ten thousand people.

"Hey, Mikki," Frank Uberman called out. "You need a hand with that?"

"I'm all set, but thanks."

Frank has known me since we were both in diapers and he's married to one of my closest friends, so he was well aware that I didn't usually wait on myself. After I replaced the hose, I sent him a jubilant grin. Amazing as it seemed, I'd not only filled my tank and convinced the credit card doo-hickey to give me a receipt, I'd also avoided spilling a single drop on the ground. For an additional minor miracle, my gloves, coat, and slacks were still as clean as when I started.

My sense of triumph was short-lived. A car door slammed. One of the people waiting in line for a pump had left his vehicle. He stalked toward me, one hand clamped down on his hat to keep erratic wind gusts from blowing it away. The only way to describe his body language was "aggressive."

"I want to talk to you, Ms. Lincoln."

If there had been a single word in that sentence with a guttural sound in it, I'd have said that Greg Onslow, CEO of Mongaup Valley Ventures, growled it at me. I took a step back, all the distance I could manage to put between us without tripping over the concrete base for the gas pumps.

"This is hardly the place." In my head, the words sounded firm and businesslike. In reality, they came out faint and squeaky.

I'm not a small person. I've shrunk a bit with age but still measure nearly five-foot-seven and my build is almost substantial enough to qualify as what my late husband used to call a BMW — a big Maine woman. Let's go with "sturdy" and call it good.

Onslow was younger, taller, and broader in the shoulders, and for some reason he was furious with me. I'd always thought his green eyes cold and calculating, but on that particular morning they blazed. I had no idea what I'd done to tick him off, but clearly something had pushed his hot button.

I had seen him lose his temper once before. At the time, I'd been told it was a rare occurrence. Whether that was true or not, I didn't like being the object of so much hostility.

Maybe, I thought, *the gas station is as good a location as any for a confrontation.*

I certainly wouldn't want to be alone with someone this volatile. In this very public place, I'd have plenty of witnesses if Onslow went so far as to issue threats or attempt to throttle me. From behind me I heard the reassuring sound of approaching footsteps. I didn't need to turn around to know that Frank had my back.

Another car door slammed shut, momentarily diverting my attention by drawing my gaze to Onslow's Porsche. Ariadne Toothaker, Mongaup Valley Ventures's head of personnel, had braved the brisk breeze to step out of the passenger side of the vehicle. She watched her boss with a guarded expression on her carefully made-up face.

My voice was steadier when I focused on Onslow again. "You want to talk? Talk."

"Call off your dogs."

I glanced over my shoulder. Frank was there, as I'd expected, but so was Joe Ramirez. He'd come out of the store as soon as he realized someone was hassling one of his customers. If his scowl was anything to go by, he'd have welcomed an excuse to go a couple of rounds with Greg Onslow.

That didn't surprise me. Onslow called himself an entrepreneur and claimed he had the best interests of Lenape Hollow at heart every time he launched a new project, but somehow his investors, including Frank and Darlene Uberman, ended up losing money while he managed, time and time again, to land on his feet. He'd skated close to break-

11

ing the law on several occasions, even if he hadn't yet crossed over that line.

"I want to hear what he has to say," I told the two men.

Violence wouldn't solve anything, and might well end with one of my friends getting hurt. Frank is tall and trim. He keeps in shape by playing endless holes of golf, but he's no spring chicken. He was a year ahead of me in school. As for Joe, a man with his wiry build could probably defeat Onslow in a fair fight, but not without damaging his standing in the community. I wasn't willing to take the chance that he'd be kicked off Lenape Hollow's board of trustees for brawling. Besides, I hoped that if I gave Onslow the chance to vent his spleen now, he'd be less inclined to try to talk to me later, when I was at home alone and considerably more vulnerable.

Nobody within hearing distance made any move to leave. Every ear was stretched in our direction. Inside the gas station/ convenience store, noses were all but pressed to the windows as customers and sales clerks alike tried to see what was going on.

Onslow didn't appear to notice. His attention was fixed on me and he was getting angrier by the minute. "You'd better stop

12

her," he said. "I won't stand for this kind of sabotage."

I took a deep breath. "Could you be a little more specific? I don't have a clue what you're talking about."

"Sunny Feldman." He spat out the name.

Well, finally! His state of mind now made *some* sense. Not a whole lot, you understand, but at least I had an inkling of what had set him off.

Greg Onslow was the current owner of what remained of Feldman's, once a giant among Borscht Belt resort hotels. The property had been neglected for decades, until only a jumble of ruins remained. He planned to raze the condemned buildings and erect something new. Speculation favored a call center, which would provide much needed jobs for local people, but no one knew for certain what he intended.

Roberta "Sunny" Feldman was the last member of the hotel's founding family to own the resort. She sold out just before the tourism boom turned to bust in the Sullivan County Catskills back in the 1970s. She walked away with enough money to see her comfortably through a lengthy retirement. At eighty-six, she's still going strong. A month ago, she hired me to edit her memoirs.

13

That's what I do to make ends meet in *my* retirement. As "Michelle Lincoln, the Write Right Wright" I offer editorial services to writers. Most of my clients send me their manuscripts as attachments to emails and I never meet them in person. There have been a few exceptions. One is Sunny. Another was Greg Onslow's first wife. After her death, he wanted me to revise a novel she'd written — ghostwrite it, really, since it needed a *lot* of work. I turned him down.

Now, apparently, he expected me to stop Sunny from finishing her book. I had no intention of agreeing to that plan, either.

"I don't know what you think I can do —" I began.

"Tell her it's crap. Convince her she'll be a laughingstock if her tall tales get into print."

"I would if that were true, but it isn't. Besides, she already has a publishing contract."

He snorted. "She's going to publish it herself. Vanity —"

"No. Not that there's anything wrong with self-publishing these days, but the truth of the matter is that she signed a contract with a traditional publisher. She's already been paid an advance against royalties." Celebrity memoirs do very well, and although Sunny

Feldman isn't a household name, back in the day she knew a lot of people who were.

"Lies. She's making it up. She's trying to ruin me."

Onslow grew more agitated by the minute and I didn't like the way he kept clenching and unclenching his fists. A surreptitious glance reassured me that we still had an audience. No one was going to stand idly by if he decided to do more than spew verbal abuse. That it had so far been directed more at Sunny than at me was probably the only thing keeping Frank and Joe in check.

The situation changed in the next instant.

"You always were a hack," Onslow said with a sneer. "How much is she paying you? I'll double it if you'll quit the project."

Low blow! And so insulting! I think I can be forgiven for getting hot under the collar in response.

"A," I said, holding up one finger, "I won't accept money from you, no matter how much you offer. And B, taking myself out of the equation won't stop Sunny's book from being published." With two fingers already in the air, I added a third and jabbed all of them in his direction to emphasize my point. "I don't see what concern it is of yours anyway."

"Her lies are sabotaging my demolition project."

Sabotage seemed a rather strong word and this was the second time he'd used it. "How?"

"Stories about the hotel. She's making it sound as if it's some kind of historical landmark that needs to be preserved. If she was so concerned about those buildings I want to tear down, she shouldn't have sold them in the first place. There's no possibility of renovation. They're too far gone."

I hated to agree with Greg Onslow about anything, but he was right when it came to the ruins of the once grand resort. Better to raze what was left than try to preserve an eyesore.

I tried to sound reasonable as I pointed out another obvious truth. "Sunny's stories about the good old days can't possibly have any effect on your plans."

"She's telling lies. Whoppers. Doesn't that frost you? Your reputation will suffer, too, when the truth comes out." His voice got louder with every word.

I didn't believe Sunny was playing particularly fast and loose with the facts, or that she was doing so as part of some desperate, last-ditch effort to stop Onslow's project. She wouldn't benefit in any way that I could see if demolition came to a grinding halt.

"What you're saying makes no sense." Given what I knew of Onslow's past schemes, *he* was far more likely to be the one who was lying. I started to turn away.

He grabbed my arm, jerked me around until we were nearly nose-to-nose, and shouted into my face. "Stupid, delusional old woman! Can't you see what she's up to?"

I've read the words *purpling with rage* in novels and always thought it an exaggeration. Onslow proved me wrong. If I hadn't been on the verge of losing my own temper, I might have been worried that he was about to pop a blood vessel or have an apoplectic fit. As it was, I was preoccupied with trying to hold on to the remnants of my self-control.

"Old woman?" I repeated in ice-cold tones.

I smacked him sharply on the hand. The moment he released me, I should have walked away, but by then I was too angry to be sensible. I held my ground.

"Lying bitches!" he bellowed. "Both of you. You're trying to ruin me."

"Oh, please!" My voice had risen to match his. "I want nothing to do with you or your schemes."

"Then you've let her dupe you." His eyes abruptly narrowed. His sneer intensified. "Wouldn't surprise me," he said in a tone of voice that conveyed his disgust. "You're nothing but a jumped-up, crazy cat lady."

That was the final straw.

I can count on the fingers of one hand the number of times I have totally lost my temper in public. Every one of them was memorable . . . and every one embarrassed the heck out of me afterward.

The first was in high school. The second time was in college. The other two were later in life. One was at a club meeting, after a totally irrational person made unfounded accusations against a friend of mine. But the angriest I've ever been was when, shortly before my father died, a clueless nurse informed me that, during the time I'd taken a short break from sitting by his bedside, I'd *once again* "just missed" an opportunity to communicate with her comatose patient. To my mind, it was unnecessarily cruel to tell me that, and quite possibly untrue, since he never gave any sign of regaining consciousness in all the hours I *was* there. I let her have it with both barrels.

When I lose control, I *really* lose control. I don't care who's listening. I yell. I tell the

18

object of my ire exactly what I think of whatever it was that set me off. I'm not proud of this. It's a character flaw, but that's not to say that the tirade is undeserved.

This fifth occasion followed the same pattern. By the time I was once more calm enough to take in my surroundings, Onslow had retreated. He drove off without bothering to get gas. Most of the other cars left quickly, too, although Frank Uberman stayed. So did the Lenape Hollow librarian, Pam Ingram.

"Shit," I muttered under my breath.

Nothing like making a fool of myself in public.

"You okay?" Frank looked as if he'd rather be anywhere else, but old friendship held strong. He wasn't going to abandon me until he was sure I was fit to drive myself home.

"I'll live."

I couldn't remember exactly what I'd said to send Onslow scurrying away with his tail between his legs, but I felt fairly certain he wouldn't bother me again.

Joe Ramirez had gone back inside the store. Now he popped out again with a bottle of water in hand. "Next time we're in someplace that serves alcohol, I'll buy you a real drink," he said as he offered it to me.

Pam finished filling her gas tank. "I'll pay for the second round," she said with a grin. "That was the finest moment of justified payback I've seen since Susan Sarandon and Geena Davis blew up that guy's truck in *Thelma and Louise.*"

Is it very bad of me that I was flattered by the comparison?

CHAPTER 2

After I left the gas station, I had a few errands to run. My original plan had been to return home as soon as they were completed and get back to work on the manuscript of a romance novel I was editing for a client. That wasn't going to fly. Even though nearly an hour had passed by the time I crossed everything off my to-do list, I was still too wired to settle. The level of concentration I'd need to catch typos and continuity errors was far out of reach.

Instead, I drove to Frank and Darlene's house. Darlene's van was in the driveway, so I knew she was home. I didn't hesitate to let myself in through the front door. I had an open invitation to do just that. I also had Darlene's spare key, in case of emergencies.

As I entered the living room from the entry hall, I shrugged out of my coat. I had just opened my mouth to let my friend know I'd arrived when I spotted her lying full-length on the floor, her neck extended at an unnatural angle and a look of acute pain on her face. Her walker stood off to one side, as if it had been shoved out of the way when she lost her balance and fell.

The coat slipped from my grasp and a horrified gasp escaped me before I could stop it. Seconds later, I was on my knees beside her. I fought the instinct to run my hands over her neck and shoulders to determine how badly she was injured. I was afraid touching her might make things worse.

"Darlene! What happened? Are you hurt?"

Her eyes popped open and her expression changed to one of astonishment. She started to sit up.

"Don't move. I'll call an ambulance."

When I tried to rise, she grimaced and seized my arm with surprising strength. "I'm fine."

I sat back on my heels to stare at her, belatedly realizing that I'd completely misread the situation. Darlene's current facial contortions were the result of trying very hard not to laugh.

"Well, this must be my day for making a fool of myself. If you didn't take a tumble, why are you lying on the floor?"

"It's called exercise. Stretching keeps assorted muscles and joints from stiffening up more than they already are. Give me some space, will you? I need lots of room to heave myself up."

Once I was on my feet and had retrieved my coat, I watched without comment while Darlene maneuvered. She sat up, grabbed a throw pillow from the sofa, and used it to cushion her arthritic knees when she shifted her weight onto them. She had to place one hand flat on the carpet to get that far and pause briefly before moving on to the next part of the process. This involved sticking her left leg out to the side, taking hold of the top of a sturdy end table with both hands, and levering herself to her feet. Something made a loud popping noise as she rose.

I winced at the sound. "Doesn't that hurt?"

Darlene shrugged. "Not really, and getting up this way is easier than the alternative methods. It doesn't make me look nearly as silly, either."

Both hands held up in surrender, I shook my head. "Far be it from me to —"

"What? Make fun of the cripple?" Darlene grinned at me.

I rolled my eyes. She could get away with a crack like that, but heaven help anyone else who dared joke about her disability in such a cavalier way.

Darlene suffers from osteoarthritis . . . in spades. As she herself says, there are worse forms of the disease, but it's still a degenerative condition. She once held Pam Ingram's job at the town library but had to take early retirement at the age of sixty-two. By that point, she could no longer get a good grip on a book, making it nearly impossible for her to shelve. She found it difficult to be on her feet for long periods, too, and walking was painful for her.

Darlene's arthritis affects the joints in her hands, wrists, neck, knees, ankles, and feet. Some days pain pills and ointments keep everything under control and she only needs to use a cane or a walker to get around. At other times, especially when the weather changes abruptly or is excessively damp, she has to rely on a wheelchair or use her scooter. She refers to the latter as her "motorized transport."

On this particular day, Darlene ignored the walker I'd noticed in the living room. She needed to rest the occasional hand against a wall or on a piece of furniture to steady herself on her way through the dining room and into the kitchen, but her balance was better than usual.

"Are you hungry?" she asked as I followed her.

"I could eat."

Darlene is a fantastic cook and usually has something yummy already prepared. Not that either one of us needs extra treats. She's a couple of inches shorter than I am and jokes that she's twice the woman she was in high school. Since strenuous exercise isn't on her agenda, she's not likely to lose weight anytime soon. Neither, sad to say, am I, although I have started taking better care of myself. As soon as most of the winter's snow melted, I started walking more. Unless I have purchases to bring home, I don't need to use the car to get around. Everything is close together in Lenape Hollow and going up and down our hilly streets is better than a workout in a gym . . . or so I keep telling myself.

A short time after I arrived, Darlene and I were settled at her kitchen table with freshly brewed coffee and ham and cheese sandwiches in front of us. The air was scented with the comforting aroma of chocolate chip cookies not long out of the oven. They awaited our attention on a cooling rack on the counter.

Just as I took the first bite of my lunch, I heard the sound of toenails tapping rapidly on the tile floor. Darlene's dog, Simon, trotted over to poke a very cold nose into the free hand I'd allowed to dangle at my side. I dutifully patted him on the head. In the eight months since Darlene and Frank had adopted him, he'd morphed from fluffy black puppy into grown-up dog of the mutt variety.

I should have been able to relax. I was with a good friend, eating good food, and being showered with affection by a good dog. Instead, the tension that had been riding me since the incident at the gas station attacked the back of my neck with a vengeance. Rolling my shoulders and turning my head from side to side did nothing to alleviate the problem. I wondered if I should ask Darlene to teach me some of her stretches.

She cleared her throat. "Are you going to tell me about it or not?"

I sent a narrow-eyed glare in her direction. The twinkle in her bright blue eyes answered one question. News of the morning's folly had preceded me.

"Who called you?" I asked. "Frank, I suppose."

"Oh, yes. And Pam Ingram. Despite the difference in our ages, we've become good friends in the years since she was hired to replace me."

"I'm not sure I want to talk about it," I muttered.

"Oh, come on." There was a note of mischief in her voice. "Take pity on the housebound."

An unladylike snort escaped me before I should stop it. Despite her mobility issues, Darlene manages to go just about anywhere she wants to. It just takes her a little longer than most people to get there. I took another sip of coffee and shifted slightly so that Simon's weight wasn't entirely on my feet.

"I don't know what to say. To tell you the truth, I'm not certain I *know* what happened. Onslow kept pushing, heaping on the insults and accusations, and I just . . . exploded."

"Yes, I've seen one of your explosions before." Strands of Darlene's short, fluffy white hair fluttered as she nodded her head in a knowing way.

"You can't possibly remember that. It was over fifty years ago."

"Of course I can. It was . . . memorable." Darlene put down her coffee mug, rested her elbows on the table, and used both hands to prop up her chin. She closed her eyes. "I can still see the shocked expression on Ginny Durland's face when you lit into

27

her and her boyfriend for making fun of majorette practice. Miss I'm-better-than-you-are-because-I'm-a-cheerleader-and-dating-a-jock didn't know what hit her."

Warmth crept up my neck and into my face. I was torn between feeling a sense of pride for standing up for myself and enduring acute embarrassment because I'd lost control. I had no idea what I'd shouted at Ginny, just as I couldn't remember exactly what I'd said to Greg Onslow. I could only hope I hadn't descended into profanity on either occasion.

"Ginny shouldn't have mocked us," Darlene said. "She deserved the put-down."

"To be fair, we were pretty pathetic."

Looking back on it, I couldn't imagine why I'd tried out for the newly formed majorette corps in the first place. The school marching band had been hoping to enter a competition that year and for some unknown reason the director had decided that adding baton-twirling majorettes to the mix would be a good idea. Wrong. So wrong.

The team was to consist of four girls. Darlene and I and two others were the only ones who showed up for tryouts. That made selection easy but led to other problems. None of us had any experience. Since I was deemed the most coordinated of the bunch,

I was put in charge of working out routines and teaching them to the others. At sixteen, I was not well equipped to take on that kind of responsibility. I was already frustrated by the time Ginny and her boyfriend wandered into the hallway outside the gym, where we were practicing, and decided it would be fun to heckle us. If memory serves, it was her use of the term "spaz" that set me off.

Perhaps it's a good thing that I can't recall what I said to her.

Darlene refilled my coffee. "Like Ginny, Onslow deserved to have his head handed to him."

"Probably, but why did I have to do it in public? I'll never live this down."

"Piffle. You're a heroine. They'll write songs about you."

I couldn't help it. I laughed. Just that quickly, I felt better about myself. Darlene was right. Anyone who'd ever clashed with Greg Onslow or been taken in by one of his moneymaking ventures would cheer my lack of control. Most of them would probably wish they'd been the ones to lash out at him.

And yet, the embarrassment remained.

"The whole incident was ridiculous," I complained. "Not only is Onslow under the mistaken impression that Sunny is gunning for him, but he seems to think I can persuade her to back off. I'm just the hired help."

"Maybe his new project isn't going as well as he wants people to think."

The jaded look on Darlene's face reminded me once again that she and Frank had been among those who had lost money on one of Onslow's get-rich-quick schemes. They'd invested in a plan to turn an old tannery into modern office space. Everything had seemed to be going well. Then, just after Onslow sold off his shares, asbestos was discovered in the walls of the original structure. That had put the kibosh on the entire project.

"Or maybe," Darlene speculated, "it's the new marriage that isn't going so well."

I felt my eyes widen. "Meow."

"That *was* catty, wasn't it, but I can't help but feel sorry for the second Mrs. Onslow. With her looks, the term 'trophy wife' springs instantly to mind."

Since I'd never met her, I didn't have an opinion, and our conversation returned to the events of that morning. By the time I left Darlene's house, she'd convinced me that if anyone took exception to the way I'd dealt with Onslow's aggression, they were the ones with a problem. It didn't take much persuasion. Although I can't completely stop caring, I learned a long time ago that it's a waste of time to dwell on what other people think of me.

CHAPTER 3

That evening I was in the mood for solitude. I didn't go near my laptop, so I wasn't tempted to go online, not even to check email, and I turned off the ringers on my cell phone and landline. I briefly considered contacting Sunny to tell her about Onslow's unfounded accusations, but I was ninety-nine percent certain she'd already heard about our set-to at the gas station. Besides, I'd be talking to her in the morning. We planned to meet at Lenape Hollow Memorial Library at ten. There would be plenty of opportunity then to discuss the ravings of the Mongaup Valley Ventures CEO, assuming either one of us cared to do so.

After supper, already changed into a comfortable nightgown, a fleece bathrobe, and wooly socks, I settled in on the loveseat in my living room with a printout of several chapters of Sunny's memoirs and a mug of hot chocolate. Nights in April can still get pretty darned chilly in the foothills of the Catskill Mountains. Since the weather report I'd seen that morning had predicted that temperatures would drop into the upper twenties overnight, I was tempted to light a fire in the fireplace. Calpurnia, my calico cat, clearly favored that idea. Standing on the hearth tiles, she stared pointedly at the stacked and ready-to-be-ignited kindling and logs.

"I'm not planning to stay up all that late," I told her.

I won't leave a fire burning when I'm not there to keep an eye on it. I have a fire screen, but even the tiniest ember can cause a disaster. I'd rather, to quote an old cliché, be safe than sorry.

Calpurnia sent an offended look my way. I ignored her and tried to focus on Sunny's account of the summer nights she'd crept out of her parents' quarters at the world-famous Feldman's Catskill Resort Hotel and into the posh lodgings occupied by a major movie star. She'd been in her late teens at the time. I did a quick calculation and placed their affair in the early 1950s.

While Sunny was generous with bits of remembered conversations and tended to overshare details of physical encounters, she was often hazy about dates. She tended to be coy about naming names, too, although she'd dropped some big ones. One of my editorial notes, for all the good it had done so far, was "be specific." The whole point of a tell-all book is to tell it all, not just hint at who and when. The where, of course, was almost always Feldman's.

"What on earth," I wondered aloud, "does Greg Onslow think she's going to write that will have any effect on his demolition project?"

As far as I could see, Sunny was nostalgic about the hotel and her life there in its heyday, but she'd stopped taking a proprietary interest in the physical complex the moment she sold the place. Then again, memories can hit you hard when you least expect it. My own experience was a case in point. I hadn't given much thought to Lenape Hollow or the house I grew up in for five decades. Then, shortly after my husband died, I found out that my childhood home was up for sale. On impulse, I bought it and moved back to my old hometown.

I don't regret my decision, but there had been unforeseen consequences. For one thing, the house had needed extensive repairs. To pay for them, I'd been obliged to eke out my retirement income by going back to work. Since the job opportunities for English teachers over the age of sixty-five are somewhat limited, I decided to go into business for myself. What I earn from editing Sunny's memoirs will pay the current year's property taxes.

Calpurnia hopped up beside me on the loveseat, landing on top of a stack of loose pages, the ones I'd already edited. I caught them as they started to slip and moved them to a slightly more cat-proof location on the end table. Satisfied with these arrangements, Cal curled up beside me, purring at full volume. I shifted just enough to put my feet up on the footstool and continued reading.

Halfway through Sunny's account of yet another illicit tryst with a celebrity hotel guest, I started to nod off. Yes, reading about sex *can* be boring. Not even a concentrated effort to put together the hints she'd dropped and deduce the identity of her lover was enough to keep me awake. It was time to pack it in and make a fresh start in the morning.

Calpurnia grumbled in protest when I attempted to get up. I gave her a gentle shove. She landed on the carpet, sent a fulminating glare at me over her shoulder, and stalked off in the direction of the kitchen. I followed her, refilled her nearly empty food dish, put fresh water in her water bowl, and rinsed the dregs of chocolate out of my mug before I turned down the thermostat and headed upstairs.

After a brief stop in my second-floor office to drop off Sunny's pages, and a longer one in the bathroom, I headed for the bedroom that had once been used by my parents. It's a big corner room at the front of the house. Two windows look out over my porch roof to Wedemeyer Terrace, giving me an excellent view of the four-classroom Catholic elementary school across the street. The room's third window, at the side of the house, doubles as a fire escape. I can exit through it onto the slanted roof of the garage and descend to a point less than seven feet above my neighbor's lawn — not an easy jump, but doable.

By the time I climbed into bed, Calpurnia had already settled for the night. For once, I didn't have to move her in order to make room for my feet. I took out my hearing aids and removed my glasses, putting everything in the proper cases on my nightstand before I turned out the light and snuggled down under the covers.

Five minutes later, I changed position.

Ten minutes after that, I rolled over to try

to get comfortable lying on the other side.

I know how much time passed because, even nearsighted, I can read the illuminated dial on my bedside clock. I sighed. It was going to be one of *those* nights. Tired as I was, my mind refused to shut down.

Unsurprisingly, the entire scene with Greg Onslow began to replay itself in my head. I had to forcibly evict him from my thoughts, but all that did was bring Sunny and her book into sharper focus. Several things about the manuscript had been bothering me.

She wasn't *always* coy about the identities of those she wrote about. She'd named over a dozen prominent figures who'd been guests at the resort. That they'd stayed there wasn't in question. It was what Sunny claimed they'd done while they were in residence that was troubling. I couldn't help but wonder, especially after hearing Onslow's accusations, if she might have exaggerated a bit in writing down her version of events.

It's not your job to doubt the veracity of her memories, I admonished myself.

Nor was I the one in danger of being taken to court after the book came out. I frowned as I plumped my pillow and shifted position yet again. Sunny didn't seem to be concerned about that end of things, and it's true that most famous people are considered public figures, but that doesn't mean the ones who are still alive won't try to sue her. Consoling myself with the knowledge that her publisher had a legal department and thus any potential lawsuits were their problem, not mine, I finally drifted into sleep.

CHAPTER 4

Despite the trouble I'd had falling asleep, I rose the next morning in time to witness a colorful sunrise. That awful, gusty wind was gone and what clouds there were showed grayish-white instead of black against a pale blue sky. As predicted, it had been cold overnight. The temperature at dawn was below freezing, but the day warmed up quickly.

After breakfast, I headed for the library to meet Sunny. I walked, since certain events the previous year had convinced me that I needed to keep myself fit. I also go up and down stairs at a brisk pace, exercise with a TheraBand to increase the strength in my arms, and ride the stationary bike I keep in one of the nearly empty rooms in my attic. I've considered investing in a real bicycle, but the ones they sell these days are a far cry from the model I had as a girl. I'm not sure I want to mess with all those speeds, let alone try to master hand brakes.

Lenape Hollow Memorial Library isn't far from my house. After I descended a steep hill, I crossed North Main Street and hung a right. By then I was within a hop, skip, and jump of my destination, which is situated between a grocery store and our century-old redbrick elementary school. My short, plump, white-haired client waited for me in front of the circulation desk.

"So," she said in the husky voice of a former smoker. "I suppose I have to thank you for rushing to my defense." She didn't sound at all grateful and the expression in her dark brown eyes was unreadable.

"I guess Pam told you what happened at the gas station."

The librarian looked up from scanning returned books to waggle her fingers at me in greeting. She'd never struck me as the gossipy sort, but if I'd witnessed such an explosive encounter firsthand, I'd have dined out on the story myself. I could hardly criticize anyone else for regaling their friends with the details.

"No one needed to tell me anything," Sunny said. "I've seen the whole absurd episode for myself."

She held up her smartphone, an app already cued. Someone had taken a video of my quarrel with Greg Onslow and posted it online. For an instant, I just stared at the tiny image of myself, paralyzed by the fear that I'd been immortalized on social media as a venom-spewing shrew. That's fine if you're Elizabeth Taylor as Martha in *Who's Afraid of Virginia Woolf?* and win an Oscar for the performance. Otherwise? Not so much.

Repressing a groan and a strong desire to cover my eyes, I watched and listened to the previous day's tirade. It wasn't as bad as it could have been. The clip caught only a portion of the whole, and some of the words we exchanged had been whipped away by the wind. It didn't appear I'd sworn or used bad language or hurled personal insults, even though Greg Onslow deserved a few in retaliation for what he called me.

If the rant had come from any mouth but my own, I'd probably have cheered, especially when I informed Greg Onslow that I'd never have pegged him as being so paranoid that he thought he had to attack little old ladies before they had a chance to hurt him. I almost smiled when I heard myself add, "You'd better watch out. If everyone who's ever had a bone to pick with you were to get together and chant your name, the windstorm they'd raise would blow you into the next county."

Huh, I thought. *No wonder he turned tail and ran. I sound like I'm threatening to gather a coven and sweep him out of existence.*

I wouldn't have pegged Greg Onslow as the superstitious type. I don't believe in hexes, curses, or spells myself, but my threat reduced him to silence. He stood there gaping at me before slowly backing away, hands upraised as if to ward off the power of my words. To add the final indignity to his ignominious retreat, a sudden gust of wind *did* come up. It whisked the hat off his head and sent it swirling out of sight just as the video ended.

"I guess it could have been worse," I said as Sunny closed the app and put away her phone.

I wasn't thrilled that I'd lost my temper in public, but I hadn't sounded totally deranged. Left with no other viable choice, I decided to cling to the positive. I could be in worse company than Thelma and Louise and the sisters in *Practical Magic.*

From the other side of the circulation desk, Pam sent me a sympathetic smile. "At least the video hasn't gone viral . . . yet."

"Do me a favor and don't give it any help."

She was chuckling as she turned away to accept a stack of books from a patron waiting to check them out. I gestured for Sunny to precede me downstairs to the area of the library where microform readers and computer workstations were housed. The reason we'd agreed to meet at the library in the first place was to look through the old newspapers in its collection.

"Onslow's gone off the deep end," was her only comment as we descended.

"Do you have any idea why?"

She shrugged. "You've read as much of the memoir as I've written. I don't even mention the demolition."

"Do you plan to weigh in on that subject in print?"

"Maybe. It depends."

"On what?"

"I won't be happy if Onslow uses the site to put up something even uglier than the few run-down buildings that are there now."

"He's never been known for his good taste, but why would he accuse you of sabotage? Your book is a long way from being in print."

"I may have shared some of my stories with the historic preservation people."

Since I couldn't think of any reason why that would upset Onslow, I abandoned the subject and we settled in to indulge in some serious research. At my insistence, Sunny had agreed to search for published accounts to back up some of the incidents she'd written about. Although her memories were vivid, they were unsubstantiated and often lacked context.

Extensive fact-checking of content wouldn't ordinarily be part of my job, although any good copy editor verifies details. As a friend, I was hoping to impress upon her the importance of collaborating evidence. At the least, she needed to find proof that the people she wrote about had been guests at Feldman's when she said they were.

After I located the month and year I was searching for and started to skim articles, my mind began to wander. Could anything Sunny have said be significant enough to undermine Onslow's project? Words can be powerful weapons. What exactly, I wondered, had she told the "historic preservation people" about the old hotel?

The remaining buildings at the resort undoubtedly created an eyesore, but Feldman's had once been the pride of the community. I supposed that rising sentiment in favor of restoration instead of demolition might cause a delay in construction. For a company like Mongaup Valley Ventures, time is money. I didn't care for Greg Onslow the individual, but I didn't want financial setbacks to bankrupt his company. It employs far too many local people in an area where good jobs are scarce.

I glanced at Sunny, wondering if I *wanted* to know more. The screen in front of her showed an article on the wedding of Eddie Fisher and Debbie Reynolds. They were married at Grossinger's in nearby Liberty — right time period but wrong hotel.

She caught me reading over her shoulder. "Are you *sure* we need to do this? I'm writing a memoir. I don't see why I need to bother with —"

"Facts?"

"They're *my* memories."

If she'd been younger, I'd have accused her of pouting.

I glanced at the time in the lower corner of the screen. "We've only been at this for fifteen minutes. Surely you can devote a little longer to the effort."

"It's a waste of time."

"No, it isn't. Come on, Sunny. You know no one, not even you, can always remember everything accurately."

"My recollections —"

"Are colored by everything you've lived through since. So are mine. Humor me. Yes, writing about your own life gives you a certain amount of leeway, but for some of the more salacious chapters, the least you can do is make sure the others involved were actually where you say they were at the time."

"Fine. I'll keep looking, but so far the only relevant stories I've come across are an article about a ribbon-cutting ceremony and another on the training camp my dad set up to attract world heavyweight boxing contenders."

I returned to scrolling. Along with the verification I felt Sunny needed, I was also looking for something else, partly for the book and partly to satisfy my own curiosity. Sunny claimed she hadn't been interested in family stories when she was growing up and had never paid any attention to her mother and father when they talked about the early days of running a small hotel in Lenape Hollow. I felt certain there must have been write-ups on the founding of Feldman's in the local newspapers. If nowhere else, some of the dates and details ought to show up in Sunny's parents' obituaries.

The better part of an hour passed before the thudding of slow, heavy footfalls broke my concentration. I glanced up from the screen, surprised to see Pam Ingram approaching. Although she's a tall woman and comfortably padded, she's not particularly overweight and ordinarily moves soundlessly through the stacks. I did a classic double take when I got a look at her face. In a complexion I'd normally describe as peaches-and-cream, the peaches had dried up and the cream had curdled. Her eyes had a glassy look.

I pushed back my chair and stood, reaching toward her when she swayed. "Pam, what's wrong?"

"I —" She cleared her throat and tried again. "I've just heard the most terrible news."

Sunny stood more slowly. Leaning on the cane that, for the most part, she used only to prod people into moving out of her way, she snapped out a command. "Spit it out, young woman. Whatever the matter is, it can't be as bad as all that."

"There's been a terrible accident at the Feldman work site. Mr. Goldfarb was at the police station when the call came in and he overheard everything. The police and an ambulance are there now."

Sunny and I exchanged a look. She left it to me to ask the obvious question. "Who's been hurt?"

47

"He's not hurt," Pam blurted. "He's dead."

"Who?" Sunny demanded.

I think we both knew what the answer would be before we heard it. There was only one person whose death could throw an otherwise calm and rational individual like Pam Ingram into such a state *and* send her straight downstairs to tell us the news. Even so, my first reaction was one of profound disbelief when she finally said his name.

"It's Greg Onslow." Pam spoke in a whisper as tears rolled slowly down her cheeks. "Greg's dead."

All the starch went out of my legs. I landed in my chair with an undignified plop. Sunny remained standing. Both hands clenched on the head of her cane, her face expressionless, she contemplated Pam's words for a long moment. Then, ever so slowly, a smile overspread her features.

"That's that, then," she said. "Good riddance to bad rubbish."

CHAPTER 5

I was people-watching the following morning, seated at a window table in Harriet's,
the small café owned and operated by Ada
Patel, a New Jersey transplant with a flair
for cooking comfort food, when I was spotted by the local constabulary. In itself, there
was nothing unusual about that. The one-
story brick building that houses the Lenape
Hollow Police Department is situated directly across North Main Street from the
eatery. Despite rain falling in a steady
drizzle, I was easy to spot when Detective
Jonathan Hazlett ventured outside. I was
not at all alarmed when he pointed me out
to his companion, but it did surprise me
that both men immediately headed my way.

"Mind if we join you?" Hazlett asked,
gesturing for the other man to take the
empty seat at my two-person table before I
had time to reply. He borrowed a chair from
an unoccupied table for himself.

49

I took another sip of my coffee and studied the two men over the rim of the mug. Even if the stranger hadn't been with a fellow officer, I'd have suspected he was in law enforcement. He didn't need to be in uniform. He had the poker face and the no-nonsense attitude down pat. I swear they must teach a class called "How to Give Nothing Away" at the police academy.

"To what do I owe the honor?" There was only the teensiest hint of sarcasm in my voice.

"Greg Onslow."

"Yet another count against him," I murmured, perhaps unwisely.

Both men leveled narrow-eyed stares in my direction, but they were prevented from commenting when Ada materialized beside us carrying a coffeepot. She plunked down two empty ceramic mugs and poured without asking what they wanted. She knew Hazlett's preferences. I wouldn't have been surprised to learn that she'd already learned his companion's, as well.

"Refill?"

I nodded. I had a feeling it would help to be fully alert during the conversation to come. As I stirred in sugar substitute and creamer, I continued to study the two men.

In some ways, they couldn't have been

more different. Hazlett is recruitment-poster material — a little over six feet tall and broad shouldered. Thick, rust-colored hair tops a craggy face dominated by big brown eyes, a beak of a nose, and a chin with a cleft in it. Those looks aren't everyone's cup of tea, but he fits my image of the upright lawman perfectly.

I may have watched too many Dudley Do-Right cartoons as a kid.

His fellow officer, although blessed with a healthy head of black hair, appeared at first glance to fit the too-many-donuts stereotype of a policeman. He wasn't flabby, but no one would ever call him trim, either. Having seen the two men walking side by side when they crossed the street, I put his height at around five-foot-eight, not much taller than I am. Like Hazlett, he appeared to be somewhere in his late thirties, old enough to have some crime-solving experience under his belt.

"This is Detective Brightwell from the sheriff's department," Hazlett said when Ada left to wait on other customers. "He has a few questions for you."

I barely repressed a sigh. "I guess that means Onslow's death wasn't an accident."

Speculation had run rampant in Lenape Hollow during the twenty-plus hours since

51

the news broke. I confess I'd wondered about the circumstances myself. Construction sites are dangerous places, but Onslow hadn't been the careless type.

Neither officer confirmed my supposition that Onslow had been murdered, but I didn't hear any denials, either. That didn't surprise me, but something else did. I sent Detective Hazlett a direct look. "Why aren't you the one investigating?"

"The *unattended death* in question took place in the hamlet of Feldman. That's outside the village limits." When I looked blank, he clarified. "I handle crimes that take place within the *village* of Lenape Hollow. If something happens outside the village but in the *town* of Lenape Hollow, the county sheriff's department is in charge."

"Ah, I see."

In Maine, where I lived most of my adult life, the towns are also made up of villages, but at least in the ones with which I'm familiar, the police force and all the other local administrative offices are part of *town* government. Villages are no more than geographical designations. I'm still getting used to the subtle differences in the way things are structured in New York State.

Detective Brightwell's chair creaked as he shifted a little closer to me. "I understand you and Mr. Onslow had a rather heated encounter two days ago."

"And I suspect you've already seen the video."

"I'd like some context."

"Good luck with that. I have no idea what set him off. I'm a freelance editor. Sunny Feldman hired me because she's writing a book reminiscing about the glory days of her family's hotel. Mongaup Valley Ventures, Onlsow's company, is in the process of tearing down the resort buildings, but that's the only connection I know of between them. Sunny hasn't been directly associated with the property for decades. As for my loss of control, I can't properly account for that, either." I shrugged. "I guess he just threw one too many insults my way and I snapped."

Out of the corner of my eye, I saw Hazlett wince at my choice of words. I frowned in return. It wasn't as if I'd pulled out a gun and shot Greg Onlsow. I might have been out of control verbally, but I'd been far short of the sort of road rage that leads to violence.

"Did you see Mr. Onslow again after that incident?" Brightwell asked.

"No, I did not, nor did I want to. I'd have been perfectly happy never to cross paths

53

with Greg Onslow again."

"I guess you got your wish," he said. "Where were you the evening after your quarrel?"

He considered me a suspect. If the situation hadn't been so serious, I'd have smiled at the absurdity of that notion. As things stood, I felt no inclination toward amusement. Although the detective's facial expression continued to give away nothing of his thoughts, his unspoken accusation hovered in the air between us.

I cleared my throat. For a fraught moment I couldn't remember what I *had* been doing that night. Then my brain began to function again and I answered. "I was at home working on the chapters Sunny had already finished writing."

"Were you alone?"

"Yes, unless you count the cat."

"Did you talk to anyone?"

I shook my head as more details of how I'd spent the evening came back to me. "I didn't want to be bothered by people who'd heard about what happened at the gas station, so I turned off the phones. I don't think anyone tried to reach me. No one left any messages."

"Were you on your computer?" Hazlett asked. "Sending email? Working on something that would be time-stamped?"

"No. I was editing by hand."

"That's too bad."

I picked up my mug and took a long swallow from it. The bitter aftertaste was a good match for the way this conversation was going.

"At the time," I said slowly, "I didn't realize I'd need an alibi." I added another packet of sweetener to my coffee, stirred it in, and took a tentative sip followed by a less cautious one. "When did Onslow die?"

The two men exchanged a look but neither answered me. Instead, after a moment, Hazlett asked, "What about your security system? Was it on?"

I brightened at the thought. "Yes. Yes, it was."

I had it installed a few months after I bought the house, when I feared I was being stalked. By the time that danger was past, I'd acquired the habit of leaving it activated whether I was at home or not.

In the ordinary way of things, deadbolts alone should have provided sufficient peace of mind. I live on a quiet street in a sleepy little town. Onslow's murder aside, there is not a lot of crime in Lenape Hollow. Then again, only last summer I'd had another reason to be glad the house was alarmed.

Now, it seemed, my precautions were about to prove useful once more.

Detective Hazlett nodded his approval. "The security company should have a record of when the alarms were engaged and when they were turned off."

"That would have been the next morning, when I left the house to meet Sunny at the library."

At that point, I should have been able to relax, but Detective Brightwell was staring at me with as much intensity as ever. It was painfully obvious that he continued to have doubts about my innocence.

I aimed my best glare at him. "Let's get this out in the open. I didn't kill Greg Onslow. Surely you have more likely suspects than a woman in her early seventies who barely knew the man. I didn't like him, but I didn't have any reason to kill him, either."

Brightwell acknowledged my statement with a brusque nod. "I'll be in touch if I need more information."

"Oh, goodie," I said, not quite under my breath.

"Thanks for your time," Hazlett said when both men were standing.

I didn't believe for a minute that I was about to be arrested for murder, but being questioned left a bad taste in my mouth. As soon as the detectives left the restaurant, I looked around for Ada. She was at my side in an instant.

"I'd like a cup of hot chocolate, please, and a slice of your homemade double chocolate layer cake."

"Coming right up," she said.

So what if it was only ten thirty in the morning!

CHAPTER 6

Veronica Rappaport was the bane of my
existence when we were in high school fifty-
plus years ago. Since my return to Lenape
Hollow, we've established a slightly less
prickly relationship. As Ronnie North, she's
a force to be reckoned with in our town,
donating to many good causes and even
volunteering her time to some of them. I
admire her civic spirit, but as far as I can
see, her attitude toward me is almost as
snarky as it was when we were teenagers.
Other than being members of the same
church and involved in some of the same
community organizations, and the fact that
we're both widows, we don't have much in
common. I'm still struggling to make a living. Each of her three husbands left her
wealthier than the one before.

Given our history, the last thing I expected
to see when I glanced out my bedroom
window that afternoon was Ronnie's flashy

Rolls-Royce pulling into my driveway. For a moment, I considered hiding out in my upstairs office and pretending I'd taken out my hearing aids so I couldn't hear her knocking on my door or ringing the bell.

"Coward," I admonished myself, and trotted down the stairs to shut off the security system. I'd already opened the front door and was waiting for Ronnie when she came up the steps to the porch and lowered her umbrella.

"Oh, good," she said, giving it a shake that spattered me with cold, wet droplets. "You *are* home."

I thought she smiled. Since she's had at least two facelifts, it's a little hard to tell. Without waiting for me to invite her in, she pushed past me. An overpowering whiff of Emeraude, her signature perfume, trailed after her.

By the time I caught up with Ronnie, she was in my living room glaring at Calpurnia. My calico cat lay sprawled across both cushions of the loveseat, the most comfortable place to sit. It was crystal clear that she had no intention of being displaced. Even Ronnie didn't have nerve enough to fight her for the prime spot.

"You shouldn't let animals sleep on the furniture."

I shrugged. "She lives here, too."

I considered adding, "and you don't," but I thought I'd better find out what she wanted before I deliberately provoked her. I suggested we adjourn to the kitchen and offered coffee. She requested tea. The bags in the cupboard were ancient, but I didn't bother to apologize.

A few minutes later, cups steaming in front of us, we settled into what my mother always called the "dinette." It's really just an alcove at the back end of the kitchen, big enough for a table that seats four and not much else. The windows look out over my backyard. In my parents' day, we always had a bird feeder in plain view. Many a meal had come with entertainment from our feathered friends and the squirrels who continually tried to steal their food. I put up a new feeder almost a year ago, but I keep forgetting to fill it with birdseed and suet.

Ronnie took only a sip of her tea before setting down the cup. She ran critical eyes over my kitchen decor but managed not to comment. That made me even more wary. She hadn't just dropped by for a casual visit. Not Ronnie North. She had something on her mind.

Lifting one wrinkly and blue-veined hand,

60

she tucked a stray strand of black hair behind her ear. As a girl, the shade had been natural. In bright lighting, her blue-black highlights had been striking. Somewhere along the line, she'd made the unwise decision to banish every trace of gray and return to her original color. Bad choice. Worse dye job. Women our age look far better if they let nature have its way.

"I'd kill for a cigarette," she said at last. "I've been trying to quit."

"Good for you." I hesitated, then plunged in. "Is there some reason you're here? Not to be inhospitable, but you usually avoid me like the plague."

Looking as if it pained her to admit it, Ronnie said, "I owe you one. This seemed a good opportunity to repay the debt."

More confused than ever, I just stared at her.

"With advice, Mikki. It appears that Greg Onslow was murdered. That means you need to watch your back and get a reliable lawyer on retainer." She suggested a firm in Middletown, one that specializes in criminal cases.

"It's . . . nice of you to be concerned," I replied, "but I think you're overreacting."

"He was *murdered,* Mikki. Right after you and he had a very public quarrel."

"I *argued* with him, Ronnie. I did not kill him." I leaned a little closer, waiting until our eyes met. "You might want to follow your own advice about that lawyer. There was no love lost between you and your former grandson-in-law."

Their quarrels were legendary, both before and after Onslow's first wife's death.

Ronnie's eyes narrowed. "I haven't even spoken with him since last summer," she said in a huffy voice.

I fought the temptation to roll my eyes. Apparently, it was okay for her to suggest that I was a suspect in a homicide investigation, but out of line for me to make the same observation about her. "Has Detective Brightwell talked to you yet?"

It didn't surprise me that she ignored the question, or that she heaved herself out of her chair and stormed out of the kitchen, the very picture of indignant outrage.

CHAPTER 7

After Ronnie left, I briefly considered the subject of suspects and motives, but what puzzled me more than the identity of Greg Onslow's killer was the question of what had set him off that day at the gas station. He'd kept talking about sabotage, yet if I was to believe Sunny, the most she'd done was share a few of her stories with someone involved in local historic preservation efforts.

I had no idea who that might have been, but I did know how to find out. A few minutes online yielded the address and phone number of the Lenape Hollow Historic Preservation Society. The website said they were open on Wednesday and Friday afternoons from one to five. I tried calling first, since this was a Friday, but the line was busy. A glance at the clock told me I had plenty of time to pay them a visit in person.

The rain had stopped, although it was still cloudy and damp. I shrugged into a lined raincoat suitable for temperatures in the mid-fifties, grabbed my bag, tucked a purse-size umbrella inside just to be on the safe side, and headed out. The first part of the walk took me south along Wedemeyer Terrace — all level ground — but it pleased me to note that I hardly huffed or puffed at all when I descended the hill closest to the Main Street address that was my destination. I might have taken another route. There were several to choose from, but every single one of them plunged downhill in a similar fashion.

Less than twenty minutes after I left the house, I made my way up a long, steep flight of stairs to the office space above Lenape Hollow's state-of-the-art sign-making company. A number of businesses are located on the second floor of this building, everything from the suite occupied by an accounting firm to the headquarters leased by the folks whose reason for being was to lobby for the preservation of old buildings.

Despite the frosted glass in the window of the door to the latter, I could tell there was a light burning inside. I knocked once and turned the knob but nothing happened. Rapping harder, I called out a greeting.

Slow, plodding footfalls sounded as someone approached from the other side. The click as the lock disengaged was followed, when the door swung inward, by a creak on a par with a special effect for a haunted mansion. As I stepped into the tiny, cramped office, I heard a muffled snort and turned to see a familiar face.

"Well," I said. "You're about the last person I expected to find here."

Ann Ellerby gave one of her characteristic shrugs, her bony shoulders moving up and down as she came out from behind the door and closed and relocked it. I've known Ann since we were children, although she's seven or eight years younger than I am. We lived in the same neighborhood growing up. When I returned to Lenape Hollow, I was surprised to discover that she worked for Ronnie North as a live-in housekeeper and cook. Looking at her now, wearing her usual uniform of jeans and a long-sleeved Henley, I had no reason to think she'd traded that position for a new job.

Ann's presence meant Ronnie was involved in this historic preservation group, and that meant it was likely that Ronnie was the one with whom Sunny had shared her stories. The pieces of one small puzzle began to come together.

The Lenape Hollow Historic Preservation Society operated out of a single small room furnished with a desk, two chairs, three file cabinets, and a shredder. One narrow window let in as much pale sunlight as there was on such a gloomy day. The glass, like everything else in sight, was spotless, leading me to surmise that Ann had a good deal of time on her hands.

I sank into the sturdier-looking of the two chairs and tried to work out what to ask first. Ann saved me the trouble of deciding on a question.

"If you're wondering what I'm doing here, I'm the official volunteer."

My eyebrows lifted. "Your idea or Ronnie's?"

"What do *you* think?"

"I think she volunteered you and you're going along with it for a change of pace. I'm also guessing I'm the first person to stop by here in months."

"You'd be wrong about that last part. This isn't exactly Grand Central Station but folks know we're here."

"Sunny Feldman?"

"She's been by, but she talked to Ronnie, not me."

Proof of my earlier guess hadn't been long in coming. Now my mind moved rapidly toward another logical conclusion.

"You don't need to keep the door locked against an eighty-six-year-old woman. Who else has been in?" I didn't give her the chance to prevaricate. "Greg Onslow, right? Complaining because he'd heard you were planning to get an injunction to stop him from building whatever it is he planned to put up to replace Feldman's?"

"Close enough. What a nasty piece of work that man was."

"This group can't have been much of a threat. I'm sure he already had all the permits he needed to start demolition."

Ann shrugged again and settled into the other chair. Her demeanor was calm, but her pale blue eyes looked troubled. "The lawsuits the society threatened would have been more of a nuisance than anything else, but with a sympathetic judge they could have held things up for months. The idea was to convince Onslow to set aside a portion of the property to build a museum celebrating the history of Catskill Mountain resorts. The location is perfect — the site of one of the premier hotels in the area. Let's face it, it doesn't hurt Bethel Woods to stand on the site of the Woodstock festival."

"But why did Onslow call your efforts sabotage? Demanding some of his land sounds more like blackmail to me."

"Who knows what he was thinking?"

"Did he realize Ronnie was involved with this historic preservation group?"

"I doubt it. The proposal was presented to him by a team of lawyers. The society was named but not any of the members."

"And that's when you started locking the door. If he'd barged in here, hoping to confront a real person, he'd have recognized you." Everyone in town knew Ann worked for Ronnie.

"Got it in one."

"It doesn't surprise me that Ronnie took the opportunity to cause trouble for Onslow," I said slowly, "but I have to wonder why she didn't want credit for it. Onslow was blaming all his troubles, real or imagined, on Sunny."

Ann answered with another snort.

"What's that supposed to mean?"

"Let's just say Ronnie may have elaborated on some of Sunny's stories in order to get Onslow's goat. One of her arguments — pardon me! — one of the Lenape Hollow Historic Preservation Society's arguments for building the Borscht Belt Museum on the site of this particular historic hotel was the claim that Feldman's inspired both *Dirty Dancing* and the resort scenes in *The Marvel-*

ous Mrs. Maisel."

"Did it?"

"No." She sent me a pitying look that said plainer than words that anyone who'd lived in the area long enough already knew the true story. "Well, I don't know about that TV show, but for the movie, that honor goes to Grossinger's. I believe the woman who taught dancing there and provided most of the authentic details to the film's writers still lives in Liberty."

I wasn't about to admit that I'd never seen *Dirty Dancing,* not all the way through at any rate. For all I know, it may do a wonderful job of portraying vacationers and employees at Catskill resort hotels in the sixties, but my own experience was far different. I was a townie. My contact with summer people was limited. They made the streets of Lenape Hollow a lot more crowded from Memorial Day to Labor Day, but otherwise had little impact on my life. While I had friends who took summer jobs at local hotels, I'd worked at the telephone company as a long-distance operator.

"Ronnie stopped by my house earlier today," I said to get the conversation back on track. "She seemed to know I'd talked to the police, but she wouldn't tell me if they'd questioned her or not. If they find out she

69

was at odds with Onslow over this museum business, they might think she had a reason to want him dead."

This time Ann did more than snort. She laughed out loud. "You've got that backward, Mikki. Look at how mad he was at you just for working for Sunny. She's lucky he didn't go after her directly. Now imagine if he'd found out it was Ronnie who was behind his troubles. Given the bad blood between them, *she'd* be the one lying in the morgue right now, not him."

CHAPTER 8

The suite belonging to the accounting firm where Luke Darbee worked was right next door to the headquarters of the Lenape Hollow Historic Preservation Society. Luke is my second cousin thrice removed. Before heading home, I stopped by his office to say hello. After one look at his pallor and the bags under his eyes, I insisted he come to my house for supper that evening. He didn't put up much of a fight and turned up on my doorstep a little more than an hour later.

"Sit down before you fall down," I ordered. "You look exhausted."

"The deadline to file income taxes for the year is only a few days away."

That was explanation enough. Although Luke doesn't need to work, having inherited a considerable fortune from his late father's family, he likes to stay busy. A few months ago he took a job with a local accountant as a tax preparer.

71

I first met this pleasant young man — he's not yet thirty — when he turned up in Lenape Hollow looking for information on the Greenleigh family. It was obvious from the first that we were related. We both sport the infamous Greenleigh nose. It's a little too big for our faces. The more unfortunate members of the clan have a profile that's distinctly ratlike.

Genealogy is only one of Luke's hobbies. He's also an amateur thespian. He majored in drama in college, but being of a practical bent, he had a double major. His other degree is in business administration.

For some unknown reason, he decided to settle down in Lenape Hollow. He says he likes the place. He was living in a high-end RV when he first arrived. He put it in storage for the winter, rented the apartment above the pizza parlor on South Main Street, and seems quite happy with the arrangement.

Neither Luke nor I ever feel compelled to chatter while we eat. That evening, I should have been content to feed him and give him a break from the demands of tax season, but I had the strongest feeling that there was something different about our dearth of conversation. I couldn't help but notice that he kept his gaze fixed on his plate, avoiding eye contact.

I didn't think the meal was the problem. I'm not a gourmet cook. For the most part, if you eat at my place you get meat, potatoes, rice, or pasta, and a vegetable or salad. Pork chops doused in cream of mushroom soup and baked for an hour is one of my standbys, and I'd served it to Luke at least once before.

Belatedly, it occurred to me that someone had probably shown him that wretched video. I cleared my throat. "I imagine you've heard about Greg Onslow."

"I heard he was dead." Luke's voice was carefully neutral.

"Not just dead. Murdered."

He kept his focus on the food in front of him. "No surprise there. Nobody liked him."

I glanced at the clock and saw that it was just going on six. "Mind if I turn on the news?"

Without waiting for a reply, I got up and retrieved the tablet I'd left on the kitchen counter. When I brought it back to the dinette table, I opened the cable TV app, selected my favorite among the stations that cover goings-on in Sullivan County, and positioned the screen so that it was visible to both of us.

73

My timing was impeccable. The anchor was just introducing the reporter assigned to cover a press conference the sheriff had called. He confirmed that the death of Gregory Onslow, CEO of Mongaup Valley Ventures in Lenape Hollow, was a homicide currently under investigation by his department. Beyond those bare facts, he gave no details, and he answered "no comment" to every question he was asked.

I closed the tablet and went back to my meal. Calpurnia, who until then had been asleep on the bench seat beneath the windows, got up, stretched, and curled up again, showing not the slightest interest in either the food or the company. She was napping on the warm spot above one of the old-fashioned radiators that still provide hot-water heat in my home.

Overall, the house hasn't changed much in the last five decades. My parents sold it and moved away from Lenape Hollow shortly after I started college in Maine, so I never came back to my hometown for summer vacations. I was sixty-eight before I saw the place again. There had been several owners in the interim, but none of them had seen fit to do more than minimal upkeep. It was left to me, after I moved back in, to replace the roof and upgrade the plumbing and wiring. While I was at it, I commissioned a few changes to the upstairs floorplan and turned the room I'd slept in as a teenager into an at-home office. I'm still working on several DIY projects, but in a few more months, at the two-year mark of my occupancy, everything should be pretty much the way I want it.

Luke broke another lengthy silence with a quiet comment. "At least your video didn't turn up on that newscast." I could hear the smile in his voice.

"So much for hoping you hadn't seen it. It didn't exactly show me at my best." I stabbed a broccoli floret with my fork and carried it to my mouth.

"Oh, I don't know. You had Onslow on the run."

"And now he's dead. Guess who the police think is a person of interest?"

"Oh, come on! You're too smart to have killed him right after fighting with him in public. If you'd wanted him dead, you'd have waited at least a month and then you'd have done a much better job of hiding the body." He grinned at me as he scooped up the last of his soup-flavored rice.

"Thanks. I think. But Detective Brightwell isn't as convinced as you are of my common sense. Unfortunately, I was home alone when the murder occurred."

"More proof of your innocence." Having finished his food, he polished off a glass of root beer before adding, "If you'd needed an alibi, you'd have figured out a way to give yourself one."

There were still a few bites left on my plate, but I'd lost my appetite. I put down my knife and fork. "I'd feel better if I knew someone else had it in for Onslow, preferably someone I don't know. I don't want Frank or Darlene to have killed him. Or Ronnie." I added her to the list as an afterthought.

"Or me?"

For a moment, I was startled. I'd all but forgotten that Luke had worked briefly at Mongaup Valley Ventures. He'd accepted a position in their publicity department late the previous fall. His employment there hadn't lasted past the first snowfall.

We'd never talked about his stint at MVV. I'd cautioned him beforehand against working for Greg Onslow's company. No doubt as a result of my obvious bias, he hadn't volunteered any information after he left. For the first time, I wondered if he'd been fired.

"You must have met quite a few people at MVV," I said, approaching the subject obliquely. "Any likely suspects?"

"Just print out the employee list and pick a name at random."

"That bad?"

"That bad."

"I'm not going to say I told you so."

"And I appreciate that."

"But I'd really like to hear your thoughts. Did anyone in particular have a grudge against Onslow?"

"There was no love lost between him and Ariadne Toothaker."

"His head of personnel?"

He gave me an odd look. "His vice president. I was supposed to be a candidate for her old position when I was hired. Temporarily, she was handling both jobs."

"If they clashed, why promote her?" And why, I wondered, had she been with him at the gas station?

"Beats me," Luke said. "All I know is that their corporate philosophies weren't a good match."

"I met her once. We didn't click. In fact, she took an active dislike to me when she realized I was only applying for a job at MVV to give myself an opportunity to snoop." I thought back to that day a year and a half earlier. In addition to Ms. Toothaker, I'd spoken to one other person.

"I also encountered a young woman named Jenni Farquhar. She was Onslow's secretary, but she wasn't very good at her job."

Luke's humorless chuckle told me he knew who she was. "A redhead, right? Chest measurement higher than her IQ? When I was hired, she'd just been demoted to payroll clerk. She couldn't have been very happy about it, especially when her replacement ended up engaged to marry the boss."

"Onslow's second wife was his secretary?"

Luke's expression turned grim. "Briefly. She went from secretary to wife in record time and now Giselle Onslow is a wealthy widow."

I was instantly intrigued. "Do —"

With an abruptness that cut me off in mid-question, Luke stood and carried his empty plate and utensils to the sink. Keeping his back to me, he rinsed them before putting them in the dishpan.

"Thanks for the meal and the company, Mikki. I'd offer to help wash and dry, but I really need to get back to the office. Tax season doesn't leave much time for socializing."

In the interest of maintaining family harmony, I dropped the subject, but I confess I couldn't help but wonder what it was he *wasn't* telling me. *Had* he been fired from Mongaup Valley Ventures or had he quit? I'd have loved to know the reason he left.

It's none of your business, I told myself as I squirted soap into the dishpan and filled it with hot water.

Doing the dishes by hand is a chore I find soothing, as long as there aren't too many pots to scrub. As I swished and rinsed and conveyed clean plates to the drying rack, I considered the lines along which Detective Brightwell, if he had any sense, must be investigating. Surely he'd consider the widow a person of interest. Those nearest and dearest to the victim always have the best reason to kill. Brightwell wouldn't have any difficulty identifying Ariadne Toothaker as a suspect, either. He might even be taking a hard look at Jenni Farquhar.

I had to be way down on his list, along with all the people Onslow had swindled over the years. Ronnie might have wanted to kill him, given how unhappy he made her late granddaughter, but I couldn't see her attacking him with anything more lethal than her razor-sharp tongue.

By the time I dumped the dishwater down the sink, I felt cautiously optimistic. With any luck, the police would focus on the widow and assorted employees of Mongaup

79

Valley Ventures. Those I cared about would be off the hook.

CHAPTER 9

I spent Saturday running errands, grocery shopping, and going over my tax return one last time before filing it online. Sunday morning, a sunny one following a night of heavy rain, found me staring at the palm frond I'd been handed as I entered the First Presbyterian Church of Lenape Hollow.

I wasn't entirely sure what I was supposed to do with it. Oh, I know the symbolic use of palms on Palm Sunday. Waving them around is supposed to recreate the reception Jesus received when he entered Jerusalem. Considering the way the next few days went back then, making all that fuss might not have been such a good idea.

Churchgoing wasn't part of my life when I lived in Maine. Since my return to Lenape Hollow, I'd attended services at First Presbyterian sporadically. I'd never become an official member of any other congregation and it had been in the Sunday school room in the basement that I'd first met both Darlene and Ronnie, so Darlene had been encouraging me to get back into the habit.

This was one of her good days. She needed only a cane to help her balance. I settled into the pew beside her to the accompaniment of softly murmured conversations as people all around us exchanged greetings and gossip. Most of them kept their voices too low for me to hear exactly what they were saying and I was just as well pleased not to be able to eavesdrop. I could guess what two of the hottest topics of conversation were. I wouldn't have minded speculating about Greg Onslow's murder, but I preferred to avoid any discussion of my own final encounter with him.

"I was invited next door for supper last night," I said, choosing what I hoped would be a safe topic of conversation.

"By the O'Days or the Frys?" Darlene asked.

"The Frys."

She rolled her eyes. I smiled. My tolerance for young children is extremely limited and Cindy and her husband have three rambunctious little boys.

"The kids were on their best behavior." Better yet, with impressionable young minds in the room, none of the adults had brought up any unpleasant or embarrassing subjects.

Unfortunately, I could think of nothing else from my evening that was worth sharing. I studied the palm frond. I thought it was real. At least it wasn't plastic.

"I wonder where they get these. Is there a warehouse somewhere just for church supplies?"

"Probably," Darlene said, "but we didn't go that route. It was cheaper to order them from Amazon."

At first I thought she was kidding, but she assured me she was not. Since she'd been an elder in the church prior to the last election, I had no reason to disbelieve her.

I was spared having to come up with another conversational gambit by the entrance of the minister. Pastor Cameron is a good man, but he's only a mediocre orator. I sang along on the hymns, although I don't have much of an ear for music, but my mind wandered during the sermon.

So did my gaze. I spotted Ronnie in her usual pew toward the front, right beneath the stained-glass window she donated to the church to replace one that was destroyed by vandals.

First Presbyterian boasts a dozen stained-glass windows, six on each side of the sanctuary. As a kid, I always found the Bible scenes fascinating. I still like looking at those, but the window Ronnie paid for leaves me cold. The Art Deco design clashes horribly with its neighbors.

After the final hymn, the usual traffic jam formed as all the parishioners tried to leave at the same time. There was a bottleneck at the door where the pastor had installed himself to shake hands with every member of his congregation, taking the time to inquire after each person's health, family, and anything else he could think of.

He means well, but after an hour sitting on a hard wooden bench, I was impatient to escape. The feeling was akin to standing in the aisle of an airplane at the end of a long flight, waiting for the passengers in the seats closer to the front to exit.

I was subjected to an additional irritant on this particular Sunday. Clarice Cameron, the minister's wife, bore down on me with a determined gleam in her eyes. Relieved that her attention was not fixed on them, other worshippers parted to let her through.

"Mikki. Darlene. What did you think of the sermon?"

"Very appropriate," Darlene murmured.

Since I hadn't listened to most of it, I said nothing. I assumed Pastor Cameron had contented himself with retelling the story from the Scriptures. He's not inclined to go off script. In spite of my silence, or perhaps because of it, Clarice zeroed in on me.

"Poor Mikki. I trust the police haven't bothered you too much."

She *sounded* sympathetic, but I braced myself all the same. Odds were good that she'd seen the video and drawn her own conclusions. Her next words seemed to confirm it.

"If you need counseling, you know we're here for you. After all, you're still one of our flock."

"I appreciate that," I murmured, "but it won't be necessary. I'm fine."

Clarice and I *should* have been friends. We're both retired teachers. In fact, she started teaching at Lenape Hollow High School when I was a senior there. That was her first year out of college, so she's only a few years older than I am. Instead of gravitating toward her, I avoid her when ever possible. She's pushy, argumentative, and judgmental. Worst of all, she's determined to get me back into the fold. My irregular attendance at church really bugs her.

"The police talked to you at Harriet's. You were seen," she added before I could deny it, not that I intended to. Given that we live in a small town, she'd undoubtedly heard from a dozen different sources that I'd been questioned by Detectives Hazlett and Brightwell. "Did they tell you how he was killed?"

"All I know is what's been on the news."

I edged a little closer to the exit, but Clarice stuck like glue. She was slender enough to squeeze herself in alongside me, even in a crowd.

"He was found at the construction site," she continued. "I wonder if the killer tried to hide the body. That place must be dotted with cellar holes from where all those buildings used to stand."

"I don't think much demolition has actually been completed yet," Darlene said, "and I believe they backfill any holes right away for safety reasons."

Clarice turned avid eyes her way. "Has your husband been out to the site? He's on the village board of trustees, isn't he? Aren't they the ones who issue building permits?"

"Feldman's is outside the village limits," Darlene reminded her, and used her cane to good effect in clearing a path toward the door, a trick she'd picked up from watching Sunny Feldman do the same.

Frustrated by our failure to provide her with any juicy details about the murder, Clarice shifted her focus from "poor Mikki" to "poor Darlene."

"I feel so badly for you. It must be so hard for you at this time of year."

Darlene's blank expression was an accurate reflection of my own lack of comprehension. "I don't follow you, Clarice," she said.

The minister's wife lowered her voice. "I'm sure your life would be much easier if you could persuade your husband to convert to Christianity."

Two spots of color appeared high on Darlene's cheeks. "Frank's beliefs have never been a problem for us," she said in icy tones. "I can't speak for *other* people."

The criticism went right over Clarice's head. Darlene looked prepared to elucidate. Fortunately for the minister's wife, another parishioner caught her arm, demanding her attention. When she turned to see what he wanted, we were able to make our escape.

"Can you believe her?" Darlene leaned heavily on her cane as we made our way out of the church.

"She's not the brightest bulb, but I don't think she's actually anti-Semitic, just clueless."

"Oh, yes. I'm sure some of her best friends are Jews."

Since I didn't have a comeback, I kept my

mouth shut the rest of the way to the parking lot. It was slow going, since we had to watch out for mud puddles. By the time we reached Darlene's van, she was over the worst of her irritation.

"You're right, Mikki. Clarice's opinions stem more from ignorance than maliciousness." She gave a short bark of laughter. "I just wish I'd thought to introduce her to Frank's mother when Mama Uberman was still alive."

"I can't imagine Mrs. Uberman would have cared much for Clarice, and she'd have alienated her right off the bat by telling her she needed fattening up."

I could just picture Frank's mother hustling our minister's wife into her kitchen and making her a pastrami sandwich on rye or trying to tempt her with a bagel smeared with cream cheese. Back when I was an underweight teenager, she'd greeted me the same way every time she saw me. "You're nothing but skin and bones," she'd say. "You should eat, already!"

Darlene tossed her cane into the front of the van and hoisted herself onto the driver's seat. "I suspect they'd have found they had a lot in common," she said. "Through all the years Frank and I were dating, and then engaged, and then married, his mom never missed a single opportunity to tell us that she'd die happy if only *I'd* convert."

CHAPTER 10

Monday was uneventful. I edited client manuscripts and did chores around the house. Laundry was the number-one priority. I have a washer and dryer in the small utility room in between the kitchen and the back porch, although I prefer to hang clothes on the line to dry when the weather cooperates. After that, a lick and a promise was the best I could muster when it came to dusting and vacuuming. If I could afford it, I'd hire a housekeeper to come in once a week to save me the trouble.

Neither Detective Brightwell nor the murder investigation rated more than a passing thought until the following afternoon, when Darlene phoned to say he'd just left her house after questioning her and Frank. She sounded upset.

"I'm sure it's routine," I said in an attempt to reassure her. "You and Frank *did* have business dealings with a murder victim."

"He asked Frank if he left the house on the night Onslow was killed."

"Did he?"

"No, but the police have only my word for that. I got the distinct impression that Brightwell didn't believe me."

"He's probably talking to everyone with the least possible motive for wanting revenge on Onslow. Lots of people lost money investing in one of his get-rich-quick schemes," I added. "Frank's unlikely to be the only one Brightwell questions."

"Do you really think so?" Darlene hesitated, then blurted, "He seemed very interested in the fact that Frank witnessed your quarrel with Onslow at the gas station."

My hand tightened on the phone. That didn't strike me as a reason to suspect Frank. Instead, it made me think the detective was taking a harder look at *my* motive. Brightwell had seen the video. Was it good or bad that he'd asked for Frank's eyewitness account of the incident? I wondered briefly if I should reconsider Ronnie's advice about hiring a lawyer.

Her voice low and uneven, Darlene said, "I don't like this. Not at all."

"Neither do I. Maybe we should ask around and find out if Brightwell has talked to any of the other people Onslow swindled."

"What a good idea. I can call a few of those who lost money in the tannery debacle, but I don't know who invested in other projects. If they reacted the same way we did, they were probably too embarrassed to admit to being conned."

"Brightwell must have found out about you from Onslow's business records. If he has access to those, then he has other names, as well." I toyed with the phone cord, an old habit I'll miss if I ever get rid of my landline. "We don't need to check with everyone who was cheated. Just a few should be enough. Why don't you make a couple of phone calls and I'll see what I can uncover? I know of one person he swindled out of her life savings."

"I'd feel a lot better if I knew we weren't the only ones Brightwell is questioning," Darlene admitted.

So would I, I thought as I said good-bye.

I replaced the hearing aid I'd removed during our conversation — it squeals if it comes too close to the receiver. Then I took it out again so I could call the Lenape Hollow Police Station. I asked for Ellen Blume, a young officer I'd met on several occasions. She'd once confided to me that her mother, who had been fond of Tiffany, Greg Onslow's first wife, invested in one of his shady business deals and ended up losing just about everything she had saved for her retirement.

Onslow's game plan was simple. He lined up financial backing for a project that looked good on paper, then sold out just before it fell though, usually due to some hidden flaw. He ended up making a healthy profit while the rest of the investors were left holding the bag. He'd come close to being arrested only once for his underhanded dealings. On that occasion, he'd managed to shift all the blame to an upper-level employee who'd been involved in even more nefarious activities of his own.

"What can I do for you, Ms. Lincoln?" Ellen asked when she came on the line.

"I just have a quick question, if you don't mind. I was wondering if all the people who lost money on Greg Onslow's schemes are being questioned in connection with his death."

"I don't have that information." She sounded annoyed.

"I thought you might know if *one* of them had been. I don't want to put you on the spot, and I don't intend to bother her, but if I knew that this particular person had been questioned, or was about to be, it would relieve my mind."

She was silent for so long that I was afraid she didn't intend to answer me. Then I heard a little sigh from her end of the line. "I shouldn't be telling you this, but yes, Detective Brightwell has talked to my mother. He interviewed her yesterday. I can't swear to it, but I think he plans to talk to everyone Greg Onslow swindled since he came to Lenape Hollow."

"I'm very glad to hear it. That will give him plenty of suspects."

This time her extended silence had a different quality.

"Ellen?"

Her voice dropped to a whisper. "He's also started a second round of questioning. He's talking to people who may not have told him everything they knew the first time around. If he's not at your house already, he'll be there shortly."

With that ominous warning, she broke the connection. I stuck my hearing aid back in and walked from the kitchen to the picture window in the living room. Sure enough, a vehicle sporting the logo of the sheriff's department was just pulling into my driveway.

CHAPTER 11

Detective Brightwell *had* to follow up. I'd made a spectacle of myself quarreling with a man who'd ended up dead the very next day. Any policeman worth his salt would wonder about my relationship with the victim.

On the other hand, shouldn't he have contacted my security company by now? If he had, they'd have confirmed that I didn't turn off the door alarms at any point during that fateful night.

I pasted a smile on my face and went to answer his knock. I didn't bother to feign surprise at finding him at my door. Neither did I offer him coffee. I led him into the living room, settled myself on the loveseat, and hauled Calpurnia, who'd been sound asleep on the other cushion, into my lap. There are times when one simply has to have something comforting to hold on to.

He didn't sit down. Perhaps he thought

that looming over me would give him an advantage. Looking up at him put a crick in my neck, and although I couldn't read anything in particular in his expression, the effect *was* a bit menacing. Beneath my nervous fingers, Cal's fur bristled. She glared at him and spat.

"Nice cat," he said. "Too bad she can't talk."

Both my eyebrows shot up in a silent question. I'd have preferred to lift just one, but I've never been able to master that trick.

"I have a few questions, Ms. Lincoln, starting with this one: Where did you go on the night Gregory Onslow was murdered?"

"I was right here all evening. I've already told you that." My cold stare and icy tone of voice didn't faze him in the least.

"Maybe you were and maybe you weren't. When you had your alarm system installed, you had keypads put on your front and back doors and had the security company fix your downstairs windows so they'll only open a couple of inches."

"That's correct." All of a sudden, I began to have a bad feeling about where this line of questioning was headed.

"It turns out there are two additional exits from this house, not counting an upstairs door that leads out onto a small balcony."

"Oh, surely you want to count that one."

His scowl warned me that he didn't appreciate sarcasm.

"I only mean that it would have been possible for me to leave the house that way. I could have crossed the garage roof and jumped down into my neighbors' yard. Of course, I'd have needed a ladder to get back inside again."

"The other two exits are the ones that are problematic."

"Yes, I can see that, but until this moment, it honestly didn't occur to me that they might be. I didn't bother to have alarms put on them because no one can get inside the house through either one."

"Show me."

Carrying Calpurnia, I led him through the open pocket doors that separate the living room from the dining room. I stopped just inside the latter to open the regular-size door immediately to my left and reveal the small sunroom beyond.

"This is located directly beneath my upstairs balcony," I said as I stepped inside and opened yet another door.

I went out onto a tiny landing at the top of a short flight of steps. A faint oily smell drifted up to me from the inside of the garage. My Taurus had sprung a leak a few months earlier, and my attempt to clean the spot where it had dripped had not been entirely successful.

"This gives me easy access to my car in bad weather," I explained. "I didn't have an alarm put on it because no one can get in from the outside unless the garage door is open."

"Show me the other exit."

"Not much of a conversationalist, are you? Follow me. We'll have to go down cellar."

Cat signaled her displeasure at being lugged around by kicking me in the ribs. I left her in the dining room as we walked through it to reach the kitchen.

Brightwell eyed the door to the utility room as we passed by.

"You go through there to reach the back porch," I said as I veered in the opposite direction.

There are two more doors at the far end of the long, narrow kitchen. My old-fashioned telephone is mounted on the wall between them. The door on the right stood open and we could see the length of the hallway, all the way to the glass-paned door that separates it from my small foyer.

In silence, I opened the door on the left and preceded Detective Brightwell down a narrow flight of stairs. We had to trek all the way back across the basement to reach the exit he was so curious about, a heavy wooden barrier with a bar across the inside for added security.

Without waiting for my permission, the detective lifted it and went through. He stopped short when he found himself at the foot of a short flight of steps blocked only inches above his head by a solid expanse of metal.

"That's the bottom of the bulkhead in the backyard," I explained. "There's a padlock on the other side."

Did I sound a bit smug? I think I can be forgiven if I did. Clearly, it would have been a waste of money put an alarm on that door.

Brightwell went up a step to give the metal barrier a hard shove, establishing that it had no give at all. He looked faintly apologetic as he turned toward me . . . until he spotted a much less solid door to one side of the steps. He lost no time opening it and poking his head into the small, shelf-lined room beyond.

"That's my root cellar," I said. "It's not currently in use, as you can see. My mother stored her Christmas candles in there and back in the nineteen-fifties my father gave some consideration to converting it into a bomb shelter."

As a youngster, I'd envisioned it as an ideal place to imprison the annoying girl — that would be Ronnie — who bullied me in school. I didn't share that memory with Brightwell. He'd doubtless see it as early evidence of criminal tendencies and decide I was the one who should be locked up.

He didn't say another word until we were back in the living room and I'd resumed my place on the loveseat. This time he sat, too, pulling one of my comfortable armchairs around so that he could face me directly. From his jacket pocket, he retrieved a tiny tape recorder, activated it, identified himself and me, and stated the date and time.

"Ms. Lincoln," he said for the record, "has just shown me the two entrances to her home that are not covered by her security system."

"And it should have been obvious," I interjected, miffed by his attitude, "why they aren't. No one is ever going to get into my house through either one of those doors."

"That's true," he conceded, "but going out through one or the other is another matter. On the night Gregory Onslow was killed, you *could* have left this house and returned without deactivating your security system."

"I could have. I did not."

"When did you first meet the deceased?"

I thought about putting off the rest of this interview until I could contact a lawyer, but I hadn't killed Greg Onslow and I had nothing to hide. I reasoned that delaying the inevitable would only make Detective Brightwell more suspicious of me.

With that thought in mind, I answered his question and a dozen more, leading up to a repetition of my account of the quarrel on the morning of April tenth. I won't go so far as to say that he appeared satisfied by the time he turned off his recorder, but he did leave without arresting me. He didn't even tell me not to leave town.

CHAPTER 12

As luck would have it, my cousin Luke drove past my house just as Detective Brightwell was leaving. He'd put his ancient Vespa in storage for the winter, along with his RV, and purchased a ten-year-old Jeep. It was instantly recognizable because the last owner had painted flame-breathing dragons on both sides. The good detective paused long enough to give the vehicle a hard stare before getting into his cruiser and backing out of the driveway.

Since I wasn't wearing a watch, I started slow-counting. At *twenty-one-one-thousand,* the Jeep reappeared and parked across the street. Given how little time it had taken him to return, my best guess was that Luke had gone only as far as the end of Wede-meyer Terrace before making an illegal U-turn. It was fortunate for him that Bright-well had headed in the other direction.

"Was that cop harassing you?" Luke

demanded as he bounded up my front steps.

"No, he was not, and even if he was, I'm perfectly capable of handling the situation on my own." I gave the paint job on his Jeep a pointed look. "Just because you drive around using dragon power, you needn't feel any compunction to play the knight in shining armor with me."

"C'mon, Mikki. I've got a right to be concerned." He looked away and added in a mumble, "You know I care about you."

"I'm fond of you, too, Luke, but let's not get carried away. Detective Brightwell is just doing his job. He has to talk to everyone who had the slightest reason to wish Greg Onslow ill."

"Boy, have you got that right!"

Something in his tone of voice put me on red alert. "Wait a minute. Did you think he was asking me about *you*? Why would he?"

"Nothing. Never mind. I shouldn't have jumped to conclusions."

I cut short his attempt at retreat by taking a firm grip on his forearm. "Come inside."

Since I used the "teacher" voice I'd perfected over decades of dealing with junior high students, he caved, but he wasn't happy about it. I'd have said he was sulking, except that there was a definite look of panic in his eyes. I steered him into the kitchen and made him take a seat at the dinette table while I pulled two bottles of Sam Adams from the refrigerator and opened them. I didn't bother with glasses.

He eyed the beer I handed him. "It's a little early in the day for a drink, isn't it?"

"It's been that kind of afternoon and it's almost four o'clock. If you have to get back to your clients' tax returns I can make coffee, but you're not leaving until you tell me what's going on."

"The beer's fine." As if to prove it, he took a long swallow. "Yesterday was the fifteenth. The deadline is past. There's more work to do for all the folks who filed for extensions, but the pressure's off. I'm actually taking a little time for myself before I have to go back in and tackle those late returns."

I settled into the chair opposite him. "That's excellent news. Now are you going to spill the beans or do I have to beat the story out of you with a wet noodle?"

My deliberately mixed clichés made him shake his head, but they got a smile out of him. "Okay. Okay. Brightwell has me on his suspect list, too."

"Why you, for heaven's sake? Oh, wait," I interrupted before he could answer. "Because Onslow fired you?"

He picked at the label. "That's part of it."

"This is like pulling teeth. What's the *other* part?"

"I was in the wrong place at the wrong time, that's all." At my impatient "hurry up" gesture, he added, "I was seen near Feldman's at the time of the murder."

"Seen by whom? And how do they know when Onslow was killed?"

"I'm guessing they did an autopsy," Luke said, answering my second question first. "And I don't know who told the cops I was nearby, but it wouldn't exactly take a genius to recognize my Jeep."

I frowned at my as-yet-untouched beer. "Why would just driving past the entrance to Feldman's be suspicious? It's on the main road into town. There's always traffic."

"Not at three in the morning." Luke took another swig.

Narrowing my eyes at him, I pondered that. "You live downtown. You work downtown. You were still on tax deadline, or whatever you call it. What on earth were you doing out there at that hour of the morning?"

"That's exactly what Brightwell wanted to know, and I don't think he believed me when I said I went for a drive to clear my head before turning in for the night." He glanced my way and frowned. "You look like

105

you've got a few doubts yourself, but it's the truth. I haven't been getting a lot of sleep the last couple of weeks. I was wound up. Tired, but not the kind of tired that was going to let me get any rest."

The truth, I thought, *but maybe not the whole truth.* Luke had reduced the label on the beer bottle to a pile of shredded paper.

"What I don't understand is why you didn't tell me about this sooner. Brightwell had already questioned you by the time you came here for supper, hadn't he?"

"I didn't want to worry you," Luke said with such sincerity that I had to believe him. "You had enough on your plate, what with that video of the quarrel you had with Onslow going viral and all."

I stared at him, appalled. "Please tell me you're not serious."

"Well, maybe 'viral' is an exaggeration, but I don't know anyone in town who hasn't seen it."

"This just gets better and better," I muttered. "Well, never mind. Spilt milk and all that. And don't think you can distract me. You still haven't adequately explained why Brightwell took an interest in you. Even in the wee hours, there must have been other people out and about."

"Have you ever been over that way at that

time of the morning?"

"Well, no. To tell you the truth, I prefer not to drive at all after sunset. The glare from headlights bothers me more after dark than it used to. But that's beside the point." I drew in a deep breath. "The important thing for both of us to remember is that neither of us had any reason to want Greg Onslow dead. Ergo, Brightwell is just talking to us so he can eliminate us from consideration."

I expected Luke to agree with me, and possibly make fun of the fact that I'd used a word like *ergo* in conversation. Instead he polished off his beer and stared morosely at the empty bottle for a long, silent stretch before abruptly leaving the table.

"I've got to get going. I need to go home and crash."

He moved faster than I could, and he didn't have to contend with Calpurnia, who chose that moment to try to wind herself around my ankles. By the time I snatched her up and carried her with me to the front door, he was already in his Jeep. With a sense of dismay, I watched him speed away.

Not for a moment did I think my cousin was guilty of murder. What concerned me was my certainty that he'd left out a few details. I could only hope that whatever the big secret was, it wasn't anything that would make Detective Brightwell even more suspicious of him.

CHAPTER 13

The next morning I had another appointment with Sunny. I'd barely entered the lobby of the library before she hustled me out again.

"I thought we were going to finish up what we were working on last week," I objected.

"Later. Right now, we're taking a little field trip. I want to visit the ruins of the hotel." She unlocked her car, tossed her cane into the back seat, and gestured for me to get in on the passenger side.

"Why?" I placed my tote on the floor between my feet and buckled up.

"Why do you think?"

"Nostalgia?" I was truly at a loss.

She started the engine. "Hardly."

"You feel compelled to return to the scene of the crime?"

She scowled at that. "Since the cops aren't sharing information, it strikes me as a good idea to find out more on my own. I figured you'd want to come along. After all, we're both prime suspects in the murder of Greg Onslow."

"You, me, and half the population of Lenape Hollow. And I, for one, could do without knowing all the gory details."

"Are they gory?" she asked.

"That," I said repressively, "was a figure of speech."

A few minutes later, Sunny made the turn onto the grounds of what remained of Feldman's Catskill Resort Hotel. A long, curving driveway led up to a series of four- and five-story ruins. Once upon a time, they'd housed lodgings and entertainment venues.

She glanced my way. "Did you ever come here back in the day?"

I shook my head. "I had no reason to."

"It was something to see. Twenty-five buildings sitting on more than eight hundred acres, like a little city all its own. Feldman's even had its own zip code. There were nearly six hundred guest rooms, but they were only part of the resort. There were two pools, one indoor and one outdoor. Three ski slopes. An ice rink. An airport. A golf course. A shopping arcade with a barbershop and a beauty salon as well as a half dozen specialty stores. A nightclub that could seat over a thousand people. Our shows featured all the best entertainers of the era. Singers. Comics. People came for the singles weekends. Families came for annual reunions. We offered dance lessons, games of Simon Says, and horseback riding, although some of the older guests preferred to play cutthroat mah-jongg or pinochle. And the food! You wouldn't believe the meals we served."

While she waxed nostalgic, covering ground with which I was already familiar thanks to reading the completed chapters of her memoir, we drove past walls covered with graffiti. Not a single window had been left unbroken. The concrete foundations were chipped. Where the siding was wooden, it showed evidence of having been used for target practice. The grounds themselves were so overgrown that without the trails plowed by heavy machinery the side roads would have been impassable.

Several of the original structures had already been demolished. A trio of dump trucks was parked beside a distant pile of rubble, but there was no work going on.

Sunny parked in a likely looking open space and got out of the car.

"I don't see any police tape," I said, following suit.

Deep ruts suggested a great many vehicles had congregated in this spot in recent days, and that one or two had gotten stuck in the mud, but that didn't necessarily mean the body had been found nearby. The road continued on past more decaying buildings.

"It's probably gone," Sunny said, referring to the tape, "but Mongaup Valley Ventures has posted guards to keep unauthorized visitors away from the site."

The growl of an engine broke the morning stillness and startled a half dozen birds into flight. A moment later an SUV with the MVV logo on its side bore down on us and screeched to a halt next to Sunny's car.

A burly young man in his mid-twenties exited the vehicle. The patch on the shoulder of his gray uniform identified him as working for Mongaup Valley Security. I knew from past experience that this was a private firm wholly owned by Mongaup Valley Ventures. Just like a real policeman, this rent-a-cop had all the usual crime deterrents attached to his heavy belt — portable radio, nightstick, pepper spray, Taser, and gun.

I tensed, expecting the first words out of his mouth would be a demand to know what we were doing there. A command to leave seemed sure to follow. To my surprise, although he sent a suspicious look in my direction, he addressed Sunny in a friendly manner.

"Ms. Feldman? Ms. Onslow said you were to look around all you like. I'm just here to make sure you stay safe."

I shot Sunny a look. "You might have mentioned you had permission to explore."

"What? You thought I'd sneak onto the property?" The ghost of a smile played across her lips. "As it happens, young Giselle was perfectly happy to let me take another look at my family's legacy."

"I didn't realize you two were on such friendly terms."

Sunny shrugged. "It didn't hurt that I hinted I might be willing to take this white elephant off her hands. With that happy prospect in mind, she was more than willing to oblige me."

"Seriously? You'd buy it back?"

"Of course not. What kind of fool do you take me for?"

The guard, whose name tag identified him only as "Keller," stood silently by throughout this exchange. If he had any opinion about the fate of the old resort hotel, he kept it to himself. Only when Sunny started walking toward the nearest pile of debris did he react by trotting after her.

113

"You want to be careful, ma'am." He gave her cane a doubtful look. "This ground's pretty uneven. Lots of nails scattered around, too," he added, "and you've got to be on the lookout for snakes."

My steps faltered as I set off in their wake. Maine has snakes, too, but none that are poisonous. New York State is a different story.

"Do you happen to know where Mr. Onslow's body was found?" Sunny asked. "If we have clear directions, that will remove the necessity of tromping all over the site and greatly reduce the possibility one of us will step on a venomous creature."

Or into a nest of vipers, I thought.

Keller snorted. "I guess I do, since I'm the one who found him."

His words knocked my concern about random reptiles to the back of my mind. While I wouldn't have elected to accompany Sunny on this expedition if she'd given me a choice, my curiosity was now fully engaged. Since we were already at the scene of the crime, and we'd had the good fortune to encounter an eyewitness, I was as interested as she was in hearing the details, so long as they weren't too gruesome.

"I take it you were on duty that night?" I asked.

Keller nodded. "There were two of us, like always, but our rounds take us all over the property and it's a big place. Usually it's pretty boring. Once in a while we have to chase off kids trying to sneak into buildings, but that's about it for excitement."

"So where was the body?" Sunny sounded impatient.

"You ladies better get in the SUV. It'll be easier to drive you there than try to walk."

Another look at how overgrown everything was convinced me he was right, although the stench inside his vehicle nearly made me change my mind. Ordinarily, I like the smells of pizza, French fries, and onion rings, but after a few hours, let alone a few days, the odors from takeout bags lose their appeal.

Sunny settled into the back, where there was more room for her cane, while I took the passenger seat. I grabbed hold of the roll bar to augment my seat belt as we set off over the uneven terrain.

It was difficult to carry on a conversation while being jounced about, but I had questions. "It must have been a terrible experience for you," I began.

The sympathy in my voice was genuine. I'd stumbled upon a murder victim myself the previous summer. I could imagine very well how shocked Keller must have been by his discovery, especially when the dead man was his employer.

"He wasn't a pretty sight, I can tell you that."

The SUV hit a pothole and kept going. I winced as my elbow connected with the passenger-side window.

"Where, exactly, was he?" Sunny asked.

"Down in a cellar hole," Keller said. "At first I thought he'd fallen in by accident and maybe cracked his skull open. He was always coming out here at odd hours, poking around and criticizing." Steering around yet another a gigantic pothole, he brought the Jeep to a stop in front of a prodigious pile of rubble. "That was before I got a good look at the bullet hole."

"He was shot?" Up until this point, I hadn't heard *how* he'd died. If I'd thought about that aspect of things at all, I suppose I'd have assumed someone hit him over the head, or maybe stabbed him to death.

"Right in the middle of the forehead." Keller mimed holding a pistol to his brow and pulling the trigger.

My stomach twisted into knots. A part of me didn't want to hear any more. I've never been fond of gratuitous descriptions of violence in mystery novels. On the other hand, this information cast Detective Brightwell's interest in me, a women of a certain age, in a clearer light. *Anyone* can fire a gun.

"Exactly where did you find his body?" Sunny had extricated herself from the back seat unaided. Instead of waiting for us to join her, she made her way to the side of the road, moving slowly only because she was taking such a keen interest in her surroundings.

Keller had parked near an expanse of overgrown grass just starting to turn green. I belatedly recognized it as the remains of a golf course. We were a fair distance from where we'd left Sunny's car and well out of sight of the road that ran past Feldman's and into the village of Lenape Hollow.

"He was down there," Keller said, pointing in the direction of a pile of rocks and dirt. A bulldozer was parked nearby. "A few hours more and he'd never have been found. This hole was scheduled to be back-filled first thing that day."

Sunny and I peered into a pit about six feet deep and of a size to have been the cellar of a small house. Large chunks of stone, probably from the foundation of the building that once occupied the space, lay scattered here and there. Had Onslow fallen

117

onto one, that alone could have caused his death, but that wasn't what had happened. The killer had made certain he didn't survive.

"This was the pro shop," Sunny murmured. Turning to the guard, she asked, "You say this hole was about to be filled in?"

"That was the plan."

"Is there any particular reason you checked this area?" I had a sneaking suspicion that most of the patrolling, especially that done during hours of darkness, was accomplished from the inside of his SUV. It had been cold that night, too. Below freezing.

A faint tinge of pink stained Keller's cheeks. "I, um, got out of the vehicle to stretch my legs."

Translation: He'd had to answer a call of nature.

"And to look around," he added hastily. "Just in general, you know. I'm paid to keep an eye on things."

"Of course," I said in a soothing voice. "Go on."

"Well, um, when my flashlight's beam swept over the area, it picked out a bit that didn't look right. It was his hand, the only part of him that wasn't hidden behind debris. If I hadn't spotted that, no one would ever have known what became of him. Where he was lying, it would have been easy to miss seeing him. They'd have covered him up and everyone would have thought he took off for some place with no extradition treaty so he could live large off the interest from his Swiss bank accounts."

Sunny choked back a laugh. "I can't think of anyone more deserving of an unmarked grave."

As I had been on the day we first heard Onslow was dead, I was taken aback by her callous attitude, but the guard's calm assumption that his boss had been the sort to run off with ill-gotten gains surprised me almost as much. I wanted to ask him what he'd heard about the way Mongaup Valley Ventures did business, but before I could get a word in edgewise, Sunny posed a question of her own.

"You said you weren't the only guard on duty that night. Where was the other guy?"

"We've each got our regular patrol routes. If you're thinking it's funny neither of us heard the shot, that's not at all surprising. Near as I can figure, at the time Mr. Onslow was killed, we were both about as far away from here as we could get and still be on the property."

His radio crackled just then, and he stepped aside to answer it.

I looked at Sunny. "What do you make of all this?"

"Not much, except that we now have an insight into what MVV employees really thought of their boss." She shrugged as she turned away from the site. "I wondered if the location might be significant, but there's nothing special about the pro shop or the golf course."

"Only that this spot is remote," I said. Whoever had lured Onslow here had been familiar with the resort and with the routes the guards took on patrol. He, or she, had chosen a time and place guaranteed to provide all the privacy necessary to get away with murder.

CHAPTER 14

The short drive from the resort to the Lenape Hollow Public Library passed in silence. I wasn't certain how to take Sunny's attitude. I didn't understand why she felt so much animosity toward Greg Onslow. He hadn't been the one who originally bought the hotel grounds from her, and I felt certain she was too smart to have invested in any of his crooked schemes.

"I'll let you out here," Sunny said, pulling into the small parking lot behind the building.

I sent a questioning look her way as I undid my seat belt. "I thought we were going to continue our research."

She just shrugged.

"If you aren't going to do it yourself, then you might think about hiring someone for the job. You have a deadline looming."

"That's still a long way off."

"You need to allow time for me to edit

your draft and then more time for you to revise it."

"Fine." Impatience made her voice sharp. "I'll pay someone to look stuff up."

"Verify facts." I smiled as I corrected her, attempting to soften the implied criticism, but she wasn't looking my way and didn't see my expression. I repressed a sigh. "When do you think you'll have more chapters ready for me?"

"It'll be toward the end of the month."

As diplomatically as possible, I said, "Sooner than that would be better." So far I'd only seen about a third of the book.

"Sorry. No." She glanced at the clock on the dashboard. "I need to get a move on. I have quite a few things left to do before Passover. You wouldn't believe the amount of housecleaning involved, or the dietary requirements, and I've invited a large group of friends to my house for the first seder."

Despite having grown up with a fair number of Jewish friends, I didn't know much about how Passover was celebrated. We'd always had that week off from school, but in my family we'd called it Easter vacation.

During all the years I lived in and taught in Maine, neither Passover nor Easter had been on my radar. Our schools closed for two weeklong "spring" vacations, the first in February, to include Presidents' Day, and the second in April, to incorporate another secular celebration, Patriots' Day, the holiday that honors the midnight ride of Paul Revere on the eighteenth of April in '75. That's 1775, at the start of the American Revolution. Until 1820, Maine was part of Massachusetts. When we broke away to form our own state, we kept the holiday. It was only by some cosmic fluke that in this particular year Easter, the beginning of Passover, and Patriots' Day would all fall during the same week.

Sunny cleared her throat, clearly impatient at my delay in exiting her car. I had to wonder if she was in such a rush only because she had cleaning and cooking to do or also because she was anxious to get away from me and my questions. It must have been obvious to her that our trip to the crime scene had made me curious about her reaction to Onslow's death.

As soon as that thought crossed my mind, I slapped it down, ashamed of myself for doubting her. I had no reason to think Sunny would lie to me. Granted, I was embarrassingly ignorant about Passover customs, but if Sunny was orthodox in her beliefs, it was certainly possible she wasn't supposed to engage in any sort of work for those seven — or was it eight? — days.

I got out of the car, taking my tote bag with me. "I can probably find someone to do the research, if you're willing to pay a little over minimum wage."

"We can talk after the twenty-seventh." The dismissal in her voice was crystal clear.

Never argue with a client, I admonished myself. I shut the passenger-side door and then had to step briskly out of the way to avoid losing a toe.

For about thirty seconds I contemplated going into the library and doing the work myself. I reasoned that it wouldn't take all that long to tie up the most obvious of the loose ends connected to Sunny's memoir.

I reconsidered because I knew it wouldn't be that simple. I'd get sidetracked reading unrelated articles and end up wasting the entire day. Instead, I headed home, where other clients' manuscripts awaited me.

Chapter 15

Detective Brightwell returned the next day for a third round of questions. Having learned that Onslow had been shot, I was not surprised to find him on my doorstep. This time I invited him into the kitchen, waved him toward a seat in the dinette, and provided refreshments. The corn muffins were almost homemade. I'd used a box mix but I'd baked them myself.

He accepted my hospitality but wasted no time getting down to business. "I have a few more questions about your previous conflict with Gregory Onslow." He took out his recorder and went through the usual pre-interview routine, then said, "You told me when we last spoke that you turned down Mr. Onslow's offer to hire you to edit his late wife's book. Is that correct?"

"Yes."

"But you'd already agreed to edit it for her."

"She hired me just before her death. If she'd lived, I would have done what's called a developmental edit, pointing out where the manuscript still needed work. Then it would have been up to her to revise her writing. She might or might not have brought it back to me for a copy edit. That's a read-through to catch typos and continuity errors."

Calpurnia chose that moment to pad into the room. She stopped short at the sight of Detective Brightwell and hissed at him. Having made her opinion clear, she did an abrupt about-face and stalked out again, tail held high. I thought it politic to hide my smile.

"Why weren't you willing to do the same job for her husband?" Brightwell asked.

"Because it *wasn't* the same job. Tiffany's novel would never have sold to a publisher without extensive rewriting and she was no longer around to do the work. Onslow needed to hire a ghostwriter, not an editor. That's not a service I offer."

I wasn't certain the detective understood the distinction. I was about to elaborate when he threw me a curve.

"According to others I've spoken to, Mr. Onslow was the one who refused to let you

continue work on his late wife's manuscript."

"If he said that, he was lying." *Typical,* I
thought. Greg Onslow had only a nodding
acquaintance with the truth.

"Can you prove it?" Brightwell asked.

"I don't suppose I can." I frowned at him.
"Unlike you, I don't record my conversations. May I ask to whom he made that
claim?"

The tiniest flicker of amusement came and
went in his eyes. Correct grammar has a
tendency to produce that response. Or
perhaps it was my tone of voice that tickled
his funny bone. Offended by Onslow's
dishonesty, I may have sounded just the
teeniest bit imperious. Unfortunately, to
properly put on the airs of a grand dame
one really needs to be sipping tea from a
delicate china cup. I was drinking my coffee
out of a *Star Wars* mug, a Christmas present from my great-niece.

"Three separate individuals shared that
information with me," Brightwell said as he
reached for his muffin. "Onslow's widow,
his personal secretary at the time of his first
wife's death, and his vice president all said
they were told the same thing."

"The vice president — that would be
Ariadne Toothaker?"

He nodded, his mouth full. He chewed and swallowed. "Do you know her?"

"Only slightly, but she didn't much like me the one time we met."

"Does she dislike you enough to make up a story that might implicate you in a murder?"

"I can't imagine that she does, although she was a witness to my quarrel with her boss. The one in the video clip."

"So she told me. What about Mrs. Onslow? The second one. Do you know her?"

"We've never met, and I'd just like to point out that having my spat with Onslow become public knowledge has turned me into an ideal scapegoat. Anyone who wants to shift attention away from his or her own guilt probably thinks it's a good idea to stir up trouble for me."

I didn't go so far as to suggest that he take a harder look at Giselle Onslow. He hardly needed me to tell him that the victim's spouse is always a likely suspect in a murder case. Giselle stood to gain as Onslow's heir. As his wife, she undoubtedly had access to the Mongaup Valley Security schedule. She'd have known what route the guards followed on their rounds and how to avoid being caught by them when she bumped off her husband.

Brightwell's expression gave nothing away. I couldn't tell if he believed me or not. He took a few more bites of his muffin followed by a long swallow of coffee.

"Was there a hefty commission associated with that ghostwriting job?" he asked.

Now it was my turn to make use of food to give myself time to think. I polished off my muffin before I spoke.

"I'm not trying to make my fortune with this job, Detective, just pay for a few extras my retirement income doesn't cover. I can afford to turn down work I don't want to do, and that's what I did. I have no idea why Mr. Onslow told a different story. Maybe he just wanted to shift the blame for his own inaction to someone else. As far as I know, he never made any further attempt to get Tiffany's novel published."

"Perhaps he didn't like you much, either."

"Oh, I'm certain the feeling was mutual. On the other hand, he was the one, last summer, who lobbied for me to edit the script for our quasquibicentennial pageant. That would seem to contradict the idea that he didn't think I was qualified to work on Tiffany's book."

"Can anyone verify that recommendation?"

"Try the entire board of directors of the

local historical society. I think you already know Sunny Feldman, Ronnie North, and Darlene Uberman." Seeing the wince he tried to hide, I added the names of two board members who, as far I knew, *hadn't* had a grudge against Greg Onslow.

Throughout the interview, Brightwell had jotted down the occasional thought in a small, spiral-bound notebook, no doubt as backup to the recording. When he flipped it closed, I assumed his questions were at an end, but I let myself relax too soon.

"Do you own a gun, Ms. Lincoln?"

"Definitely not. I hate guns and so did my late husband. He wouldn't have one in the house." Remembering that I wasn't supposed to know Onslow had been shot to death, I affected curiosity. "Is that how he was killed? There hasn't been anything about the murder weapon on the news."

His eyes narrowed. "I think you already know the answer to that, Ms. Lincoln."

"I *was* told he was shot," I admitted. "Then again, I also heard he was stabbed, bludgeoned, and strangled, and those are just the suggestions people voiced in church last Sunday."

Now that I thought about it, I realized that Clarice Cameron had advanced a theory that turned out to be very close to the truth.

A lucky guess? I found myself wondering, absurd as the notion seemed, if the pastor's wife could have had a reason to kill Greg Onslow.

After warning me that he might have more questions at a later date, Detective Brightwell left. I closed the door behind him, still thinking about Clarice. I didn't know that she'd ever met Onslow, but what if she had? What motive might she have had to murder him?

I had no intention of meddling in an official investigation. This third interview, however, and the possibility there could be another, had convinced me I needed to take my status as a suspect more seriously. I began to think about all the other people who'd been at odds with the victim and wondered if I should talk to some of them myself. I knew I had one advantage over Detective Brightwell when it came to asking questions. I didn't have to limit myself to formal interviews. Whether an encounter with a suspect took the form of a casual conversation or a confrontation, interesting tidbits of information were sure to emerge.

CHAPTER 16

I started my investigation by driving to Darlene's house. Frank was just leaving, golf bag slung over one shoulder.

"Isn't the ground a little soft for that?" I asked. It had rained again overnight.

"That just makes it more of a challenge to play a few rounds," he assured me with a smile. "Darlene's on the back porch."

I joined her there and settled into a second wooden rocking chair. Although I'd seen a few people out and about in shorts, I left my sweater on. It was enough to be able to be outside without gloves and a hat. While we watched Simon race around the backyard, I filled Darlene in on my most recent interviews with Detective Brightwell and the field trip Sunny and I had taken to the scene of the crime.

"All that made me think that if I can find a way to talk to other people at odds with Greg Onslow, I might pick up on something the police have overlooked."

Darlene listened without comment, but by the time I stopped talking she was frowning. "You really should stay out of it. You know that, right?"

"I'm not going to interfere, but I can't help but wonder who killed him. Don't tell me you haven't thought about that, too."

"Not to the point of making a list of possible murderers, but I'll bet *you* have."

"Maybe." I hadn't written anything down, but Darlene knew me well enough to guess that I'd compiled one in my head. Suspect everyone — wasn't that the rule of thumb for detectives, both amateur and professional, in all the best crime novels?

Simon joined us on the porch, tongue lolling and a look of adoration in his big brown eyes. Darlene stroked his head while I stared into space, barely seeing the low hedge that separates Darlene and Frank's lawn from their next-door neighbor's yard.

"So," Darlene prompted, "are you going to keep me in suspense?"

I repressed a smile but I couldn't contain a little flutter of pleasure at her question. I'd been right. She was as curious as I was. Well, why not? Wanting answers is a normal human reaction when one is plunged into the middle of a mystery.

"It will take less time to name the people I've already ruled out."

"You, me, and Frank, I assume?"

"Yes. And probably Clarice."

"Clarice Cameron?" The look she gave me suggested I'd taken leave of my senses. "Why on earth would you think she's capable of murder? She's as upright and uptight as they come."

"Remember what she said in church? About the body being dumped in a cellar hole? How did she know that?"

Simon left Darlene's side and trotted over to plop his head into my lap. I tickled him behind one silky ear while I waited for Darlene to come up with an answer. Craving more attention, the pooch flopped himself down and rolled over, offering up his tummy for a rub. Naturally, I obliged.

"I'm sure she was just speculating," Darlene said.

I let the doubtful note in her voice pass without comment. "You're probably right. After all, what would her motive be?"

"Well . . ."

My attention sharpened. I stopped tickling Simon's belly and sat up straighter. "Are you kidding me?"

"Remember how, when Tiffany died, her funeral was held in the church?"

I nodded. I'd been there. That sad occasion was the first time I set eyes on Greg Onslow.

"Onslow *said* he was going to make a monetary donation to the food pantry in his late wife's memory. He was even specific about the amount — five thousand dollars — but he never followed through. Clarice was livid. She'd gone ahead and made several pricey purchases on the strength of his promise."

"Ouch. Was she able to find the money elsewhere?"

"Ronnie came through for her. Since Tiffany was her granddaughter, I suppose she felt obligated."

I gave a low whistle. "Ronnie's on my list."

"Of course she is. She never forgave Onslow for making Tiffany so miserable or for trying to open a theme park on the property next door to her house. And don't forget that she took him to court over Tiffany's shares in Mongaup Valley Ventures."

"Did they ever sort out which of Tiffany's wills was the real one?" There had been two, one leaving everything to her husband and the other naming her grandmother as her heir.

"I've never heard. That's odd, now that I think about it. Do you suppose the case was settled out of court?"

"If Ronnie lost, that would give her one more reason to hate Greg Onslow."

"Hate, yes. But kill? Can you *really* imagine it, Mikki? For one thing, why on earth would Onslow agree to meet Ronnie in the middle of the night at the demolition site? And can you picture Ronnie with a gun?" She held up a hand to stop me from answering while, frowning, she attempted to visualize the scene. "How did his body get into that cellar hole? Was he standing on the edge when he was shot, so that he fell in, or did someone drag his body over to the pit and toss him into it after he was dead?"

I stopped the gentle back and forth of the rocker, wondering why that question had never occurred to me. Yes, anyone can fire a gun, but it requires a certain amount of physical strength to move a dead body.

"The security guard said he was hidden behind some rubble. I don't think he could have fallen into that spot on his own. Well, that narrows the field. We're looking for someone younger and stronger than Ronnie."

"And for someone more mobile than I am." Darlene chuckled. "Will wonders never cease? I guess I should be grateful that I'm so old and decrepit."

I barely heard her. At the words "younger and stronger," Luke's face had popped into my mind. I pushed it right back out again.

"I certainly couldn't schlep Onslow very far, either," I said.

Darlene's brow wrinkled in concentration. "Frank can swing a golf club, but he's not particularly strong otherwise, and Clarice may have a heck of a grip when she buttonholes you, but she's even older than we are. And skinnier. Onslow was . . . bulky."

"We must be missing something," I said. "Detective Brightwell clearly hasn't ruled me out. What does he know that we don't?"

"Maybe he's factoring in a rush of adrenaline. Or he thinks the killer could have had an accomplice."

"Then everyone we've just eliminated has to go back on the list of suspects, and I'm adding Sunny, too."

"Oh, please — she's what? Eighty-five?"

"Eighty-six, but age hasn't slowed her down much. I wish I had her stamina. Besides, like Ronnie, she can afford to hire muscle."

"There's still the problem of the murder having taken place when it did," Darlene reminded me. "Why would Onslow agree to meet anyone at that hour?"

I'd started to rock back and forth again,

finding the steady rhythm conducive to thought. Beside my chair, Simon snored softly. "Maybe it's the location that's significant for some reason. I need to talk to Sunny again, but I don't suppose that's going to happen anytime soon."

"Why not?"

"Passover."

Darlene frowned. "Passover hasn't started yet."

I shrugged. "Sunny told me she had preparations to make, and then she said she wouldn't be able to do any more work on her book until after the twenty-seventh. Is writing on the forbidden list or something?"

"That would depend on how religious she is."

I made a mental note to do some research on Passover before I saw Sunny again, if only to prevent myself from making some ignorant remark in her presence.

"Let's move on to other suspects," I suggested, "like the three women who steered Brightwell back to me by repeating Onslow's story that he was the one who nixed my opportunity to ghostwrite Tiffany's book. I hate knowing that he lied about me."

"He was a thoroughly despicable human being," Darlene said. "Who did Brightwell talk to?"

"Giselle Onslow, Ariadne Toothaker, and Onslow's private secretary at the time. That would have been a young woman named Jenni Farquhar. I met her the same day Ms. Toothaker interviewed me for a job. Jenni didn't strike me as the brightest bulb. For one thing, she really seemed to believe she was in the running to become wife number two. I suppose she could have wanted revenge after Giselle scooped the pot, but if so, she chose a peculiar way to get it. Too complicated, for one thing."

"Still, it might be worthwhile to talk to her, and I agree that the other two belong on the list of suspects, especially Giselle. Can you think of anyone else?"

"Legions, I imagine, if we consider how many people Onslow swindled over the years."

I should have mentioned Luke, but I deliberately withheld his name. If I told Darlene he'd been questioned by the police and that I'd thought he was keeping something back when he admitted as much to me, she'd push me to find out what he was hiding. I rationalized my omission by telling myself his secret was most likely something entirely benign.

"I'll see what I can find out about the three of them online," Darlene offered, "but it might also be a good idea for you to meet Giselle face-to-face."

"Would she agree? She has no reason to do me any favors."

"She doesn't have to. I know where she'll be next Monday. She's a member of the Friends of the Library. Our annual business meeting is scheduled for that evening."

"She may not attend, given that she's a new widow."

"She has to be there. She's our treasurer." Darlene rocked contentedly, a smug expression on her face.

"Okay. Let's say she shows up. What excuse do I have for being there? I'm not a member."

"It's easy enough for you to join and I'm sure you can find some innocent reason to speak with her and get her talking. You're a good listener. Given a sympathetic ear, who knows what she might say?"

"I think you're being overly optimistic," I said, "but if I don't manage to cross paths with Giselle Onslow on my own between now and then, I'll give your plan a try."

CHAPTER 17

Two days later, at nine on a gloomy, overcast Saturday morning with thundershowers in the forecast, I was at home trying to work on a short story sent to me by a new client when I was struck by a wave of nostalgia. For once, this was not prompted by a memory of growing up in Lenape Hollow, but rather by the realization that it was the third Saturday in April and for the second year in a row I was going to miss seeing the Kenduskeag Stream Canoe Race on TV.

James and I didn't live close enough to Bangor to attend in person, and we had never been tempted to participate, but it had been one of our annual traditions to watch the race from the comfort of our living room. The last time had been shortly before his death.

It's a little hard to explain the fascination of seeing canoes and kayaks wipe out in the rapids at Six Mile Falls. The crowds lining the banks at that point in the race are called *river vultures.* There are rescue crews there as well. Everyone who falls in is quickly pulled out again. For many years, another of the highlights was watching a retired librarian in a white tuxedo go over the falls while standing up in his canoe. He always made it safely through.

Yes, I know. It's a silly thing about which to have regrets, but knowing I'd miss this annual rite of spring made me long for the family I'd left behind. The upshot was that I made a phone call to James's younger sister Allie, who still lives in rural Maine.

After we'd exchanged the usual pleasantries, she brought me up-to-date on what her two children and their three youngsters were up to. Susan, although older by two years than her brother Nick, had married and had children later, so her Josie and Patrick are a decade younger than his boy, Bradley.

"Brad spent the last week looking at colleges," Allie announced.

"Stop making me feel old! I remember when he was born. Heck, I remember when his father was born."

"He's sixteen and he already knows he wants to be a doctor."

"Good for him."

I was wondering how to ask if he'd need financial help — I'm not wealthy, but since I don't have children of my own, Allie's descendants are my heirs — when my sister-in-law let out a yelp.

"My goodness, will you look at the time. The race is about to start! Rob, turn on the TV."

My sigh must have been clearly audible. During the short silence on the other end of the line, I could hear the announcer in the background as he reported on the fact that the end point of the race would be north of downtown Bangor this year. The paddlers wouldn't have enough clearance to go under the last bridge before the usual finish line. Depending on how much snow there had been during the winter, when spring thaw had begun, and recent rainfall amounts, conditions could vary a great deal. The previous night's full "pink" moon had apparently influenced the high water level, as well. The Penobscot River, into which Kenduskeag Stream flows at Bangor, is tidal that far upstream.

"You know, Mikki," Allie said, "you can watch the race online. Just go to WABI's website. They always stream it live."

I don't know why that had never occurred to me. I use the Internet all the time. Just the previous day, I'd spent an hour looking up Passover traditions.

I lost no time saying good-bye to Allie and reaching for my laptop. Sure enough, there it was. I spent the rest of the morning happily curled up on the loveseat with the cat, watching spills and rescues to my heart's content.

CHAPTER 18

All dressed up in a sky-blue skirt with a matching jacket and a pale blue blouse with a pussy bow, I drove to the First Presbyterian Church of Lenape Hollow the next day for Easter Sunday services. I'd topped off the outfit with a plain but pretty beige hat with a brim, one I'd bought at a gift shop on the coast of Maine several summers earlier but had rarely had occasion to wear. For the second week in a row I was prepared to sit through one of Pastor Cameron's boring sermons.

That was something of a record for me as an adult, although when I was growing up in Lenape Hollow, I rarely missed Sunday school or church. That pattern changed when I went away to college in the sixties. Later I fell in love with a man who'd had no religious upbringing at all. We were married in our nondenominational college chapel, and the only time we set foot in a

145

church after that was to attend weddings or funerals. I suppose I might have begun attending the church of my childhood on a regular basis after my return, if only for the social contact, had Clarice Cameron not tried so hard to herd me back into the fold.

Darlene noticed the way I was dressed as soon as I got out of my car in the parking lot behind the church. She hit the lock button on her key fob, angled her walker toward the paved path that led to the front of the church, and said, "Lose the hat."

"But it's Easter," I protested, "and I *like* hats."

"Do you see anyone else wearing one?"

I had to concede her point. Most of the other women heading toward morning worship were not only hatless, they were decidedly casual in their choice of attire. Ronnie North was the only one I could see who was wearing a dress, a brilliantly flowered wraparound that screamed both "vintage" and "designer original."

With a sigh, I plucked the hat off my head and tossed it into the back seat of my car. I was tempted to make a quick return trip to the house and trade the clothes I was wearing for slacks and a blazer. My skirt was a trifle snug, since it dated from my pre-retirement days, and the pantyhose I'd put on that morning felt downright alien. Thank goodness I hadn't gone completely crazy and worn heels. My feet were happy in beige flats that matched the small clutch I carried in one hand.

Suck it up, I told myself. *In a little over an hour you'll be home and back in jeans and a sweatshirt.* In my job as a work-at-home freelance editor, I never have to dress up.

Since it was Easter, there were more people in church than usual. Most of them were in a sociable mood, and I was feeling quite cheerful by the time I took my place in a pew. The hymns were uplifting. The choir was in good voice. I had every intention of paying attention to the sermon until Pastor Cameron began to speak.

Five minutes into his long-winded oration, delivered in a droning voice, my mind began to wander. My thoughts drifted to his wife. Had Clarice simply been speculating the week before, or did she actually know something about Greg Onslow's death?

After the final benediction, as the congregation began to inch its way toward the back of the church to shake the minister's hand, the object of my interest saved me the trouble of looking for her. She was impossible to miss as she bore down on me. The glaring yellow of her Easter outfit, a simple A-line dress trimmed with a white ruffle at the throat, had me squinting against the brightness.

"Just the person I wanted to see!" The determined look in her eyes made me wish I could turn tail and run.

"Which one of us?" Darlene had opened her walker, but she had to wait for a path to the aisle to clear before she could make her escape.

"Why, Mikki, of course. You already do much too much for the church, Darlene. I worry sometimes that you overextend yourself."

Behind Clarice's back, I made a face and mouthed "teacher's pet." I had to take a hasty step back when the minister's wife abruptly turned her laser-like gaze on me.

Hold your ground, I reminded myself. *You want to talk to her.* This was the best chance I was going to get to question her about the murder.

"You taught junior high school." It was a declaration, not a question.

I gave a cautious nod. My former occupation wasn't a secret, but I'd retired years ago.

"The church needs your particular skills."

"Do you have grammar that needs to be

corrected?"

I risked a glance at the departing parishioners and saw an opening. The cowardly thought that I could abandon Darlene and make a run for it crossed my mind. I quickly squashed it. It was too late anyway. Clarice moved sideways, blocking my exit.

"Oh, you're such a kidder!" she said. "No, Mikki, we need someone to help out with our youth program. The group meets one evening a week. They're perfectly lovely but, well, they're *teen*agers. They're a bit much for one person to handle. It would be such a blessing to have an individual with your experience assisting Pastor Cameron."

I couldn't think of anything I'd like less, except possibly being incarcerated for a crime I hadn't committed. Teaching had been a fulfilling career, but I'd been more than ready to leave the classroom when I hit sixty-five. These days the only teens whose company I enjoy are my great-niece and two great-nephews.

"I'm sorry, Clarice, but I'm not as young as I used to be. Riding herd on young people requires way too much energy."

From behind me I heard a poorly muffled snort. Darlene managed to turn it into a cough.

"Piffle," Clarice said. "You're younger

than I am."

But not as dedicated, I thought. Aloud, I changed that sentiment to, "I'm hardly the best role model. It isn't as if I'm in church every Sunday."

"You'll do better in the future, I'm sure. There are homemade refreshments after every meeting," she added, as if that might entice me to change my mind.

I shook my head. "I'm sure the snacks are delightful, but I can remember what youth fellowship was like when I was in my teens. We weren't bad kids, but we were rowdy."

In other words, we'd been normal teenagers with little else on our minds besides fantasies involving the opposite sex.

"We threw the best dance parties in town," Darlene said with a reminiscent smile.

They had been well attended, but that was mostly because our church has a nice big meeting hall attached to it. It was one of the few places, back in the day, where more than a few dozen people could congregate at the same time.

Clarice was undeterred by my lack of enthusiasm. She waxed positively poetic about the sterling qualities of the current crop of young people, which seemed to beg the question of why the minister needed

help controlling them. I watched parishioners trudge past the row of stained-glass
windows toward the exit, all the while growing more and more desperate to join the
exodus.

*Get her off this topic and onto how Onslow
was killed,* I reminded myself. Accordingly,
I lowered my voice to a conspiratorial whisper.

"Things are a little unsettled right now,
Clarice, if you know what I mean."

It took her a moment to catch on. When
she did, her eyes widened. "Oh, you mean
the *murder*?"

"I'm afraid so. I'm sure you've seen that
video, the one in which I made such a
dreadful fool of myself."

"Well, I —"

"I'm beginning to wonder if there's anyone who *hasn't* seen it."

"Well, yes. It's . . . it must be terribly
embarrassing for you."

"Oh, it is. Believe me. And because of it,
the police have been asking me a lot of
questions. This isn't a good time for me to
make commitments." Before she could
argue, I rushed on. "Of course, I had nothing to do with Greg Onslow's death. I'm
the picture of a law-abiding citizen, just as
you are. I'm sure you remember that I was

able to be of some small assistance to the local police in the past."

Clarice Cameron has the memory of an elephant. She drew in a sharp breath. I could almost see the gears shifting as she underwent the transformation from recruiter to sympathetic listener.

"Oh, my dear, you must be careful. On those other occasions, you put yourself in terrible danger. You were lucky to escape with your life."

"I'm sure no one wants to harm me, Clarice, but I am in an awkward position so long as the murder goes unsolved. You must know exactly what that feels like. Didn't the police want to know why you were so certain that the body would be found half-hidden in a cellar hole?"

Once again, I heard a muffled snicker.

"I wasn't certain of any such thing!" Indignant, Clarice tried to back away, but Darlene's walker was in her way.

"I'm sure I heard you say so just last week."

"I was only speculating."

"Did you know Onslow?"

"No."

"You never met him?" I let her hear my skepticism.

A pink stain spread from her neck into

her face. "Well, only the once, at his first wife's funeral. He never had anything to do with the church after that."

"You didn't contact him about the food pantry?"

Clarice directed an accusatory look at Darlene before she answered me. "I was never able to get through to him by phone and my emails and letters went unanswered. And for your information, the police have *not* questioned me. Only someone with a nasty, suspicious mind would expect them to."

I rested my hand briefly on one of her bony shoulders. "I'm relieved to hear it. I wouldn't wish a police interrogation on anyone."

With that parting shot, I slipped out of the pew and followed Darlene down an aisle now empty of parishioners. She can make excellent speed using her walker when she wants to. She didn't slow down until we reached the parking lot. By then we were giggling like a couple of schoolgirls.

"That was very bad of you," she said when she had control of herself again.

"I know, but I wanted to be certain she didn't kill him. Now I am."

"I did that research we talked about," Darlene said as she got into her van.

"What did you find?"

She closed the door and lowered her window. The parking lot had emptied rapidly. We could continue our conversation without fear of being overheard.

"Nothing all that helpful, and I ran into a roadblock when I tried to look into Giselle's history before she came to Lenape Hollow. The piece in the paper about her wedding to Greg Onslow gave her name as Giselle Wyncoop, but Wyncoop isn't her maiden name. It was the second marriage for both of them."

"Where did she live before she moved here?"

"I don't know. The article didn't say."

"Can you check vital records?" I asked. "Don't you have to put your maiden name and place of birth on a marriage license?"

"I'm not sure just anyone can request a copy, but I'll see what I can find out."

"What did you learn about Ariadne Toothaker? She's low on my list of suspects, but I've been told she and Onslow clashed repeatedly over work issues."

"I had better luck finding information on her. Her bio at the Mongaup Valley Ventures website says she was originally from Danvers, Idaho, and that she worked for several different corporations before she was hired as director of personnel at MVV."

"Danvers? Why does that sound familiar?"

"It turned up when we were digging for dirt on Onslow after Tiffany died. Danvers is the town he lived in before he moved to Lenape Hollow. He ran his usual scam there, cashed in, and got out before the company he persuaded people to invest in had to declare bankruptcy."

I perked up at that news. "Was Ariadne bilked?"

"It doesn't appear so, but she could have met Onslow while he was still living there. A few months before he moved on, she took a leave of absence from her job in Chicago to settle her father's estate, and it wasn't long after Onslow set up shop in Lenape Hollow that she took the job as head of personnel. Now she's a vice president. She strikes me as being eminently qualified for that position, and I couldn't find anything to suggest that butting heads with her boss over company business gave her a reason to bump him off. Other people have much better motives."

I was glad to be able to rule someone out. "Will you keep digging?"

Darlene grinned at me as she started the engine. "Count on it."

CHAPTER 19

As Darlene had predicted, Giselle Onslow showed up at the Friends of the Library meeting on Monday evening. I'd never seen her close up before and studied her with intense interest as she read the treasurer's report in a low-pitched, pleasant voice. Despite being so soft-spoken, her enunciation was perfect and I had no trouble understanding her. I didn't even have to turn up my hearing aids.

First, second, and third impressions were all identical — she looked like a fashion model with her tall, slender build and the kind of face a camera loves. Large, clear blue eyes were set in a perfect oval and topped by extraordinarily long lashes. She had perfectly regular features. Her hair was long and ebony-colored. Simply describing it as black would never do it justice.

I admit I looked for flaws. Eventually I found a small one. The pinkie on her left hand looked like it had once been broken. It stuck out a bit from the other fingers on that hand. I smiled to myself at the thought that in an earlier, less-enlightened age superstitious people might have labeled that a "witch's mark."

"Not exactly the picture of a grief-stricken widow, is she?" whispered a woman seated behind me. I didn't recognize her voice.

Pam Ingram answered her. "She's had practice. This is the second time she's had a rich husband die on her."

The undertone of venom surprised me, but I didn't give it much thought because the vote to accept the treasurer's report was immediately followed by the introduction of new members. I was one of two. Both of us were promptly conscripted for committees.

The meeting concluded with a period of socializing. The Friends of the Library was a varied group. Darlene and I were at the upper end of the age range. The majority of the members were closer to Pam's years, somewhere in their early to mid-thirties.

After sampling a few of the cookies set out along with coffee, tea, and a bowl of punch, Darlene volunteered to clear a path through the milling attendees to Giselle. Since the weather lately kept snapping back and forth between warm and partly sunny days and periods of pouring rain, her arthritic knee and ankle joints had gone into a meltdown, forcing her to use her scooter. She caught Giselle's attention by tooting the horn at her.

I was uncertain how Giselle would react when Darlene introduced us. She had to have heard about the quarrel I had with her late husband at the gas station and she'd probably recognize my name, if not my face. She blindsided me by apologizing.

"I'm so sorry Gregory was rude to you, Ms. Lincoln."

"Call me Mikki, please."

With a tiny nod, she agreed to the request. "My husband was under a lot of stress during the last week of his life. I'm afraid he took it out on you."

If she was aware that I was a suspect in his murder, she gave no sign of it. I couldn't read a thing in her facial expression. Even her eyes remained neutral.

"I should have done a better job of hanging on to my temper, too," I said, coming as close to expressing my regret as I could manage. I forced a smile. "If you don't mind my asking, was there something in particular that was troubling him?"

"Oh, you know how it is when you're a successful entrepreneur. There's *always* a

158

crisis brewing." She dismissed the subject with a casual wave of one hand.

"He seemed particularly upset that Sunny Feldman was writing a memoir."

"I suppose so. I don't know why. Gregory didn't talk to me about business."

"Really?" Darlene interrupted. "I thought you were his private secretary before your marriage."

Giselle's laugh, like the rest of her, was quietly sexy. Not all that many men belong to the Friends of the Library, but every one of their heads turned our way at the sound. The testosterone level in the room shot through the roof.

"I stopped working after the wedding."

Out of the corner of my eye, I saw Pam Ingram hovering nearby. The librarian was careful to keep her distance, but it was obvious she was interested in our conversation. Reminded of her reaction at the gas station, when she'd applauded my put-down of Greg Onslow, I wondered what her history had been with Mongaup Valley Ventures. Had she, like so many others, been conned out of her hard-earned money? Did she blame Giselle as well as Giselle's late husband?

"Not to be tactless," Darlene said, drawing my full attention back to the widow, "but won't you have to take charge of the company now that he's gone?"

"How perceptive of you. Since Gregory left everything he had to me, I now own a controlling interest in MVV." Her cat-that-ate-the-canary smile spoke volumes. She intended to take over, all right, and she'd enjoy being the CEO.

"Will the demolition of Feldman's go forward?" I asked.

"It's too soon to say. Mongaup Valley Ventures is involved in a number of different projects. In addition, there will have to be a few personnel changes." She looked positively smug when she added that last part, making me wonder if Ariadne Toothaker's head was about to go on the chopping block.

"Who is your director of personnel?" I asked, ingenuously. "I understand Ms. Toothaker was promoted."

That struck a nerve. Giselle's expression hardened and so did her voice.

"Gregory may have made her his vice president, but he soon regretted it. That dreadful woman disagreed with him about almost everything he wanted to do."

So much for Giselle not knowing what was going on at MVV after her marriage. She'd taken an interest all right.

A sip of punch from the cup she'd been holding seemed to restore her equilibrium. Before either Darlene or I could pose any more intrusive questions, she narrowed her eyes at me and asked one of her own.

"You're the woman they call the book doctor, aren't you?"

"I'm a freelance editor," I corrected her. "I dislike the term 'book doctor,' but for most people it's convenient shorthand to sum up what I do." I took a swallow of the coffee I'd clung to throughout our conversation and repressed a grimace when I realized it had gone cold.

"I understand you worked for Gregory's first wife."

I nodded, wondering where she was going with this topic. After all, Giselle was one of the three women who'd told Detective Brightwell that Onslow claimed he'd fired me after Tiffany's death. If Giselle had believed him, she couldn't have a very high opinion of my professional abilities.

"There is a short-term proofreading job coming up at Mongaup Valley Ventures," she said. "I wonder if you'd be interested in applying for it?"

"I'm a little surprised you'd consider me." That was putting it mildly!

"Perhaps I'm trying to make up for how

badly my husband treated you. It was unfair of him to refuse to let you finish editing Tiffany's book."

"I might consider working for you, but not as long as you continue to labor under a misapprehension. Your husband wanted to hire me as a ghostwriter for his first wife's novel. I turned *him* down."

She gave a graceful shrug of her shapely shoulders. "Perhaps I misunderstood what I was told. Tiffany died some time before I moved to Lenape Hollow."

"What brought you here in the first place?" Darlene asked.

Giselle smiled down at her. "Oh, I just wanted a change from the city."

To anyone living in Sullivan County, the City is only and always New York, but I wasn't sure Giselle knew that. I'd just opened my mouth to ask her for confirmation when we were interrupted by a man I recognized as the principal of the elementary school. He whisked Giselle away, claiming he needed to talk to her about the library's finances.

"Maybe that's what they're discussing and maybe not," Darlene murmured, watching the two of them with eagle eyes.

"She *is* the treasurer."

"And he's recently divorced. Can you

blame me for thinking he may have a more personal reason to monopolize the merry widow?"

"I wish he'd waited a few more minutes. I was hoping to find a subtle way to ask her why her husband would go to the demolition site in the middle of the night."

"Just as well you didn't get the chance. She might have reconsidered that offer of a job." She aimed her scooter toward the exit and I followed her out.

"You're probably right," I conceded.

"Are you going to apply for that proofreading gig?"

"I think I should, don't you?" As it had on a previous occasion, an interview at MVV would give me an excuse to snoop around inside the company's headquarters.

CHAPTER 20

I'd visited Mongaup Valley Ventures only once before. It's housed in what, fifty years ago, was a discount superstore that sold surplus goods and fire-sale items. I spared a glance for the bright red letters, ten feet tall, on the sign on top of the flat roof. One thing was certain — no one would ever have to guess who occupied the building.

The receptionist was a stranger to me, although I recognized her type. Every woman I'd seen working as a classified employee at MVV was blessed with a pretty face and a shapely body. There were blondes, brunettes, and redheads, but neither their physical nor intellectual attributes displayed much variety.

A phone call first thing Tuesday morning to Matthew Donnelly, the current head of personnel, established that Giselle had already spoken to him about me. I had just time enough before being ushered into his office to ask a few questions of his secretary and discover that he was a new hire himself. Since Donnelly didn't strike me as the type to listen to gossip, let alone repeat it, I didn't try to wheedle information out of him. Brusque and businesslike in a three-piece, pinstriped suit, he looked over my résumé, asked a few questions, and then informed me that I appeared to be more than qualified to take on the job of proof-reading MVV's new employee manual, mission statement, annual report, and brochures.

"They're all being redone?" I asked.

"Ms. Onslow insisted."

I got the distinct impression that Ms. Onslow had also insisted he hire me. That seemed a tad peculiar, given that she and I had only just met, but perhaps Greg Onslow's widow really was trying to make up for her late husband's bad behavior.

"Some of the material is unchanged," Donnelly continued, "but the rest reflects Ms. Onslow's new initiatives. She is anxious to implement certain changes as quickly as possible. And, obviously, her name will now replace her husband's on all the paperwork."

"Have there been any other personnel changes?" I asked, remembering Giselle's words the previous evening.

165

My question had his face pruning up. "None to speak of."

He didn't elaborate.

When we'd settled on a deadline for completion of the job and I'd filled in the requisite paperwork, I rose to leave. The project would give my income a nice boost, but so far I hadn't managed to advance my real agenda in visiting Mongaup Valley Ventures.

"I'll see you out," Donnelly said.

That was the last thing I wanted. "Please don't trouble yourself. I know the way. And I need to make a brief stop in the nearest restroom before I leave." I flashed a smile. "I really must cut back on the coffee."

Looking ever so slightly embarrassed, he walked me as far as the outer office and pointed the way to the ladies' room.

A few minutes later, I was back in reception, prepared to take the bull by the horns. I asked where I could find Ariadne Toothaker.

To reach her office, I had to pass the one Greg Onslow once occupied. Now it belonged to Giselle. Since I didn't want her to know I was talking to her VP, I walked rapidly past that door. I needn't have bothered. Both the outer and inner offices were dark. At ten o'clock in the morning, the new CEO of MVV had yet to make her appearance.

Ariadne's name and the title EXECUTIVE VICE PRESIDENT were etched on the glass panel of the door to another of MVV's suites. Her secretary was middle-aged and male. Within minutes of giving my name and asking to see his boss, I was shown into the inner sanctum.

Unlike the majority of MVV's female employees, Ariadne Toothaker was in her fifties. Tall and a little on the heavy side, she wore a bright red dress-for-success pantsuit and sat behind a desk clear of papers but boasting just about every computer accessory known to man. Her short-cropped brown hair framed a face perfectly made up to accentuate strong features, but nothing in her expression gave me any clue to her thoughts.

"I heard you were in the building." She waved me into one of the plush guest chairs. "Giselle appears to think a good deal more of your abilities than Greg did."

Next to eyes — hers were dark brown and unrevealing — lips are the most likely facial feature to reveal a person's feelings. Ariadne's were on the thin side but they were neither pursed, twisted, nor pressed tightly together. I couldn't tell if she disapproved

167

of hiring me or not.

"Greg Onslow had no problem with my work," I said. "He just didn't like being told no."

Ariadne's brows beetled. "What do you mean?"

"Your boss misrepresented my dealings with him. I turned him down, not the other way around. He wanted a ghostwriter. I edit. The two things are mutually exclusive."

"Interesting."

"Was he the one who told you otherwise?" I asked.

"I don't remember where I heard it, but I don't suppose that matters now."

"Only to me."

"I'm sure the fat paycheck you're about to earn from Mongaup Valley Ventures will make up for any harm to your reputation. Is that why you wanted to see me? To set the record straight?"

"That was one reason."

I debated only a moment before deciding to level with her. What did I have to lose? The worst she could do was refuse to answer my questions.

"Thanks to the timing of my quarrel with your boss and the lie he told about me, I've come in for scrutiny by the police. I'm a person of interest in the investigation of his murder."

"I imagine you find that troubling, but I don't understand why you think I'd be interested in your problem." She sat perfectly straight and absolutely still, both hands resting lightly on the surface of her desk.

"I can't help but be curious about how he spent the rest of that day. You were with him in the car at the gas station. Perhaps you can fill in those blanks?"

Her lips twitched slightly. I felt my shoulders tense. If she laughed at me for having lost my temper, I was very much afraid I'd say something I'd regret.

"We were on our way to an on-site meeting with a contractor," Ariadne said. "After we returned here, I didn't see Greg again. And just in case you're wondering, I wasn't the one who killed him."

"I didn't think you were, but you worked closely with him. Do you have any idea why he'd go out there at two or three in the morning?"

"I assume he was checking up on the security guards. Greg was very hands-on when it came to supervising personnel." She hesitated, then added, "At a work site like that one, there's always a chance that material will go missing. Sometimes it's an inside job."

I tried to envision the guard I'd met — Keller — as a thief, let alone a killer. Possible, but not likely.

"Will demolition of the old hotel buildings continue?" I asked.

"At the moment, that project is on hold."

"For how long?"

"Indefinitely."

"Your decision?"

That question got an immediate reaction. "Giselle has taken charge of day-to-day operations on all Mongaup Valley Ventures projects. She fancies she's executive material." Ariadne Toothaker's hands were no longer relaxed. They held on to the edge of her desk with a white-knuckled grip.

"I take it you don't agree with her decisions."

"MVV needs to be run by an *experienced* CEO, not an amateur. She'll be the ruin of this company."

The intensity behind the statement gave me a much better perspective on the dynamics at Mongaup Valley Ventures. Ariadne Toothaker and Greg Onslow might have clashed repeatedly, but he'd promoted her and kept her on because working together helped make the business successful.

"Is Giselle's decision to hire me one of the reasons you think she can't handle the job?"

"That's the least of my problems with her. It hardly matters to me who she's hired *or* fired."

"Who has she fired?" Not Ariadne, obviously. At least, not yet.

The eagerness in my voice prompted the hint of a smile. "So far, just one person, a poor foolish payroll clerk named Jenni Farquhar. I suppose Giselle had cause. Jenni was notoriously incompetent."

"Jenni Farquhar," I repeated. "Wasn't she the secretary Giselle replaced?" I pictured Jenni in my mind — ginger hair down to her waist, big blue eyes, and a figure that would do credit to a Barbie doll. "I'd think the only surprise there would be that it took Giselle so long to get rid of her."

Once she'd married Onslow, she could have insisted he fire Jenni. What was the point of taking petty revenge at this late date?

"You seem to have tapped into some of the less salubrious office gossip." Ariadne looked even more amused.

"Someone *did* mention Jenni's demotion to me," I admitted.

It had been Luke who told me that Giselle

replaced Jenni as Onslow's private secretary. I'd come to my own conclusions about whether or not Jenni had been sleeping with her boss before Giselle came along. Nothing less seemed adequate to explain why she'd lasted as long as she had. She was barely capable of handling word processing, let alone the more complicated aspects of a secretarial job. Then, too, the one time I'd talked with her, she'd clearly thought she had a shot at marrying her boss.

Ariadne cleared her throat. "I trust you won't repeat anything you hear while you are an employee of MVV." All trace of amusement had vanished, replaced by a look stern enough to qualify her for a job as a junior high teacher.

"I don't tell tales out of school. On the other hand, should it ever become an issue, I won't lie to the police."

She rose abruptly, signaling that it was time for me to leave.

I stood more slowly. "If Giselle is arrested for her husband's murder, what happens to the company?"

"That would be a disaster."

"Worse than leaving her in charge?"

A bitter laugh was her only answer.

CHAPTER 21

My landline rang at eight o'clock that evening. A quick glance at the caller ID told me the person on the other end was my sister-in-law, Allie, so I had no hesitation about picking up.

Big mistake!

Her shrill voice was so loud that I had to hold the phone away from my ear. "You should never have left Maine!"

"What on earth —"

"I saw that video clip."

"Oh."

"Oh? Is that all you have to say?"

"What do you want me to say, Allie? I'm not the one who uploaded it." I wondered, not for the first time, who had, but I didn't suppose I'd ever know the answer to that question. There had been too many people around that day. Any one of them could have used a cell phone to record my quarrel with Greg Onslow.

173

"You might have warned me."

"I was hoping you'd never see it. In fact, I assumed you wouldn't."

Allie had never been one to spend much time online. In contrast to most people, including me, she never allowed herself to get trapped into following one link after another. She went in, got the information she was after, and got out. She used her tablet to read books and for little else.

The deep sigh I heard at the other end of the line reassured me, if only slightly. I pictured James's sister, legs curled beneath her as she sat in the comfortable easy chair she kept pulled up close to the cast-iron stove in her big farmhouse kitchen. She'd been burning wood chips for heat for the last few years instead of running an oil burner and I had no doubt that, even this late in April, she still had a fire going. Allie was Maine born and bred, but that didn't mean she liked to be cold. It was also a given that she'd have at least one dog curled up at her feet and one or more cats on her lap. Allie and her husband owned three of each.

I looked around for Calpurnia. For once, she was nowhere in sight. That was a great pity. I could have used a cuddle just then, although I had no lap to offer her. To use the wall phone, I had to perch on the high stool situated just beneath it.

Installing that wall phone, a reproduction of a 1950s model, complete with rotary dial, had probably been a mistake, but there had been one just like it in the house when my parents owned it and I was in the throes of a bout of nostalgia the day I arranged for my landline.

There's a modern extension on the end table in the living room, and of course I have a cell phone, too, although I'm still getting used to 24/7 access. The house James and I lived in for so many decades is located in a deep valley. On a good day, a cell phone would show one erratic bar. Most of the time we had to accept that we were in a dead zone.

"Okay, Allie," I said in the most soothing voice I could muster. "Here's the thing. You saw a video of me yelling at an obnoxious man, but it could have been far worse. None of my words had to be bleeped and there was no physical violence."

"What was the argument about?"

"Truthfully, I don't have a clue. He was upset about something he claimed a client of mine was doing. It really had nothing to do with me. If he hadn't started hurling personal insults . . ." I shrugged, realized

175

she couldn't see me, and tried to verbalize the movement. "It was no big deal. You've just never seen me lose my temper before. Most people haven't. It's embarrassing to have been caught on camera like that, but I'll survive the humiliation."

Silence greeted this explanation.

"Allie?" I toyed with the cord while I waited for her to say something.

"Gregory Onslow. That's the name of the man you argued with, isn't it?"

"It is," I agreed in a cautious voice. I had a bad feeling about where our conversation was headed.

"He was murdered the very next day."

Or that same night, I thought, but I didn't correct her. My sigh was loud enough that it would probably have been audible in Maine even without the aid of a telephone.

"Well you can't blame me for being worried about you." Allie sounded defensive. "It wasn't hard to find newspaper articles on the investigation, but they certainly didn't tell me much. If there's a cold-blooded killer on the loose in Lenape Hollow, you need to get away from there, at least until he's caught."

"There's nothing for you to be concerned about, Allie. Yes, someone did murder Greg Onslow, but that doesn't have anything to

176

do with me."

"But that video —"

"These days people put their whole lives online and then film perfect strangers' embarrassing moments and post them, too, right alongside photos of food and pictures of cats. Personally, I don't care what anyone else had for lunch and I seriously doubt there's a great deal of interest in a short clip that shows a retired schoolteacher trading insults with a small-time entrepreneur."

I realized I'd twisted the phone cord around my fingers and carefully unwound it. I had no reason to be nervous. What was Allie going to do? Ground me for a week for bad behavior? Hundreds of miles separated us. All I had to do was convince her that I was in no danger.

"I wish you weren't so far away," she said. "If I could just *see* you, I'd know if you were really all right."

"Allie, I just spent Christmas with you in Maine. I'm fine. I'm healthy in mind and body. I didn't lose my marbles, just my temper, and that isn't likely to happen again."

"Of course it won't." Allie's voice had a snap in it. "The man's dead."

"I mean I won't lose my temper again with *anyone*. Really. I average less than one meltdown a decade. I should be good now until I hit eighty."

This poor attempt at humor fell flat, but another ten minutes of repeated assurances finally persuaded my sister-in-law that she couldn't convince me to leave Lenape Hollow and take refuge with her in Maine. Although I occasionally experience a bit of homesickness for my adopted state, I could honestly say I was back where I belonged. I had, and have, no intention of uprooting myself again, not even temporarily.

Allie's phone call did accomplish one thing. It prompted me to organize my thoughts. Too much time had passed with no arrest. That infamous gas-station quarrel had taken place thirteen days earlier. If the police hadn't yet caught the killer, maybe they *did* need a little help from an interested civilian.

I sat down at my laptop, created a new document, and began a list of unanswered questions. I wrote them down in random order, starting with *Is there a way to discover who posted that video . . . and does it matter?*

Second was *Why did Sunny dislike Onslow so much?*

Next came *Why would Onslow go to the demolition site in the middle of the night?* I deleted *middle of the night* and substituted *wee hours of the morning.*

I lifted my fingers from the keyboard as another thought occurred to me. How had Onslow gotten there? No one had mentioned seeing his car and a Porsche is hard to miss.

I thought back to what the security guard had told us. If there hadn't been a vehicle, that opened up the possibility that Onslow had been murdered somewhere else and taken to the site to be dumped. Detective Brightwell must know if that was the case, but he wasn't likely to share the information with me.

I typed *Where was Onslow killed?* Then I scrolled up to the top of the page and inserted what had to be the key question: *Why kill Onslow?*

As his heir, Giselle benefitted financially.

Anyone Onslow had swindled got revenge.

That old standby, thwarted love, might be the motive. Someone could have killed him thinking *If I can't have him, no one will.*

Although that motive seemed to stretch credulity, I was determined not to leave any stone unturned. I resolved to track down and talk to Jenni Farquhar first thing the next morning. Even though she wasn't a likely suspect, she might be able to tell me something about the inner workings of

Mongaup Valley Ventures.
It was even possible she had incriminating information about the company's new CEO.

CHAPTER 22

It didn't take long to find Jenni Farquhar. She lived in nearby Hurleyville with her parents. When I talked to her mother on the phone, I learned that after leaving Mongaup Valley Ventures she'd taken a job more suited to her skill set. She was working at the pickup window of the local burger joint.

That made initial contact easy. When I reached through my car window to take the bag containing my burger and fries, I feigned surprise at recognizing her.

"Jenni? Jenni Farquhar, is that you?"

Please note that I pronounced her surname correctly. In these parts, at least, it's Forker.

Her blank look was familiar. During our previous encounter, she'd been stymied by a simple word processing problem. I'd been able to solve it for her with a few keystrokes.

I'll never understand what makes otherwise reasonably intelligent males hire office staff based on appearance. If you want your business to run smoothly, brains should win out over beauty every time. It remained to be seen if Giselle Onslow possessed both.

After tossing the food bag in the general direction of the passenger seat, I said, "We met when you were Greg Onslow's secretary."

The change in her expression startled me. Her eyes filled with tears and the entire lower portion of her face started to quiver.

"Oh, my dear, I'm so sorry. I didn't mean to upset you."

I lied.

I'd hoped for some reaction. Now that I had it, I wasn't sure what to do with it. I didn't have much time to decide, either. The driver of the car behind me in line leaned on his horn, impatient to collect his lunch.

"When do you get off work?" I asked.

If she thought my question odd, she gave no sign of it. Sniffling, she fumbled in a pocket for a tissue, dabbed at her eyes, and blew her nose. "My shift ends at two."

"I'll wait for you in the parking lot, okay? We need to talk."

Another car horn joined the first. Against the background music of discordant blatting and beeping, I pulled forward without waiting for a definitive answer. If the look of confusion on Jenni's face was anything to go by, she wasn't capable of providing one.

Two o'clock was nearly two hours away, but instead of driving home, I circled the restaurant and found a parking space with a good view of the door. I ate the burger and fries. Then I fished in the glove compartment for the paperback novel I stash there for emergencies.

I'd started to reread this particular Charlotte MacLeod mystery a couple of months earlier. I always choose novels I've read before for my "waiting room" reading. My familiarity with the plot allows me to slide easily back into the story. At the same time, since it's been a while since the last time I read the book, I've conveniently forgotten the details, including the identity of the villain. To my mind, that's a winning combination. I use the same rationale to select audiobooks to listen to on long drives.

Jenni exited the building at five minutes past two. Shoulders hunched, her movements almost furtive, she scanned the parking lot. Spotting me didn't appear to lessen her anxiety, even after I sent her a little finger wave and got out of the car. That made me wonder if she might be smarter than she seemed.

"I'd just like to talk to you for a few

minutes," I said as I crossed to where she stood frozen.

"Why?" She had a deer-in-the-headlights look about her, but at least she didn't panic and run.

"You don't recognize me, do you? We met some time ago, when I applied for a job at Mongaup Valley Ventures." That I'd only pretended to apply for it wasn't anything she needed to know. "I helped you fix a problem with your computer."

A furrow appeared between her perfectly plucked eyebrows. "I *think* I remember you."

"Well, good. My name is Mikki Lincoln. Shall we sit down?" I gestured toward a half dozen small picnic tables set up on a rectangular patch of grass. They'd only been there for a week or so and the weather was still too unpredictable for them to be much in demand. On this cloudy day, when meteorologists gave rain a forty percent chance of falling and the temperature would have trouble getting past fifty-five degrees, we had the area to ourselves.

There are advantages to looking like a harmless little old lady. Seeing nothing in my manner or appearance to threaten her, Jenni's caution dissolved. She trotted along at my side like an obedient spaniel. Once we were seated opposite each other, she tucked a lock of ginger hair behind one ear and stared at me with big vacant eyes, patiently waiting for me to start the ball rolling.

"I don't mean to pry into your personal life, Jenni," I said, "but it would be a big help to me if you could tell me a little about your time at Mongaup Valley Ventures."

She stared off into space, blinking rapidly. I was afraid she'd start crying again, but after a moment she turned her head and met my gaze head-on.

"I was so happy when I got the job working for Mr. Onslow. He was so nice to me. Mostly I just typed and made coffee and answered the phone and ran errands, but sometimes he asked me to work late, and every time he did, he'd send me a gift the next day. Flowers or candy mostly, but one time it was a necklace."

"Did he ask for . . . favors in return?"

A hint of color came into her cheeks. "No, but I kinda hoped he would, especially after he took me out to dinner that once. We went to a real swanky place. He was a widower by then, and for a little while, I thought —" She broke off and shrugged.

"You thought he might be looking for a second wife and that you were in the running," I finished for her.

185

She nodded, rubbing absently at the top of the picnic table with one finger. "If he was, it wasn't me. All the time I thought he was interested in me, he was seeing someone else."

"Giselle?"

She shook her head. "Someone else," she repeated. "I don't know who she is, but I've seen her around town." When she looked up, she was pouting. "I don't know what he saw in her! She's not at all pretty, and she's old. At least thirty."

I hid a smile. According to his obituary, Onslow had been thirty-seven when he died. Jenni was in her early twenties. I could remember being that age. The mantra of my generation had been "don't trust anyone over thirty."

My amusement faded when the import of Jenni's words sank in. Her revelation meant there was yet another suspect to add to my list, a mystery woman with no name.

"Can you describe her?"

Jenni shrugged. "There's nothing special about her, except that she could stand to lose a few pounds. "

"Hair color?"

"Brown. *Ordinary* brown." Looking as if it killed her to praise anything about her rival, she added, "She has nice skin."

I asked about eye color and height, but Jenni was unable to provide any further identifying details. Moving on, I said, "Tell me about Giselle."

Jenni went still. "What about her?"

"I understand she replaced you as Mr. Onslow's secretary."

Jenni nodded. "I got a job as a payroll clerk instead."

"And then she *married* him," I said, hoping to prompt a reaction. In my opinion, Jenni'd had a lucky escape. Greg Onslow had not been a nice man.

I felt my eyes widen slightly at the abrupt change that came over her face. All of a sudden, she looked . . . sly. Instead of showing resentment at the way Giselle had won the prize she'd coveted, Jenni looked pleased with herself, as if she was glad things had turned out the way they had.

"Did you like working as a payroll clerk?" I asked.

She giggled. "It had its perks."

Slowly, the pieces started to come together. At first the picture forming in my mind was difficult to imagine, but the more I thought about it, the more sense it made.

"Giselle befriended you, didn't she? After her marriage, you fed her all the gossip you heard at Mongaup Valley Ventures."

"We talked." Jenni's eyes sparkled.

I'd wondered how Giselle kept tabs on the company. Now I knew. With Jenni as her spy, she'd also have heard about it if her husband had ever shown undue interest in another of his female employees. Only one thing still had me confused.

"Why did she fire you?" I asked.

"She didn't." Jenni's huffy tone told me she was tired of people thinking that she'd been let go. "I was ready for a change and she gave me a big bonus so I could start saving up for my wedding."

"I didn't realize you were engaged to be married." A closer examination of her ring finger revealed a minuscule diamond. "Who's the lucky man?"

"His name is Brian Keller. He's a security guard at MVV."

My antenna quivered. "Keller? Not the same one who found Greg Onslow's body?"

"Oh, no. That's his brother, Bob. Brian works at headquarters. The hours are still terrible, but at least he gets to stay indoors."

Careful, I warned myself, as another possibility occurred to me. If Giselle killed her husband and one or both of the Keller brothers helped her dispose of the body, then saying too much to Jenni could be dangerous.

Almost immediately, I talked myself out of that notion. If either of the Kellers had conspired with Giselle, Bob Keller would never have reported finding the dead man. As he himself had pointed out, if no one had noticed the corpse, Onslow would have been buried in backfill first thing the next day. His sudden disappearance would have caused a stir, but given that he'd left other towns without warning, leaving behind bilked investors and businesses faced with bankruptcy, everyone would have assumed he was up to his old tricks.

I wondered if Mongaup Valley Ventures was facing financial difficulties. It wouldn't surprise me if it was.

"Would you say you and Giselle are friends?" I asked Jenni.

"Not really. I just worked for her."

"And now she's head of the company. Do you think she'll be able to run Mongaup Valley Ventures on her own?"

Jenni shrugged, uninterested in that aspect of things.

Nothing ventured, nothing gained, I decided. "Do you think she might have killed her husband to get control of the company?"

Jenni blinked at me in surprise. "Why would she? She got everything she wanted when she married him. Ms. Toothaker, now,

I can see *her* doing away with Mr. Onslow."

"Really?" I sent her an encouraging smile. "Why do you say that?"

"She hated the way he was running the company. They yelled at each other about it all the time and they didn't care who overheard them. I can't understand why he didn't fire her. Mr. Donnelly's secretary said it must be because she has one of those golden parachute things. You know — where the company would have to pay her big bucks to get rid of her. That would make it cheaper to keep her around, even if she was a bitch."

I found Jenni's logic interesting, but as far as I could see, it didn't give Ariadne a motive for murder. She wasn't the one who'd taken over MVV after Onslow's death. Giselle had inherited controlling interest in the company. Ariadne must have known that would happen, and known, too, that there would be no benefit to her in a change of command.

"I'm still curious about why Giselle paid you for information," I said. "Maybe she wasn't satisfied just to be Mrs. Gregory Onslow. Did she . . . seem unhappy to you?"

Jenni picked at a loose splinter on the wooden tabletop. "Well, maybe. I guess she might have wondered sometimes if she'd have done better to stick with her old boy-friend."

I leaned closer, intrigued.

"What old boyfriend?" This was the first I'd heard that Giselle had one. An earlier husband, yes, but no one had mentioned another love interest. First a mystery woman, now a mystery man — as if I needed *more* suspects! "Was this here in Lenape Hollow?"

Jenni nodded. "He started working at Mongaup Valley Ventures about the same time Giselle did. They really hit it off. I mean, you could almost see the sparks fly when they passed each other in the hall. He wasn't there long, though. Mr. Onslow fired him a couple of weeks later."

"To get rid of the competition?"

"I guess so. He left. She stayed. It wasn't very long after that when she got engaged to Mr. Onslow, and it was a real short engagement."

"Does this ex-boyfriend have a name?"

Jenni's entire face puckered up with the effort to remember, but after a moment she produced an answer. "Luke something," she said, sending my heart plunging to my toes. "He's a tall guy with brown hair. He'd be really good-looking if his nose wasn't too big for his face."

CHAPTER 23

I spent that evening and half of the next day trying to contact my cousin. Luke wasn't at the accounting firm where he'd been working. They told me he was on vacation, as were many of those who'd been swamped with tax returns right up until the April fifteenth deadline.

My calls to his cell phone went straight to voice mail. No one answered when I went to his apartment and banged on the door. I even drove out to the RV storage place where he'd parked his oversize camper, but no one had seen him there, either.

Discouraged, I went home, arriving back at my house around noon. With my thoughts fixed on my cousin, I didn't notice there was a car with Maine license plates parked in my driveway until I nearly rear-ended it with my Taurus. I hit the brakes, then stared in disbelief at the large, male person who emerged from the driver's side.

"Nicky? What on earth are you doing here?"

He engulfed me in a bear hug before I could pepper him with any more questions. Nick Carpenter is a big boy, built like a linebacker and easily topping the six foot mark. My nose hit at about shoulder level and his kiss, as always, landed on the top of my head.

When he finally released me, his familiar, beloved face wore a broad grin. "Can't a guy visit his favorite aunt for no reason at all?"

"I'm your *only* aunt."

I narrowed my eyes. Since I moved to New York State, I'd returned to Maine on several occasions and spent a few days with my husband's family on each one. This was the first time any of James's relatives had visited me. Nick's arrival on my doorstep, less than two days after I'd fielded an anxious phone call from his mother, set off all kinds of alarms.

"I've missed you." He sounded ever-so-slightly embarrassed, but I wondered if that was due to the sentiment or because he was trying to hide the real reason he'd come to Lenape Hollow.

"Right back at you."

I was perfectly sincere about having

missed him. Since James and I chose not to have children of our own, we'd always made the most of the time we spent with Allie's two. Some years we got together only for Thanksgiving and Christmas, despite the fact that all of us lived within a twenty-mile radius of one another, but I treasured those gatherings. Now that Nick and his sister Susan were both married and had children themselves, I had years of fond memories to look back on.

"You'd better come inside," I said. "Do you have luggage?"

He did. The size of his soft-sided roller bag made me wonder how long he intended to stay.

Nick gave the exterior of the house a once-over as we walked along the sidewalk that runs the entire width of my front porch. The wheels of his suitcase bumped heavily against each riser when we climbed the steps.

"Nice," he said, taking note of the small, comfortably padded wicker sofa and two matching chairs grouped around a low table. "I bet you spend a lot of time out here in good weather."

"Yes, I do. When I want a break from working in my upstairs office, this is the place I most often come to. There's room to set up my laptop, but for variety I occasionally edit by hand."

My porch is surrounded by a waist-high knee wall. When I'm seated I can see into the street but passersby remain unaware of my presence. That makes it sound as if I spy on my neighbors. I don't. In fact, no one lives directly across from my house. My head-on view consists of the top end of what I've always called The Alley — a private drive that runs downhill to Main Street — the adjacent two-car garage, and a four-room, one-story schoolhouse operated by the Catholic diocese.

I unlocked the front door. "Come on in. I'll give you the grand tour." I quickly punched my code into the security panel, preventing an alarm from going off.

Nick eyed the keypad askance but made no comment. Such things aren't often found in rural Maine, and he certainly didn't have one in the cape with dormers that Allie refers to as his "starter house" even though he and Julie have lived there for the last twenty years.

While we still stood in my tiny foyer, I indicated the stairs to the second floor. "You can leave your suitcase at the bottom. We'll take it up later."

Moving into the hall, I pointed out the

kitchen at the far end, but led him there by the circuitous route, passing through the living and dining rooms first. I even showed him the way to reach the back door through the utility room. As I did so, I was not entirely successful at blocking the memory of the last time I showed someone around my house. I hadn't seen Detective Brightwell since then, but that didn't mean he'd forgotten about me.

"Have a seat in the dinette while I throw together some sandwiches for lunch," I suggested.

At the mention of food, Calpurnia appeared out of nowhere. She'd always been fond of James's relatives and immediately began to strop herself against Nick's legs.

"Hey, girl." He reached down to scratch between her ears. A huge grin split his face. "She remembers me."

"Of course she does. You used to slip her bits of turkey every Thanksgiving." The last few years James had been alive, we'd hosted the family for that holiday while Allie and her husband, Rob, did the honors at Christmas.

It didn't take me long to make peanut butter and grape jelly sandwiches — Nick's favorite — and add glasses of milk and a few store-bought ginger snaps to the menu.

While we ate, we stuck to small talk: family; the chances of another title for the Red Sox; the weather. All the while, I kept waiting for the other shoe to drop, although I wasn't particularly anxious to hurry it along.

Once we'd eaten, we returned to the foyer to collect Nick's suitcase. He brought Cal with him, not that he had much choice. She'd commandeered his lap during lunch.

He paused long enough to give the security panel next to the front door a pointed look. "Do you need to reset that?"

"I'll do it later, when we turn in for the night." I caught his arm in a firm grip, attempting to pull him up the stairs.

He didn't budge. "Why do you need a security system at all?"

"Don't you think it's a good idea?" I started to climb, expecting him to follow me. "Lenape Hollow is a quiet little town, but a woman living alone can't be too careful."

I was treading a fine line. I didn't want him to think of me as someone in need of protection. On the other hand, it *was* sensible to take precautions. I wanted him to appreciate the fact that I'd made the effort.

"There's crime in Maine, too," I added. "If I'd stayed where I was after your uncle died, way out in the country, I'd have been far more vulnerable and much more nervous about living alone than I am here."

I glanced over my shoulder to make sure he'd stopped staring at the keypad. I smiled when I saw that he was still carrying the cat as he came up the stairs. He held her cradled in one arm and hauled the roller bag after him using his free hand. He caught sight of my expression and frowned. He hadn't been won over by my logic. Not in the least.

"Nowhere is completely safe." My tone was sharper than I'd intended. "Didn't your mother tell me their camp was broken into last winter?"

Nick's parents own a rustic little cabin on a lake about fifty miles from their year-round home. They both enjoy swimming and boating and plan to do more of both after they retire, although just when that will be is anybody's guess. Allie and Rob are the proprietors of a small convenience store in a tiny Maine village. Rob is already old enough to collect social security, but that hasn't slowed him down any or per-suaded him to cut back on his hours. I'll be surprised if Allie doesn't follow suit when she qualifies for retirement. They're both happiest when they're busy.

A sheepish look replaced Nick's frown. "Heard about that, did you? Mom was some ticked off. Whoever it was stole everything that wasn't nailed down, even the old board games she kept in a cupboard."

Upstairs, I pointed out the bathroom first, since it was directly across from the landing. Turning in a counter-clockwise direction, I identified the doors to my office, the attic, my bedroom, and what passes as my guest room.

"This used to be the nursery," I said of the latter. "There was a door into the master bedroom, but that's since been walled up. The space is cramped, but I think you'll fit. I slept in this room until I was a teenager."

It was furnished with a twin bed, a dresser, and a small armchair. Nick filled most of the remaining space. I sidled past him to open the door to a minuscule closet where he could hang a few of his clothes. The floor inside was at knee level and the back slanted up at an angle to accommodate the stairwell on the other side of the wall.

"I didn't buy this house with any expectation of entertaining overnight guests," I said apologetically. "I converted the original guest room, the bedroom I moved into when I was thirteen, into my office. There are two attic chambers, but they're unfinished and unheated. I use them for stor-age." I didn't mention the exercise bike.

"This will suit me just fine," Nick assured me. He looked down at the loudly purring ball of fur, now held securely in both arms. "I just won't try to swing any cats in here."

Leaving his suitcase behind but bringing Calpurnia along, we embarked on a quick tour of the other upstairs rooms. I was particularly proud of the way my workspace had turned out. I'd enlarged the original bedroom by incorporating what had been a walk-in closet and reconfiguring a section of the central hallway.

"I like the balcony." Nick peered out onto the small covered porch. It was only big enough to hold a folding chair and a tiny table. "Nice view."

Anyone looking out across the roof of my garage, has a view that encompasses the school across the street and, behind it and downhill, the roof of the Catholic church. It fronts on North Main Street. In the dis-tance, the land rises steeply upward again with neat rows of houses interspersed with trees making an attractive backdrop. The scenery is even prettier once leaves and apple blossoms appear.

On the way downstairs, I finally worked up enough courage to ask Nick how long he intended to stay.

"Trying to get rid of me already?" he teased.

"That's not an answer." I led him back to the kitchen. "Don't you think it's about time we stopped dancing around the subject? I'm delighted to see you, but I want to know why you're really here."

"I told her you'd see right through her clever plan."

"*She* being your mother, I assume?"

"What can I say?" He resumed his seat at the dinette table, the cat once again on his lap. "Mom's worried about you and I had vacation time coming so she suggested I drive down here and check things out in person."

Rather than snap at him and tell him he and Allie should mind their own business, I began to rummage through the refrigerator. I had no idea what to make for the two of us for supper. Living by myself, I don't even eat at regular hours. I just grab whatever strikes my fancy whenever I feel hungry.

"I watched that video," Nick said.

"It's no big deal, Nicky. I told Allie that when we spoke on the phone."

"She thinks it is, since the guy you fought with got himself murdered right afterward. Have the police arrested anyone yet?"

I had to admit that they hadn't.

"So that means you're still a suspect, right?"

I turned, freezer-wrapped package of ground sirloin in hand, and glared at him. "*Everyone's* a suspect until they catch the person who killed Greg Onslow."

"But you *were* questioned?"

"Of course I was."

"More than once?"

"Do you seriously think anyone believes I'd kill a man just because he yelled at me?"

"Answer a question with a question. Good tactic."

I stuck my tongue out at him. "I'm not proud of losing my temper, but since you saw the video, you know I gave back as good as I got. I won that argument. I had no reason to take things further. End of story."

"No, it isn't." Finally putting Calpurnia down, he got up and took the casserole dish I'd just retrieved from an overhead cabinet out of my hands. "I think you're in more trouble than you're willing to admit."

"I'm not in any trouble, Nick." I reclaimed the dish and plunked it down on the counter with a thump and a rattle. "Read my lips. I did not murder Greg Onslow."

"But you *are* a suspect. You'd just admitted that much."

I opened my mouth to assure him that the local police knew me and had probably already convinced Detective Brightwell that I was an innocent bystander. Just in time, I remembered that I'd never told my Maine family about the two previous occasions when I'd been involved in the investigation of a murder. I hadn't wanted to worry them and I didn't want Nick fussing over me now.

I opted for a nonchalant shrug of the shoulders. "Half the residents of Lenape Hollow are suspects. Onslow had a lot of enemies and most of them had much better reasons than I did to bump him off. Besides," I added, inspired, "he was shot. You know I won't have anything to do with firearms."

Nick winced at the reminder of a heated discussion we'd had at Christmas, during my most recent visit to Maine. My late husband and Rob, Nick's father, never saw eye to eye on the subject of guns and I shared James's opinion. When Nick's sixteen-year-old son, Brad, had casually informed me that he'd completed a grand slam during hunting season, I'd managed to congratulate him, but I'd felt sick inside. That sweet-natured young man was proud of the fact that he'd killed a turkey, a bear, a moose, and a deer in the same year.

I'd had a few choice words to say on the subject once Brad was out of the room. Nick had weighed in, reminding me that none of the meat had gone to waste. He'd argued that hunting feeds many Maine families who would otherwise suffer from food insecurity, and that it serves a humane purpose by culling herds of wild animals so they don't overrun the state. I'd had to concede those points, but I find it hard to condone a "sport" that glorifies stalking and slaughtering a living creature. I don't like the firearms hunters use and have even less liking for handguns. The ease with which people can get their hands on the sort of automatic weapons so often used in school shootings makes my blood run cold.

It was probably fortunate that a loud, demanding yowl interrupted us before we could resume that debate. It was unlikely either of us would change the other's opinion.

"Her food bowl is empty." I busied myself opening a fresh can of cat food and checking that Calpurnia had plenty of water. A feeder full of kibble is always available, but she prefers variety.

The respite didn't last. In case I'd missed his point, Nick leaned against the counter, arms folded across his chest, and reiterated that since he was on vacation, there was no need for him to rush back home.

"I'd really like to see a bit of the area while I'm here," he added in a gently coaxing tone of voice. "You've always said this part of New York State and the western Maine mountains have a lot in common."

When he hit me with the goofy grin he'd perfected by age ten, I caved.

"You're welcome to stay through the weekend. That will give me plenty of time to show you the sights. However, unlike yours, my job doesn't come with paid vacation days. I can't spare a lot of time to entertain you."

"I didn't come here to be entertained."

"No, you came to check up on me."

"I came to make sure you were okay, and because you shouldn't have to deal with an upsetting situation like this on your own, not when you have family ready and willing to support you."

While I appreciated that his concern was genuine, the idea of Nick becoming a long-term houseguest didn't thrill me. Fortunately, what he'd just said about family gave me ammunition to dissuade him.

"You know, Nick, I have a relative right here in Lenape Hollow. I'm sure I've mentioned my cousin Luke. He works for a local accounting firm and lives just a short distance from here."

Was it just my imagination, or did Nick look relieved by the reminder? Could it be that he wasn't as determined to stay as he'd seemed? That he'd just as soon head home on Monday and had only made the drive to Lenape Hollow in the first place because his mother had nagged him into it? I'd just begun to relax when he threw me a curve.

"I'd like to meet him," Nick said. "Why don't you see if he's free to join us for supper?"

I forced a smile. "What an excellent idea."

On the positive side, getting to know Luke ought to convince Nick that he didn't need to stay. On the negative was the fact that I'd been trying since the day before to get hold of my cousin. If he remained elusive, Nick would have grounds to doubt Luke's ability to "support" me in my hour of need.

It came as a pleasant surprise when Luke not only answered his phone on the first ring, but accepted my invitation with apparent delight.

Chapter 24

A few hours later, after a pleasant meal during which Luke and Nick got along famously and no one mentioned murder, Luke excused himself, explaining that he'd promised to meet a friend for drinks at eight.

When Nick volunteered to take care of the cleanup, I accepted his offer. I don't have a dishwasher, so washing, drying, and putting away dishes always takes up the best part of a half hour, enough time for me to have a private chat with my cousin. I allowed Luke to get as far as the front porch before I took a firm grip on his forearm and tugged him over to the wicker sofa and chairs.

"This friend — male or female?"

He was the picture of innocence. "Wouldn't you like to know?"

"In fact, I would, especially if you're meeting a certain recent widow."

"How did — ?" His start of alarm confirmed way too much about his relationship with Giselle Onslow.

"I think we'd better sit down."

Instead, he broke free and took a step away from me. "I'm not going to talk about this with you, Mikki. And I've really got to go."

I'd had years of experience outmaneuvering recalcitrant students. Ducking around him, I positioned myself so that I blocked his path to the porch steps. With my arms folded across my chest, I assumed the stern, don't-mess-with-me stare I'd developed through decades of teaching seventh and eighth graders.

"Not yet, Luke. I won't keep you long, but you need to level with me. It's important."

The tense way he held himself warned me he wanted to bolt. That he didn't suggested that he understood why it was so crucial that I hear his side of the story. After a long, tense moment, he relented, flinging himself into one of the wicker chairs and sprawling there in the manner of a rebellious teenager. I ignored the way he glowered at me and reminded myself that, despite present appearances, he was a responsible adult in his late twenties.

"Did you lie to the police?" I asked.

"About what?"

I perched on the edge of the sofa cushion, sitting so that the light filtering out onto the porch through the living-room window behind me gave me a clear view of his face. "About why you were out near Feldman's on the night Greg Onslow was murdered there. Had you been with Giselle?"

"No!" His denial sounded sincere, but he avoided meeting my eyes.

I waited.

"I drove by her place, okay?"

"Is it located near Feldman's?"

I knew Onslow had built a house for his first wife, Tiffany, but not where it was. All she'd told me was that he'd insisted everything in it be brand-new — no antiques allowed. Since I hadn't heard otherwise on the Lenape Hollow grapevine, I assumed Onslow had continued to live there after her death.

"It's out on the River Road," Luke said, "set back from the street and very private. There weren't any lights on, but then I didn't expect there would be, since it was two o'clock in the morning."

"Do you often go out there?"

He shrugged. "I used to swing by every once in a while. Stupid, huh?"

"Not smart," I agreed.

"It was sheer bad luck that I was spotted driving past the entrance to the resort on my way back to town." He shifted to sit forward in his chair with his head down and his hands clasped between his knees.

"And now we come back to my first question." I reached across the distance between us to rest my fingers on his wrist. "Do the police know about you and Giselle?"

"There's nothing for them *to* know."

I persisted in the interest of clarity. "So you didn't tell them you'd just been out to the Onslow house?"

"No. Giselle's name didn't come up. There was no reason for me to mention her."

"You were attracted to her, back when you both worked at Mongaup Valley Ventures, before Onslow set his sights on her."

"She's gorgeous and smart and funny. What's not to like?" He continued to stare at his hands. "We went out a couple of times. Then she decided the big boss had more to offer her."

"Did you quit or were you fired?"

"Six of one, a half dozen of the other. I saw the writing on the wall. End of story."

"Not quite. Not if you're stalking her."

His head shot up. "I'm not —"

I gave his arm a light slap. "I hate to tell you this, Luke, but driving by a woman's house in the middle of the night to see if you can catch a glimpse of her straddles the line between besotted admirer and stalker, especially if you've done it more than once." *And especially if she's married,* I added to myself.

His silence was telling.

Making my voice as gentle and sympathetic as I could manage, I asked, "Do you know why Giselle chose Onslow over you?"

The stifled sound he made might have been a rueful laugh. "Oh, yeah. I know. She wanted financial security."

"But you have —"

"She didn't believe me when I told her I wasn't just your average poverty-stricken low-level employee."

"You *told* her?"

Luke rarely confides his true financial status to anyone, but he is, in fact, the sole beneficiary of a substantial inheritance. An ancestor of his invented a widget used in manufacturing. Since subsequent generations were careful stewards, never squandering a penny more than they had to, the result was that Luke didn't need to work for a living. He did so because he disliked being idle.

"How's that for irony?" he asked. "The one time I willingly admit to being heir to a fortune and she thinks I'm making it up!"

Since I sympathized with his frustration, I refrained from telling him irony didn't mean what he thought it did. I may call myself "The Write Right Wright" on my business cards and flyers, but this wasn't the time to fuss about word choice.

"Let me get this straight," I said instead. "Giselle came right out and told you she was marrying Onslow for his money?"

"That's about the size of it."

"And that didn't give you an instant dislike of her?" It did nothing to improve the impression she'd made on me.

"She has a right to look out for herself."

Sometimes love is not only blind, I thought, *it's also deaf and stupid.* No matter how shallow and self-centered I found Giselle, Luke had clearly lost his heart to her.

Warning myself to proceed with caution, I continued to probe. "Wasn't she married before? Surely her first husband provided for her."

Once again staring at his clasped hands, he shrugged. "She doesn't like to talk about him. I don't think it was a very happy marriage."

From what I'd heard, husband number

one had left Giselle a wealthy widow. Luke was lucky she *hadn't* believed him, but now I had to worry about what would happen if he pursued the dubious honor of becoming husband number three.

"I'm sorry you're so unhappy," I said after a brief silence, "but given that the police have not yet arrested anyone for Greg Onslow's murder, it's probably not a good idea for you to renew your acquaintance with Giselle."

"We've agreed to be careful."

So much for there being nothing for the police to find out about!

"How long have you been seeing her?"

"Only since her husband died. I called to offer my condolences and one thing led to another, but we aren't . . . I mean . . . I'm just going to meet her for a drink, okay?"

"Oh, Luke. Imagine how it will look to the police if you're seen together."

He bounded to his feet, hands curled into fists at his sides. "Damn it, Mikki, don't you think I've thought of that? But she needs me. She's upset and confused and all alone."

I opened my mouth to tell him she'd looked perfectly capable of coping when I'd seen her at the Friends of the Library meeting, but he talked right over me.

"She knows it was a mistake to marry

Onslow. She was in love with me all along."

I wondered if she'd told him that before or after he'd convinced her he was wealthy, but criticizing Giselle was no way to convince Luke to look out for himself.

"If you care about her, that's all the more reason not to see her again until Onslow's killer is caught. If Detective Brightwell hasn't already uncovered your history with her at MVV, he soon will." I held up a hand when he tried to contradict me. "Office gossip. If I've heard it, it will inevitably reach his ears. Brightwell is the thorough type." He'd proven that by the way he'd hashed over every little detail of my alibi.

"You really think he'd believe I killed Onslow if he knew about us?"

"You'd be near the top of his list, either as the murderer or as Giselle's accomplice." Getting to my feet, I went to him and placed my hands on his shoulders. I could feel the tension beneath my fingers. He was practically vibrating with it. "Look at me."

I waited until he complied before I continued. Given his feelings for Giselle, I couldn't come right out and say what I really thought, that *she* was the most likely person to have murdered her husband, but I was determined to do my best to warn him of the danger he was in.

"The spouse of a murder victim always comes in for close scrutiny. It won't do either of you any good if the police discover that you two are romantically involved. I know you don't want my advice, but I'm going to give it to you anyway. Call her. Break tonight's date and tell her that you can't see her or talk to her again until someone is behind bars."

Pulling away from me, he ran agitated fingers through his light brown hair and blew out an exasperated breath. "I know you're right, but she needs *someone.*"

I resisted the urge to roll my eyes. "Do you want me to talk to her? I might be able to convince her that it's in her best interest, as well as yours, to avoid the appearance of collusion."

A smile flickered across his face at my choice of that particular word. Concern for me quickly banished it. "Won't that put you in the spotlight? The last I heard, you were pretty high up on Brightwell's list of suspects yourself."

"Let me worry about that." I planted a light kiss on his cheek. "Call Giselle. Explain the situation. Then convince her to meet me for lunch tomorrow at Harriet's."

Reluctantly, Luke agreed.

CHAPTER 25

"So," I said to Nick as we were finishing a light breakfast of coffee and toast the next morning, "have you thought about what you'd like to do today? I'm afraid you're on your own until after lunch. I have a couple of hours of work to complete first and then I have an appointment I need to keep at noon."

Luke had called late the previous evening to tell me Giselle had agreed to meet me. He swore he hadn't kept his rendezvous with her but had only spoken with her on the phone.

"You're self-employed," Nick mumbled into his coffee mug. He's not a morning person and his eyes were at half-mast. "Take a long weekend."

"People who work for themselves don't keep regular hours." I shouldn't have needed to remind him of that, since his parents often put in twelve-hour days and seven-day weeks at their tiny convenience store.

"Even my folks take a vacation now and then."

He must have been reading my mind! Now there was a scary thought.

"I'm *not* on vacation," I reminded him, "and I have deadlines to meet. Cheer up. I'll be available to play tour guide by mid-afternoon."

A glance through the dinette window into my backyard, past the bird feeder currently occupied by two squirrels, showed me an expanse of green beneath an overcast sky. All the rain lately had been good for new growth. The trees hadn't leafed out yet, but there were buds showing. It wasn't going to be the best weather for sightseeing, but Nick and I would still be able to go for a drive around Lenape Hollow. It wouldn't take long to show him the highlights. My hometown isn't a very big place and the surrounding landscape is much the same as what Nick sees every day at home. The biggest difference I noticed, way back when I first moved to Maine, was the complete absence of billboards there.

"I'm headed upstairs to my office," I announced.

"I guess I can find something to watch on TV while you're working."

Taking his coffee with him, he set off in the direction of the dining room. As my parents had, I used it as a continuation of the living room. I'd tucked the drop-leaf dining table into the window alcove and furnished the rest of the space with comfy chairs and an entertainment center. I'd barely reached the foyer before I heard a plaintive cry for help.

"I can't find the clicker."

"Once upon a time, people had to get up to change the channel," I called back, but I took pity on him and changed course.

Nick was already ensconced in the easy chair in front of the television, his feet on the hassock and a bewildered expression on his face. I gave his legs a shove.

"This is meant to be used first and fore-most as a footrest, but it's also a handy-dandy storage compartment."

I opened the top to reveal a space big enough to hold a dozen remotes. I've managed to limit myself to three — one for the cable box, one to turn on the screen without cable so I can watch movies, and one to control the DVD player. What can I say? I rarely buy the newest thing in technology until I'm forced into it by the demise of whatever I've been using.

Leaving Nick happily channel-surfing, I

cocooned myself in my office with the door closed and my hearing aids out. I accomplished a fair amount of editing before it was time to leave to meet Giselle. When I went back downstairs, Nick was engrossed in a *Storage Wars* marathon.

"I could come with you," he offered when I told him I was about to leave. "After all, I've got to eat, too."

He started to heave himself out of the chair but I waved him back.

"Sorry, sweetie. This isn't a social occasion. You'll find bread and sandwich meat in the fridge, or you can polish off that jar of peanut butter. We can go out to a restaurant this evening if you like. Somewhere nice. Your treat."

"Gee, thanks."

With a laugh and a little wave, I left him to continue binge watching.

Since I was the one who'd planned to leave first, I'd had Nick park his car in the garage and had left mine in the driveway overnight. I'd barely slid into the driver's seat when I realized I'd left the notebook I'd intended to take with me — a nice one, diary-sized, with a floral cover — on the hall table. With a sigh, I got out of the Taurus and went back inside for it. Among other things, I planned to ask Giselle to help me work out a timeline for the period between the gas-station quarrel and the discovery of Onslow's body. I learned years ago that it's best not to trust anything important to memory alone.

I didn't intend to linger in the house. In fact, I was hoping to slip in and out without Nick noticing me. Notebook in hand, I was already turning to leave when I heard his voice. It took me a moment to realize he was talking on the kitchen extension. I needed considerably less time to grasp that when he used the words *elderly* and *confused* he was referring to his dear old auntie.

Annoyed, I decided Giselle could wait a few minutes. I crept closer. Nick had his back to me. As I listened to the rest of his side of the conversation, I had to fight against a strong urge to smack him upside the head with my trusty notebook. The minute he ended the call, I stalked into the kitchen and confronted him. I stood with my hands fisted on my hips and my weight on the balls of my feet. If he suspected just how badly I wanted to haul off and kick him, so much the better.

"So you think I'm incapable of looking out for myself, do you? Too old and decrepit and possibly senile?"

He rolled his eyes. "You know that's not

what I meant."

"Oh, you meant it all right. I just wasn't supposed to overhear what you said. I suppose that was your mother you were talking to. May I just point out that Allie is only six years younger than I am?"

"Calm down, Aunt Mikki. I've been *worried* about you. That's all. You've got to admit that some of the decisions you've made since Uncle James died have been pretty . . . impulsive."

For *impulsive,* read *crazy.* No one in the family had been shy about telling me so at the time. I'd informed them that it was none of their business if I chose to pull up stakes and move to another state. I'd thought I convinced them that my decision was the right one, but apparently, Allie and Nick had lingering doubts about my sanity.

"You listen to me, Nick Carpenter. I am not yet in my dotage. I'm dealing perfectly well on my own with fallout from that stupid video."

"Except for the police considering you a suspect in a murder case."

I should have lied and told him they'd already cleared me. Because I was debating the wisdom of doing just that, I hesitated a few seconds too long.

Nick's eyes widened, telling me he'd taken

a shot in the dark and accidentally hit his target. "That tears it, Aunt Mikki! I'm not leaving until you're officially in the clear."

I recognized the look on his face. It was one with which I was very familiar.

When my late husband got that stubborn set to his jaw and that determined glitter in his eyes, there was no point in arguing with him. My nephew takes after his uncle. In the heat of an argument, nothing less than a nuclear blast would change Nick's mind.

"We will talk about this again when I get home." I used my "strict teacher" voice, not that I thought it would make any impression on him.

I cut short further debate by leaving the house.

CHAPTER 26

I'd calmed down by the time I reached Harriet's and pulled into a parking space just down the street from the café. I was no longer envisioning a scenario in which, aided by a rush of adrenaline, I tossed Nick out on his ear.

I could simply order him to leave and never come back, but even as ticked off as I was, I had to acknowledge that he truly believed he was acting in my best interests. In the hope of avoiding a rift with James's family, I convinced myself that if I was patient with Nick, I could eventually persuade him to change his mind. James had been capable of seeing reason. On occasion, he'd even admitted to being wrong. If Nick really was like his uncle, a little time and some delicate handling might yet bring him around to my way of thinking.

My heart sank when I walked into Harriet's and did not at once spot Giselle

Onslow. I was only a few minutes late for our appointment. I'd assumed she'd wait for me.

At noon on a Friday, the place was bustling. Harriet's was popular with those who had shops and other businesses in what was left of Lenape Hollow's downtown. It was also a favorite haunt of the men and women who worked across the street at the police station. I wondered if that was why Onslow's widow hadn't wanted to stick around. I spotted both Jonathan Hazlett and Ellen Blume in Ada Patel's lunch crowd, scarfing down burgers and fries.

I was about to turn around and return home when I heard the sound of a throat being cleared. It came from the table farthest from the front windows and out of Detective Hazlett's line of sight. Situated in an alcove to one side of the podium that held the restaurant's cash register, this small, out-of-the-way table was easy to overlook.

The person seated there had taken pains to disguise herself. Most of her luxuriant ebony hair was tucked up beneath a Yankees cap, so that only a long ponytail stuck out through the opening at the back. In a further attempt to appear nondescript, she was dressed in blue jeans and a plain, navy blue sweatshirt. She'd have done better to leave off the oversize sunglasses. Wearing them indoors on a cloudy day while sitting in the darkest corner of the room made her look decidedly peculiar.

"Lose the shades," I whispered when I reached her. "They're too conspicuous."

Giselle hesitated. I understood why when she removed the glasses. On Monday evening at the library her large blue eyes had been clear and bright, almost sparkling. Now they were dull and lifeless, and no amount of carefully applied makeup could conceal the bags beneath them.

"Are you okay?" It was a stupid question, but I asked out of genuine concern.

She managed a weak smile. "I've been better. I haven't been sleeping well. Shall we order? Then we can talk."

Ada Patel materialized at my elbow. She avoided looking directly at Giselle, although it was obvious she recognized her. Given that the café is such a popular gathering place, I had no doubt that Ada was up-to-date on all the latest gossip, and that included whatever her neighbors from across the street might have discussed while having their lunch. I didn't dare glance toward Detective Hazlett for fear I'd catch his eye. One look at my face and he'd know something was up. Then he'd probably tattle to Detective Brightwell.

I ordered a club sandwich and a ginger ale. Giselle opted for the house salad with no dressing and bottled water. I wasn't surprised. To maintain that runway model figure, she'd have to be on a perpetual diet.

Once upon a time, back in junior high, I was so thin that one of the other kids gave me the nickname Rail because I was as skinny as one. In reaction to that, I was thrilled when I first started putting on a little weight. I actually had curves! Sadly, the euphoria didn't last. As any female over the age of forty knows, once the pounds start to pile on, it's the very devil to take them off again.

By the time our food was placed in front of us, the customers at the tables closest to us had finished eating and left to return to their jobs. Giselle speared a chunk of iceberg lettuce with her fork, but instead of lifting it toward her mouth, she glanced quickly around to assure herself that no one was showing any undue interest in our conversation. Although her normal speaking voice was low and throaty, she turned the volume down even more.

"I understand why it looks bad that I want to spend time with Luke just now, but he's

226

been such a comfort to me. I don't know how I would have survived the past few days without his support."

"He's a suspect in your husband's murder," I said bluntly. "For that matter, so are you, unless you have an alibi I don't know about."

She shook her head. "I was home in bed. Asleep." Briefly she looked up and our eyes locked. "Alone. I wish Luke *had* been with me. Then we'd both be in the clear."

"In that case, the police would be looking very hard for evidence that you acted together to murder your husband. They probably are anyway, but the less you and Luke communicate with each other until after the real killer is caught, the better."

"Thank you for that," she whispered.

"For what?"

"For believing that I didn't kill Greg. Luke said I could rely on you."

Oh, thank you so much, Luke!

I wasn't at all certain of Giselle's innocence, but I didn't disillusion her. She'd be much more cooperative if she thought I was on her side, and I had a lot of questions I wanted to ask her.

"I'll be honest with you, Giselle. We're all under suspicion. Until your husband's murderer is arrested, the police are going to make our lives miserable. They're good at what they do, but maybe, if we pool our resources, we can come up with a few clues they've missed."

She looked doubtful. "How?"

I reached into my tote and pulled out my notebook. "We can start with a timeline — figure out where various people were leading up to the discovery of the body."

"How will that accomplish anything?" She dug into her salad. In some hard-to-define way, I felt she'd put a barrier between us.

"It may not, but I won't know until I have all the information. We'll start at the gas station. That . . . encounter took place around ten-thirty on the morning of the tenth. Afterward, I ran errands for about an hour and then went to Darlene Uberman's house and had lunch with her. Do you know what your husband did during that same time period?"

"No." She kept eating.

"Okay. What were you doing that day?" I took a bite of my sandwich.

"The police already asked me that."

"Then you shouldn't have any trouble remembering what you told them."

Her fork clattered to the tabletop. With obvious impatience, she used her fingers to tick off each item she listed. "In the morning I was at the fitness center for a yoga class and a massage. In the afternoon I had an appointment at a salon in Middletown. I had a facial, the hairdresser touched up my highlights, and the nail specialist gave me a manicure."

They still looked pretty good to me, but I'm not much of a judge of such things. I make do with a pair of nail clippers and a file and haven't put on nail polish for decades.

"When did you get home?"

"It must have been five or five-thirty. Gregory arrived a little while later, before six. We had pre-dinner drinks and then went out to eat at that new restaurant in Monticello."

I'd been scribbling notes as she spoke, sketching out the roughest of timelines by making boxes for AM, PM, and evening and filling them in for both Onslow and his wife.

"What did you talk about over dinner?" I asked. "Did he tell you about his day?"

"He never even mentioned his set-to with you." Giselle's smile was wry. "I had to see that online, along with everyone else in town. To tell you the truth, we hardly talked at all that evening. Gregory was in one of his uncommunicative moods. It was nearly eleven by the time we returned home. I was tired, so I went straight up to bed. I never saw him again."

"He didn't join you?"

"I don't know. I was asleep. Back then, getting my beauty rest wasn't a problem."

Clear conscience versus guilty one? I wondered about that, but I knew better than to ask such a question aloud. There was no point in alienating Giselle before I learned all she could tell me.

"Did you hear his phone ring during the night? Someone must have contacted him to convince him to go out to the construction site."

She shook her head. "The police asked that, too." She hesitated, then added, "From something that detective said, I think his phone must be missing. Do you suppose the person who murdered him took it?"

Well, there was a clue, but I didn't know what to do with it.

"What about his car?"

A small frown line appeared in her perfect forehead. "What about it?"

"Did he drive to Feldman's?"

"Oh. No. The Porsche was still in the garage the next morning. I don't know how he got there."

Another dead end.

"Let's go back to the beginning of the

timeline again. Your husband wasn't alone in his car at the gas station. Ariadne Toothaker was with him. Do you know why?"

"I suppose they were on their way to a meeting of some kind, but I really have no idea. Does it matter?"

"I don't know."

I thought about that as I ate the rest of my sandwich, wishing I'd asked Ariadne more specific questions when I'd had the chance. Giselle stared off into space, her expression unrevealing.

Time to play hardball.

"If you didn't have anything to do with the business after your marriage, aren't you a little out of your depth now that you've taken over as CEO?"

"I'm a fast learner, and I wasn't entirely out of the loop. I made friends when I worked at MVV. They kept me informed."

Friends? Or a spy or two?

"Forgive me for saying so, but from what you've said, it sounds to me as if you and your husband barely communicated. Why did you marry him if you had so little in common?"

"He swept me off my feet." She sounded just a trifle defensive. "Gregory was a very charismatic man."

231

And a rich one.

"And yet, apparently, you still had feelings for my cousin. Luke's carried a torch for you since before your marriage to Greg Onslow. You must have given him some encouragement. You two reconnected awfully quickly after the murder."

She leaned across the table, the very picture of earnestness. "Once Gregory was gone, I saw him more clearly. He . . . manipulated people. I loved him. I did. But with his death, it was as if a veil lifted and I saw how much better Luke would be for me."

"And the fact that he finally convinced you he has money has nothing to do with it?"

Her head snapped back as if she'd been slapped. "I'd love him whether he had money or not."

Her voice had risen loud enough that Ada, her waitress, and most of the remaining lunch customers turned to look our way. There was passion behind Giselle's avowal, but I wasn't convinced of her sincerity. Maybe she wasn't a black widow — the jury was still out on that issue — but I felt certain she was a gold digger.

"If you love my cousin, you'll cut all ties with him until after the police figure out who killed your husband."

Sounding testy, she said, "I've already agreed that you're to act as a go-between while we're apart."

It was time to regroup. I forced a smile, remembering too late that before questioning her relationship with Luke, I'd meant to ask her about her life prior coming to Lenape Hollow. Darlene still hadn't had any luck discovering where Giselle had come from or who she'd been before she married the mysterious Mr. Wyncoop.

"I apologize for doubting your feelings for Luke. I care about him, too. I couldn't bear it if you broke his heart a second time."

"I guess you have a right to be concerned about his happiness." She stopped toying with her napkin and glanced up to meet my eyes. "In the meantime, it's good that you and I have a legitimate reason to meet. How *are* you coming with the proofreading?"

I put down the glass I'd been about to sip from to send her a puzzled look. "I haven't begun. So far no one from Mongaup Valley Ventures has sent me anything to work on."

Her lips pursed in annoyance. "You should have received an email with attachments by now. I'll have a word with my vice president."

"Would that be Ms. Toothaker?"

Giselle grimaced. "She was against hiring you. She said it was because you wouldn't have time for us, what with all your other clients, but I think that was just an excuse. Surely you can't have all that many of them."

Ouch!

"Don't worry. I finish all my editing jobs on schedule."

Giselle pushed her empty plate aside and signaled for the check. "Are you still working for Sunny Feldman?"

"I am. As you know, she's writing a memoir, but she's not, as your late husband believed, trying to derail the demolition of Feldman's Catskill Resort Hotel."

"I don't know where he got that idea. She met with him at least once, but as far as I know, their business had nothing to do with the hotel."

"Your husband and Sunny had a meeting?" I couldn't keep the surprise out of my voice. "When was this?"

Ada's arrival with the bill delayed her answer.

"It was a few weeks before he died," Giselle said when we had privacy once more. "She came to the house, not the office. Perhaps it had something to do with some charity or a community project. Gregory was always anxious to be seen as a philanthropist."

I knew that was true. Onslow, Sunny, and I had all been involved with the local historical society the previous summer. I hadn't had the impression that they were at odds then, but no one on the society's board had liked him much. They'd tolerated him only because he'd offered free use of a venue for the quasquibicentennial pageant.

"Sunny is quite something, isn't she?" Giselle said after Ada returned her credit card and gave her the receipt. "She must be in her nineties but she's still so active. When I saw her at the library yesterday, she was on her way to look at old newspapers. I expected her to take the elevator, but she trotted down those stairs like a woman twenty years younger."

"She's only eighty-six," I informed her, once again struck by the assumptions people make about what "old" people can and cannot do.

Giselle stood to signal that our lunch, and my interrogation, had come to an end. Distracted by a new train of thought, I remained seated at the table in Harriet's after she left. Had I been too hasty to dismiss Sunny as a serious suspect? Maybe Nick wasn't the only one guilty of ageism.

I'd looked at Sunny, sixteen years my senior, and stereotyped her as an elderly woman with a cane. Because of that, I'd placed her in the "harmless" category, ignoring the fact that she more often used her cane to prod people into moving out of her way than as an aid to walking. Sunny Feldman could give Ruth Bader Ginsburg a run for her money.

Something else bothered me about Giselle's sighting of Sunny at the library, too. I'd been under the impression that, for religious reasons, Sunny couldn't do any work on her book until after Passover. If I was wrong about that, it raised a troubling question, something I'd wondered about at the time she'd given me that excuse. Had Sunny deliberately misled me to stop me from delving more deeply into her relationship with Greg Onslow?

Giselle remained at the top of my list of suspects, but now I had to move Sunny up a few notches. I returned home in a troubled state of mind.

CHAPTER 27

Nick and I declared a truce and went ahead with the agenda we'd agreed upon the previous day. Ducking in and out of scattered showers, I gave him the grand tour of Lenape Hollow and its environs, stretching it out by including Bethel Woods in the itinerary. It is, after all, the site of that legendary music festival, Woodstock, a name familiar to people even younger than Nick.

We returned to my house on Wedemeyer Terrace around four that afternoon to find Detective Brightwell waiting for me. He'd parked across the street and got out of his car as soon as I pulled into my driveway. A second sheriff's department vehicle arrived on the scene just as I slid out from behind the steering wheel and opened my umbrella.

"Detective," I greeted him. I nodded to the deputy, a man I dimly recognized but whose name I couldn't recall. "Has something happened?"

"You could say that." He shifted his gaze to Nick. "And you are?"

"Nick Carpenter. Mikki is my aunt."

"Nick is visiting me for a few days. What's going on?" I lifted my umbrella in an attempt to persuade my nephew to share it, but he ignored the offer.

"Why don't we all go inside?" suggested Detective Brightwell, who was getting equally wet. "I'm sure you don't want to provide entertainment for the neighbors."

"Now you sound like my mother. Do you really think no one has noticed the patrol cars?" A Lenape Hollow police cruiser rolled to a stop behind the others as I spoke and Ellen Blume got out.

I headed for the porch. Nick hung back, heedless of the drizzle, to pepper the detective with questions.

"What's this all about? Haven't you badgered my aunt enough? She's told you everything she knows."

"Oh, for heaven's sake, Nick. He's not badgering me." I scurried up the steps and unlocked the front door. "Come in, gentlemen. Just give me a second to shut off the alarm system."

Once it was deactivated, I gestured for them to precede me into the living room. I thought about offering to make coffee, but

238

since I was pretty sure this wasn't a social call, I decided it would be better not to draw it out.

Detective Brightwell didn't keep me in suspense. "We've had an anonymous tip, Ms. Lincoln. I can get a search warrant if necessary, but I'm hoping you'll simplify matters by giving us permission to search your house."

"Why should she?" Nick demanded.

"Hush, Nick. I have nothing to hide." I just hoped they wouldn't make too much of a mess and that no one would comment on the dust bunnies under the bed and elsewhere. I'm not the world's greatest housekeeper. "Go ahead, Detective. Do you want us to leave while you have a look around?"

"That won't be necessary, but I would like you two to stay in this room."

He left Ellen behind to stand guard over us while he and the deputy, assisted by two more, newly arrived, spread out through the house. I settled down on the loveseat to wait, certain they would find nothing incriminating. Nick paced. After a few minutes Calpurnia, roused from a nap by the searchers, appeared in the hall doorway.

Ellen had met my cat on previous occasions and was quick to shower her with the attention Calpurnia felt was her due. Holding my fur-baby against her like a shield, Ellen fielded the questions Nick threw at her, answering with shrugs and the occasional "I really can't say." I kept my mouth closed, but I felt certain that if my nephew hadn't been in the room with us, I'd have been able to persuade her to be more forthcoming.

Not much more than a quarter of an hour passed before Detective Brightwell opened the pocket doors between the living room and dining room and beckoned to me. "If you could come in here for a moment, please, Ms. Lincoln?"

"Certainly."

Nick was right behind me, all but breathing down my neck.

At first I didn't understand what had captured Brightwell's attention. Nothing appeared to be out of place. Then a deputy shifted slightly and I saw that the lid of the hassock was open. A second survey of the room showed me that Nick had left the clicker lying on the end table instead of replacing it when he turned off the TV. That meant the storage space inside the hassock should contain only two remote controls.

I stepped closer, coming to a halt when Brightwell signaled for me to stop. Even at that distance, I had a clear view of the interior. I blinked, but the extra object was still there.

"Is that your gun?" Brightwell asked.

"No." My denial was fierce but barely audible. My heart raced. For just an instant, I felt dizzy.

"Are you certain?"

I cleared my throat. "I've never owned a gun in my life and I've never seen that one before. I have no idea where it came from."

Nick slung a comforting arm around my shoulders. His voice was quietly furious. "Someone put it there, Detective. Someone who's trying to frame my aunt for murder."

"We don't know that this is the murder weapon." Brightwell steered us back into the living room, closing the pocket doors behind us and leaving his men to process their find.

I sank down onto the loveseat once more, confused and a trifle weak in the knees. Nick sat next to me, offering silent support, and Calpurnia hopped into my lap. Stroking my hand over her fur in a slow, deliberate motion helped regulate my heart rate, but my mind continued to race.

Nick was right. Some unknown person had to have planted that gun on the premises. But how could anyone have gained entry to my house? And why try to frame me? Out of all the people who might be considered suspects in Onslow's murder, why pick me to implicate?

I looked up to find Detective Brightwell leaning against the fireplace. He was staring at me with a perplexed expression on his face.

"You didn't expect to find anything, either, did you? You were as surprised as I was when you saw that gun. You thought your anonymous tip would turn out to be a crank call."

He neither admitted to nor denied any of these charges, but his next words confirmed that I'd guessed correctly. "Do you have any idea how long that gun has been in the hassock?"

Nick chimed in before I could answer. "It wasn't there this morning when I removed the remote so I could watch TV. Someone must have broken into the house while we were out."

He was about to bound to his feet when I caught hold of his arm to stop him. "That theory won't fly, Nick. The security system was on." I turned my head to lock eyes with Brightwell. "You saw for yourself that I had to turn it off when we came in."

His gaze shifted to Nick. "Mr. Carpenter, can you verify that your aunt armed her security system when you and she left the house?"

Something subtle changed in Nick's manner. He was no longer so belligerent and he stumbled over his words when he assured Brightwell that he'd watched me set it. All my junior high school teacher instincts rushed to the fore. Naughty preteens have their tells. So do grown-up boys.

"Nick," I asked. "Is there something you'd like to share?"

He stared at the carpet, holding himself so stiffly that in a gale he'd have been the tree that toppled because it could not bend. It was left to me to inform the detective that the alarm had not been on during the middle part of the day.

"I turned it off when I went out to keep a luncheon engagement," I explained. "Since Nick stayed here, there was no need to leave it on while I was gone."

Brightwell's attention remained fixed on my nephew. "Mr. Carpenter, were you in the house the entire time Ms. Lincoln was gone?"

Nick fidgeted, earning a glare from Calpurnia when he bumped against her. "Not exactly. But I set the alarm when I went out and turned it off again when I returned.

Aunt Mikki gave me the code and a house key."

"That's right. I did." I just hadn't known he'd used them.

"Where did you go?" Brightwell asked. "How long were you gone?"

"I just drove around for a bit." Nick sent me a look of apology for what he was about to share. "We'd had words before Aunt Mikki left and I was . . . agitated. I needed to get out of the house. I didn't go far. I don't know the area at all, so I —"

"Is that your car in the garage?" Brightwell interrupted.

Nick nodded.

"The garage was locked when we got here, as was the house. Did Ms. Lincoln also give you her garage door opener?"

I wouldn't have thought a forty-year-old man capable of blushing, but the back of Nick's neck colored. Even the tips of his ears turned red.

Once again, I had to answer for him. "No, I didn't. The opener was with me in my car. Nick? Did you leave the garage door up when you went out?"

"Of course not. I closed it. I just didn't lock it. Anyway, I don't see why that should matter. The *house* was secure."

"Tell me your exact movements," Brightwell said.

In a disgruntled voice, Nick complied. "I entered the garage from the house first and opened the garage door. Then I came back inside, set the alarm, and left by the front door. I wasn't gone more than half an hour," he added defensively.

"Let me make sure I've got this straight," Brightwell said. "You're saying the garage door was unlocked for about a half hour early this afternoon?"

"Well, I had to be able to put my car away again when I got back, didn't I? What's the problem? Aunt Mikki has alarms on all the entrances to the house. No one could get inside without setting off the security system."

Brightwell and I exchanged an exasperated look.

"Not *all* the doors are alarmed, Nick."

"Stay here." Brightwell's tone brooked no disobedience.

I didn't need to follow him to know he was checking the door from the dining room into the sunroom and the one between the sunroom and the garage. He returned less than five minutes later.

"There's no sign of tampering," he reported, "but it wouldn't have been necessary for someone to break in. Neither door was locked."

"Well, I guess that explains how the gun ended up in my hassock."

"It provides one possible explanation," Brightwell conceded. "I'll need formal statements from you both, and I'm afraid you're going to have a mess to clean up. We'll be dusting for fingerprints anywhere an intruder is likely to have touched."

When he left us to give orders to his men, Nick turned to me with a sheepish expression on his face. "I'm sorry, Aunt Mikki. If I hadn't gone out, no one would have been able to get in."

"I'm the one who didn't notice that I'd left the door between the sunroom and the garage unlocked."

Thinking back, I did a quick mental calculation. It had probably been that way ever since the day I showed it to Detective Brightwell. That had been well over a week ago.

"Sometimes I leave the garage unlocked myself," I said to console Nick. "After all, the car isn't the only thing I keep in there. It's also where I store my snow shovel, assorted gardening tools, and the lawn mower. I need easy access to all of those."

"You're just saying that to try to make me feel better."

"Is it working?"

Nick managed a self-conscious smile. "Yeah."

I could hardly be mad at him when his testimony was the only thing keeping me out of jail. He was my witness that the hassock contained nothing more incriminating than three remote controls until after we'd both left the house. Assuming that gun was the weapon used to shoot Greg Onslow, and I didn't see how it could be anything but, the fact that Nick had given the killer a window of opportunity to plant it provided yet another argument against believing I was the one who'd committed the murder. It didn't escape my notice that if Detective Brightwell asked, Nick could also confirm that I hadn't gone anywhere near the dining room between the time I returned from lunch and the time the two of us went out together. Thanks to my favorite nephew, there was plenty of evidence that I couldn't have hidden anything, let alone a gun, where the police had found it.

Be grateful for small favors, I told myself.

CHAPTER 28

"Why don't you let me take care of the cleanup," Nick offered after the police finally left. "You look done in."

"Oh, thank you so much. You certainly know how to flatter a woman."

"Do *you* want to tackle that fingerprint powder?"

"No. No, I don't. Between all the excitement today and the nasty weather, I have a bit of a headache. I think I'll just go lie down for a while and hope the thunderstorms the weatherman predicted don't wake me."

"Do you still want to go out to eat? I can make supper."

I shook my head. "I'm not really hungry. I know it's still early, but I'm going to call it a night. Fix yourself whatever you want."

The pounding in my head was quite genuine; the lack of appetite — not so much. What I needed most, rather desperately, was solitude. It worried me more than I was willing to let on that someone had deliberately set me up to be charged with first-degree murder.

I retreated to my room, removed my hearing aids, and took off my glasses. Still fully clothed except for my shoes, I collapsed onto the bed. All the energy abruptly drained out of my body. I longed for the oblivion of sleep, but my mind refused to settle. My thoughts kept circling back to one question — why had Onslow's killer tried to frame *me* for his murder?

Had it simply been because that video identified me as a likely scapegoat? Or was there more to it than that? Had I, without realizing it, come close to discovering the identity of the person who really shot Greg Onslow?

"I should be so lucky," I muttered.

I lay on my back, staring at the ceiling. Darkness descended, broken now and again by distant flashes of lightning. As far as I could tell, I hadn't uncovered any significant clues, nothing that pinpointed any particular person as the villain. I might believe Giselle had the best motive, and suspect that Sunny had misled me, and wonder if Luke had told me everything about his relationship with the merry widow, but so far I had no proof of anything. My guesses were as likely to be wrong as right.

One thought nagged at me, throwing my suppositions about Giselle into confusion. She'd been with me at the time my house was invaded. When we'd written our formal statements for Detective Brightwell, it had come out that Nick arrived back at the house only a few minutes before I returned. Giselle would have had to move at warp speed to beat me home from Harriet's and get in and out before Nick showed up . . . unless she had an accomplice.

Although Luke was obviously smitten with Giselle, I couldn't imagine him in the role, not when I was the one that gun was intended to implicate. Still, his infatuation with her troubled me deeply, especially when I thought about the details I had yet to add to my written timeline.

Luke had initially told me it was around three in the morning when he was seen passing the entrance to the hotel grounds. Later he'd said that it was two o'clock when he drove by the Onslow house. That left the best part of an hour unaccounted for.

Both Luke and Giselle denied having an affair while Onslow was alive. I was inclined to believe them, if only because being together during that missing hour would have given them an alibi for the time of the murder. Unfortunately, I liked other possibilities even less. Luke might have been lurking outside the Onslow house at the crucial time, hoping for a glimpse of his lady love. Or one or both of them could have been up to something more sinister.

At some point, I drifted into a restless sleep. When I opened my eyes again it was pitch black in the room. For a moment, I couldn't think why I was lying on top of the covers. Even more unusual was the absence of the cat.

Then the afternoon's events came back in a rush. I remembered everything, including the fact that I'd closed the bedroom door as a signal to Nick that I didn't wish to be disturbed. The only surprise was that Calpurnia hadn't stationed herself on the other side, yowling a blue streak until I woke up and let her in.

I was reaching for the clock on my nightstand when my mind circled back to the question of why someone would try to frame me. On the surface, the answer was glaringly obvious. Anyone who'd seen that infamous video must think I'd make an ideal patsy. Thank goodness for Nick's testimony that there had been no gun in the hassock before I left to meet Giselle for lunch. Even so, I expected the police would keep looking into my movements. They wouldn't completely rule me out until they'd dug into my past, asked intrusive questions of my friends, and found additional reasons to believe in my innocence. They were probably checking Nick's background, too.

At that thought, I sat up straight, swaying a little when the abrupt movement made my head swim. My headache was better, but it had not entirely been vanquished.

Background, I thought. *Is that the key?*

Although I'd initially included them on the list of suspects, I'd been inclined early on to rule out certain people — Darlene, Frank, even Ronnie — because I was familiar with their history. I knew a lot about Sunny's past, too, although I still had questions for her. But what did I really know about Jenni, even though she was a local girl? And Giselle's history was still largely blank.

Time to remedy that, I decided. Gingerly, I got off the bed and padded to the door. It was after ten, earlier than I'd thought but late enough that it was likely Nick had already retired for the night. I peered into the stairwell, confirming that no lights showed from downstairs.

My stomach growled. The sound was so loud I was afraid it would wake my nephew, but nothing stirred behind the door to his room. Cautiously, careful to avoid the treads that squeaked, I descended the stairs.

Nick had closed the glass-paneled door between the foyer and the downstairs hall, trapping Calpurnia on the other side. She let me know in no uncertain terms how she felt about that and followed me into the kitchen to demand that I refill her dish before I foraged for food for myself.

My nephew had kept his promise to clean up after the police. Then he'd dined on frozen pizza, polishing off three-quarters of the pie. Fortunately, I like mine cold. Since I'd left my laptop on the dinette table earlier in the day, I didn't have to go back to my office to get started on my research. I settled in with the leftovers and a cold glass of milk and began my online search with Jenni Farquhar.

There wasn't much to find, and none of it seemed incriminating. Her family had been in the area for generations. They all appeared to have been hard-working, salt-of-the-earth types. I already knew she still lived at home and I was aware of her work history. I also knew she'd been delusional enough to think she had a shot at marrying the boss. That was really the only reason she was still on my list of suspects.

Next I tried searching online for Giselle, but I had no better luck than Darlene had in discovering what her life had been like before she became the Widow Wyncoop. It was nearly one in the morning before I gave up. By then my head was pounding so hard that I could barely think straight.

I took a couple of Tylenol and went back to bed.

CHAPTER 29

Since the next morning was Saturday, I indulged myself and slept in. Nick was already up when I drifted into the kitchen and headed for the coffeepot. He knew me well enough not to try and make conversation until I'd had my first hit of caffeine.

My mug was half empty by the time my toast had popped and been slathered with butter substitute, which I honestly think tastes better than the real thing. I sat down across from my nephew, for the first time taking note of the serious expression on his face.

Something was up.

"Did you sleep okay?" I asked.

He answered me with a scowl.

I reached across the table and patted his hand. "You don't need to worry about me. Detective Brightwell doesn't really think I'm guilty."

"I know I don't *need* to. That doesn't

255

mean I can stop." He drained his coffee mug, grimacing when he realized the dregs had gone cold. He got up and poured himself a refill. When he resumed his seat, the look he aimed my way contained equal parts of concern, frustration, and determination.

"I kept waking up, wondering when we'll see that detective again. I don't think he believed me."

"Why wouldn't he?"

"I'm a stranger. I'm your nephew. He probably thinks I lied to protect you. I guess I can't fault him for that. As it turned out, I didn't have to make anything up, but I might have if I'd thought they were about to arrest you."

I wasn't sure how to respond to that. *Thank you* didn't seem appropriate. After a moment, I said, "I'd never want you to perjure yourself on my account. And you mustn't worry. Given time, this whole mess will straighten itself out. Detective Brightwell will track down Onslow's killer."

"You have more faith in him than I do."

I let his assumption stand. It would have been counter-productive to tell Nick I intended to assist the good detective in his investigation. He wouldn't approve. Worse, he might insist on helping me.

"What if the police harass you again?" Nick asked.

"I don't think the local constabulary is about to rush in and slap the handcuffs on."

He ignored the sarcasm in my voice. "You don't *know* that, which means it's not a good idea for you to talk to them again without a lawyer present. You need to hire someone with experience in criminal cases, someone to represent your interests and give you legal advice."

"Oh, please. Detective Brightwell is not going to try to railroad me just to get an arrest."

"Innocent people are arrested all the time. Some of them end up being convicted and sent to prison. I don't want that to happen to you."

I bit back my automatic response, which would have been both rude and ineffectual. *He means well,* I reminded myself for what seemed like the hundredth time.

"I doubt I'll be interviewed again. I've already told the police everything I know."

Since I'd finished breakfast, I reached over to the window seat to scratch Calpurnia behind the ears. One of them twitched, but that was the only sign she was still among the living. She'd slept through the entire meal, missing the opportunity to check for scraps and making me suspect that Nick had fed her as soon as he got up. On top of what I'd given her in the middle of the night, she was fully fortified to commit to a long day of napping.

"I have to leave for a little while," I announced when I'd dumped my dishes into the sink. I was already dressed to go out in jeans and a long-sleeved, flowered top. "Make yourself at home. I'll be back soon."

That went over like the proverbial lead balloon.

"Where are you going?" Nick fixed me with a look better suited to interrogating a teenage son than a septuagenarian aunt.

In the interest of family harmony, I humored him. "I need to check on something at the library."

"Can't you find what you need online?"

"Not everything is on the Internet."

"I'll come with you."

"That's not necessary." I didn't snap at him, but it was a near thing. "Please believe me when I tell you I'm not about to be arrested. There's no need for you to hover."

"That detective isn't the only one I'm worried about. Maybe a bodyguard isn't such a bad idea."

That statement stopped me in my tracks.

"What on earth are you blathering on about now?"

His eyebrows lifted at my rudeness, but it wasn't enough to deter him. "That guy's killer was in this house yesterday, Aunt Mikki. What if he's stalking you?"

That possibility honestly hadn't occurred to me. A finger of ice ran up my spine at the thought, but I managed to put on a brave face.

"That seems highly unlikely, Nick. At worst, he — or *she* — was watching the house, looking for an opportunity to get inside and leave the gun. The person who did that won't risk being seen nearby again." Inspiration struck. "Besides, if the police are supposed to believe I'm the murderer, it defeats the whole purpose of the frame-up to recast me as victim number two."

His scowl was fierce. "This isn't a joking matter."

"I'm not kidding, and I really need to get going. You may be on vacation, but I still have work to do." Without giving him a chance to come up with another reason to accompany me, I grabbed a sweater to ward off the morning chill and headed out.

CHAPTER 30

The police have many more ways than civilians do to check into suspects' backgrounds, analyze clues, and solve crimes. I wasn't about to set myself up in competition with Detective Brightwell, but I hoped to satisfy my curiosity about one or two minor matters. I thought I might be able to tie up one loose end by talking to Pam Ingram.

The library was quiet when I arrived. A bored-looking part-time library volunteer was at the circulation desk. I found Pam in her tiny office, a space barely large enough to hold a desk, two chairs, and a file cabinet. Another small room served as the command center for processing new materials and mailing out books borrowed through the interlibrary loan system.

When I moved aside a stack of publishers' catalogues so I could close the door, Pam looked up and frowned. I knew I was being pushy, but I didn't want our conversation to be overheard. I plunked myself down in the guest chair so that we were eye to eye and watched her expression change to one of mild puzzlement.

"I have a question about Sunny Feldman," I said. "Was she here in the library on Thursday?"

"It may have been Thursday," Pam said. "I know I saw her sometime during the past week. She was in one of the carrels in the basement. I assumed she was continuing with the research you two have been doing."

Pam shuffled the papers on her desk, avoiding my gaze. I wondered if she was remembering her display of emotion on the day she interrupted us with the news of Onslow's death, but I didn't give the subject much thought.

It was Sunny's behavior that interested me. Had she taken my advice to verify details in her memoirs with facts from newspaper articles? It was possible. Once Passover was officially at an end, I'd ask her. I'd also try to find out why she'd told me she couldn't work on her memoir until after the twenty-seventh. It was a small anomaly, but it nagged at me.

"Is that all you wanted?" Pam asked when I'd been silent too long.

I hesitated. She didn't look all that anxious to get back to what she'd been doing when I interrupted her, and she was in a position, as town librarian, to observe the activities of many of Lenape Hollow's citizens, including Sunny Feldman.

"Do you think she really needs that cane?"

Pam's smile was wry. "Sure she does. How else would she convince people to get out of her way? She whacked me a good one with it once, just because I wasn't moving fast enough to suit her."

"Usually she just pokes people with it."

"Whatever works, I suppose. She can get away with it because she's such a fixture in this community. People excuse her by saying she's eccentric or 'just Sunny being Sunny.' If you want my opinion, it's a miracle she's never misjudged her swing and caused a serious injury. I keep expecting her to crack open someone's skull."

"Surely she can't put much strength into her swing. Maybe her blows aren't that hard."

"I can tell you from personal experience that her cane leaves a bruise. She's stronger than she looks."

"In that case, I'm surprised no one's ever had her arrested for assault or sued her for damages. She's rich enough to make a "lawsuit worthwhile."

"But Mikki, the woman's a local legend."

I ignored the sarcasm in her tone. "What do you know about her background, apart from her family connection to the resort the Feldmans used to own?"

"What else is there? She sold out at just the right time with the upshot that she's wealthier than Ronnie North. She's never married. She's active in the historical society — but you already know that — and in a few other civic and charitable organizations around town."

"What about her church? Synagogue, I mean. Or do I mean temple?" It had belatedly occurred to me that although Sunny's memoir dealt with growing up at a resort catering to Jewish guests and serving kosher food, she had never once mentioned attending religious services of any kind.

"The local synagogue was Congregation Beth Israel. It closed its doors a few years ago because not enough people were attending services there anymore. They have to drive to Monticello now and I assume Sunny does. I know she's active in the Catskill Mountain chapter of the Hadassah. She puts up posters in the library for events they sponsor. She never asks permission first, either. She just pins them to the community bulletin board." Pam winced as she listened to herself. "I'm not being fair, am I? I guess I resent that bruise she gave me more than I realized."

"Perfectly understandable." I couldn't contain a chuckle.

She smiled in return.

Smiled? No, that's too pedestrian a description. Pam's face blossomed as genuine amusement shone through. Combined with her peaches-and-cream complexion, the expression made her otherwise ordinary features striking.

I stared at her, trying to pin down why the transformation left me feeling unnerved. According to Darlene, Pam had been twenty-four, relatively young for the position, when she took over as head librarian. That was eight years ago, so that made her about thirty-two. For some reason, I'd thought she was older. Although she was far from glamorous, she wasn't unattractive even when she didn't smile, and when she did . . .

All of a sudden, a picture of Jenni Farquhar, sitting across a picnic table from me, popped into my mind. She'd told me that all the time she thought Greg Onslow was interested in her, he'd been seeing someone else — someone whose name Jenni didn't know; someone she'd seen around town; someone who was old — at least thirty — and could stand to lose a few pounds; someone with ordinary brown hair but *nice skin.*

The rest of the pieces of the puzzle slid rapidly into place. Pam had been delighted when I'd routed my opposition at the gas station. She'd been glad to see Greg Onslow run off with his tail between his legs. Given her obvious dislike of him, the news of his death shouldn't have made her cry unless . . .

The accusation burst out of me before I could stop it. "You were involved with Greg Onslow!"

Every vestige of color drained from Pam's cheeks. "How did you know?"

"Someone described you to me."

"Someone *else* knows?"

Her agonized whisper had me reaching across the desk to put my hand over hers.

"No one you need to worry about. She doesn't even know your name." I hesitated. "Is there some particular reason you two kept your relationship secret?"

"I'm not married, if that's what you mean, but I'd really prefer not to have the whole town know he dumped me."

"When?"

"Right after he met Giselle." She managed a humorless half smile. "Like I could compete!"

"But you still had feelings for him." It wasn't a question.

She sat back, pulling free of my grip. "I suppose you think that was poor judgment on my part. I guess it was. I knew he had a reputation as a . . . well, to be blunt about it, as a crook and a cheat, but he could be charming and I was . . . physically attracted to him. He was a widower. I was single. There was no reason we shouldn't date. And yet . . ."

"And yet?"

"I always wondered why he was interested in me. I'm not beautiful or rich. I decided it must have been because I was respectable and he was trying to improve his public image. That was certainly his motivation last summer when he offered to provide the venue, free of charge, for the historical society's pageant."

"If that was his reason," I said slowly, considering what I knew of Onslow, "why would he keep quiet about dating you? Wouldn't he want everyone to know you were going out with him so they'd think better of him?"

"I was the one who insisted on secrecy. I

was afraid of what people would say about me, and I wasn't at all confident about the depth of his feelings. Then, just when I was beginning to believe he was sincere —" She broke off, too choked up to continue.

"He dumped you," I finished. "Cad. Louse."

A small, muffled laugh issued from behind the hands she'd lifted to cover her face.

Making my voice as nonthreatening as I could, I asked, "Do the police know about the two of you?"

"No!" Her head came up, eyes wide. "Please, Mikki. Promise me you won't tell *anyone.*"

"I can't do that, Pam. Don't you see? You had reason to hate him and now he's dead. Sooner or later, the police *will* find out, and the fact that you didn't volunteer the information will make you look even more suspicious."

"But I didn't kill him. I might have been tempted to push Giselle down a convenient flight of stairs, but I'd never have harmed Greg. The months we had together were the most exciting time of my life."

I tried and failed to picture Pam Ingram shooting Greg Onslow and throwing his body into an open pit, especially right after she'd had the satisfaction of seeing me

267

knock him down a peg in public. I couldn't imagine him agreeing to meet an ex-lover at the construction site in the wee hours of the morning, either, nor could I think of a single reason why she'd ask him to. The idea that she'd later sneak into my house, plant the murder weapon, and phone the police with an anonymous tip struck me as even more preposterous.

"Do you have an alibi for the time of the murder?" I asked.

She shook her head. "I was home. Asleep. Alone."

"Me too. Except for the cat, and she's not talking."

"I don't have any pets." Her smile was weak but genuine. "I've thought about adopting a pair of kittens, but the old maid librarian who keeps cats is such a cliché."

I sighed. "I'm not going to rush right over to the police station and rat you out," I promised, "but you need to talk to Detective Brightwell soon. Take it from someone who knows. In a murder investigation, neglecting to mention even the smallest detail can come back to haunt you."

CHAPTER 31

"We're going back out," Nick announced as soon as I returned home from the library.

"Oh?" I packed a lot into that one word — suspicion, mild irritation, amusement, even affection.

"I've found you a lawyer. We have an appointment with her in half an hour."

"You what?" The words came out as a bleat. I couldn't believe he'd gone behind my back like that.

"You heard me."

I took one look at his outthrust chin and mulish expression and decided there was no point in arguing. I told myself it couldn't hurt to talk to an attorney, even if I didn't really need one.

"What kind of lawyer works on a Saturday?" I asked as he hustled me outside and into the passenger seat of my car.

He didn't answer. He was too busy searching for a starter button. When it finally dawned on him that he'd need an actual key to insert into the ignition, he also realized that getting hold of one required my cooperation.

I tucked my bag between the seat and the door and crossed my arms over my chest. "Let me phrase that another way. Since when do lawyers have weekend hours? Aren't they all off playing golf?"

"I called around until I found someone. You're right. It wasn't easy to talk her into seeing us today. She's already got a full caseload, too."

"So why did she agree?"

"I told her the police are harassing you. That detective had no right to badger you, and you never should have allowed him to search your house without a warrant."

"First of all, he was just doing his job. More to the point, cooperating with the police is always a good idea. I'm not under arrest, am I, even though he found what he was looking for?"

"Stop being so stubborn, Aunt Mikki. What will it hurt to talk to someone who knows the legal ins and outs?"

"*I'm* stubborn?"

"As a mule."

"It takes one to know one," I muttered. In a slightly louder voice, I said, "This was not

270

your decision to make, Nicky."

"*Someone* had to do something." He held out a hand for my car keys.

My glare didn't faze him in the least.

He's worried about you, I reminded myself. *You're lucky to have someone who cares.*

Although I still wasn't happy about the situation, I fished my key ring out of my bag and handed it over. "What can you tell me about this lawyer we're going to see?"

Nick started the car and backed out of my driveway. "Her name is Ashley Mills. She really knows her stuff. She's got a great reputation."

"How do you know that?"

"I researched her online." He drove to the south end of Wedemeyer Terrace and turned left, heading downtown along the aptly named South Street.

"Oh, *that* inspires confidence!"

He rattled off details of a couple of prominent cases she'd handled. One of the defendants had been found guilty, but he'd been given a much lighter sentence because of her advocacy.

"She's going to demand a hefty retainer," I warned him. "I'm doing okay in the freelance editing business and I have my retirement income, but I'm not exactly wealthy. I have to keep to a pretty tight

271

budget."

"I'll take care of it." Once he reached South Main, he turned right and continued on past the Presbyterian church and the road that led to the cemetery.

"I can't allow you —"

"Would it kill you to let someone else shoulder the responsibility for once?" Nick made a sharp right onto Elm Street and a few moments later pulled into a curbside parking space. "The retainer's already taken care of. You may as well get the good out of it."

Those were words to warm the heart of any frugal New Englander, even a transplanted one like me. I left the car and followed him into the law office of Ashley Mills.

She ran her one-person practice out of a first-floor room in her home. It was simply but comfortably furnished in neutral shades. The only hint of color came from a vase full of tulips on the credenza, a pleasant reminder that in spite of there having been a murder in our small town, it was spring, a time of renewed hope for the future.

The sun is shining, I thought. *The temperature is mild. Soon all will be right with the world.*

Fat chance!

In reality, it was forty degrees outside and cloudy and windy, too. A little north of us they'd had over six inches of snow during the night.

Ashley Mills turned out to be the down-to-earth practical type. She was in her late thirties with mud-colored hair, hazel eyes, and a square jaw. Since it was the weekend, she could be excused for meeting us wearing a tunic and yoga pants. Nick looked dismayed by her choice of attire, but I felt certain she dressed more conservatively when she was in court. That was something I devoutly hoped I'd never have occasion to witness firsthand.

"Your nephew has already provided me with the basic facts of your involvement in the case," she informed me when he and I were seated on one side of her desk and she'd taken the position of power on the other. "Now I'd like to hear the whole story directly from you."

She took me through my various encounters with Greg Onslow and then asked me to recount the details of each of my sessions with Detective Brightwell. She made copious notes. Nearly an hour passed before she ran out of questions. She flipped through the close-written pages, pondering, before she finally looked up and met my eyes.

"Honestly, I don't think you have anything to worry about. It sounds to me as if the police are just checking into all the possibilities."

I couldn't help myself. I looked at Nick and smirked. Wasn't that just what I'd been telling him all along?

"What about that gun?" he demanded.

"If they thought your aunt hid it in that hassock, she'd have been arrested. Clearly, someone tried to make her look guilty. They failed. In fact, the attempt to frame her probably went a long way toward clearing her of any lingering suspicion." She glanced at me before shifting her focus back to Nick and sending him a reassuring smile. "I doubt she was ever a serious suspect, given the way she's helped Detective Hazlett in the past."

Before I could stop her, Ms. Mills launched into an abridged version of my previous involvement in not one but two murder investigations. Most of the details she supplied never appeared in print or online. After Nick made the appointment for me, she must have talked to someone, probably several someones, at the Lenape Hollow Police Department.

"Aunt Mikki, is all this true?" Under different circumstances, the expression of shocked disbelief on Nick's face would have amused me. He was having a hard time picturing his dear old auntie engaged in physical feats of derring-do.

"There were one or two occasions when I was in a position to provide useful information to the police," I conceded.

"It sounds like you did a lot more than that. You put yourself in mortal danger."

"It isn't as if I set out to be targeted by a killer, let alone two of them, and that's not the point anyway. What Ms. Mills was trying to get across to you is that the police have good reason to believe that what I tell them is the truth."

The lawyer cleared her throat. "Ms. Lincoln is correct. Because she had a quarrel with the victim the day before he died, Detective Brightwell had to follow procedure in order to rule her out, but I doubt he'll trouble her again."

"I don't trust him."

Nick had no need to add that he no longer trusted me, either. Keeping my previous encounters with killers to myself counted against me.

Ms. Mills repeated her reassurances, backing them up with the reminder that she dealt with criminal cases on a regular basis and knew what she was talking about.

"Why don't we leave it at this," she suggested. "You'll call me if anything new develops."

"I can agree to that." I stood and shook hands with her before my nephew could get another word in edgewise. "Come along, Nick."

Going home, I drove. He brooded in the passenger seat beside me.

"Cheer up," I said as I made the turn onto Wedemeyer Terrace. "You hired a lawyer to look after my interests and she doesn't think I have anything to worry about. You can go back to Maine with a clear conscience. Are you planning to leave for home tomorrow, or do you want to wait until Monday to head out?"

"I'm not convinced it's safe to leave you alone."

"Honestly, Nick, what more do you think you can do? I promise I'll keep Ms. Mills's number handy." His recalcitrant attitude brought out the worst in me. "I'll tuck her business card into my bra, so I'll be sure to have it with me when I'm arrested. You know — to make my one phone call."

Unable to decide if I was being facetious or not, he frowned. A moment later, his expression cleared and he blurted, "You never wear a bra."

276

I had to chuckle at the abashed look on his face. That wasn't something a forty-year-old nephew thought he should say out loud to his aunt, but it didn't bother me in the least. "Every brassiere I owned went straight into the trash the day I retired from teaching," I informed him. "I considered a ritual burning, but that seemed a bit much."

I was hoping for a laugh. No such luck.

"Aunt Mikki, you aren't taking your situation seriously. You know it isn't just Brightwell I'm concerned about. Someone tried to frame you for murder. You have an enemy — a dangerous one."

"I know you believe that, but I don't agree. I just made a handy scapegoat because of the video. Now that the attempt to frame me has failed, I'm in no danger. I'll be fine on my own."

"If even half of what Ms. Mills just told me is true," he muttered, "you haven't done a very good job of looking out for yourself since you moved here."

"I'll have you know that I have a keen sense of self-preservation." I was rapidly losing patience with my overprotective nephew. Telling myself he meant well no longer had the desired effect.

"C'mon, Aunt Mikki. Let me stick around a while longer, just to make sure you're really safe. I have another week of vacation coming. With any luck, the police will have caught the killer by the time I have to leave."

His arguments were beginning to wear me down. Moreover, I knew that if I didn't accept his offer, I'd never hear the end of it from him *or* his mother.

"Fine!" It wasn't as if having him as a houseguest was any hardship. I was fond of Nick, despite his obvious flaws. "Stay. But I warn you, you'll be bored to tears. I still have to work, and hard as it may be for you to believe, it *is* possible to run out of episodes of *Storage Wars.*"

"Don't worry," Nick assured me. "When I start hitting reruns, I'll just switch over to watching *American Pickers.*"

CHAPTER 32

Almost at once, I regretted caving in to Nick's demands. When I mentioned my plan to go out in a little while to visit Darlene, he invited himself along.

"There's no need for you to come. She's not the one who killed Greg Onslow."

I was kidding when I added that last part, but he didn't crack a smile. An all-too-familiar mulish expression hardened his features.

"She's your best friend here, right? I'd like to meet her."

His words sounded inoffensive, but the intent behind them was anything but. My nephew really believed Onslow's murderer had me in his sights. He wasn't prepared to let me go anywhere without a bodyguard.

I bit back what I really wanted to say to him, settling for a curt, "Never mind." As I retreated toward my office, I added that I'd just remembered I had some work I needed to finish.

It did not involve editing. First I composed a lengthy email to bring Darlene up-to-date on the latest developments. Then I went online. Ever since my talk with Pam Ingram, I'd been itching to find out more about her. I didn't really believe she killed Greg Onslow, but it would have been remiss of me not to check into her background.

It wasn't difficult to discover where Pam came from or where she'd gone to college. Her work history was also an open book. That she'd been married and divorced before moving to Lenape Hollow took me by surprise, but that certainly explained why she'd decided to relocate. When the library job opened up, she'd seized the opportunity to make a fresh start.

I spent a fair amount of time fiddling with my timeline for the day of the murder, but came to no new conclusions. Next on my agenda had to be a chat with Sunny Feldman, but if Nick didn't change his mind about sticking to me like glue, that was going to be difficult to arrange. My only option was to give him the slip. The plan I came up with was simple but devious.

"I'm going to church tomorrow," I informed him just before I turned in for the night. "You don't have to come along."

Predictably, Nick insisted on accompanying me.

The next morning he was already dressed in the best clothes he'd brought with him, chinos and a light blue shirt, by the time I came downstairs for breakfast.

"Have you ever *been* in a church for a regular Sunday service?" I asked as we drove downtown. Knowing the Lincoln family history, I had my doubts.

"Hey, I was married in a church."

That didn't exactly answer my question. "Of course you were. I was there. But have you been back since?"

"I've thought about it from time to time, especially with the big coincidence and all."

"What big coincidence?"

"Didn't my mom ever tell you?" He sounded surprised. "It's a neat story. She married my father when he was in the army. She went to meet him where he was stationed and the base chaplain performed the ceremony."

I signaled for the turn into the church parking lot. "All I remember is that no one in the family was invited to the wedding. Allie simply took off on her own and got hitched."

"Flash forward twenty-five years," Nick said. "Dad's sitting in the church, watching

281

me take my vows with Julie, and he keeps thinking there's something familiar about the minister. Turns out he was the same preacher who married them. Different state, different church, but the same guy. Dad talked to him at the reception and confirmed it."

"That's a nice story." I parked and turned off the engine.

"I always figured it was a good omen. Mom and Dad have a happy marriage and so do I." He followed me along the path from the parking lot and into the church.

"The pews aren't assigned," I explained, "but when I was young, my grandfather always sat in the third pew from the front on the right-hand side and I'd join him there after Sunday school. Fifty-plus years later, I still catch myself looking that way, as if I might find him waiting for me."

"Also a nice story," Nick said.

We joined Darlene, who was already settled in her accustomed pew, and I introduced them. Darlene was having a good day and had left her walker, wheelchair, and scooter at home, but she sent me a questioning look when I told her to shove in so that Nick could sit between us. That left me on the aisle, the spot she usually took.

While Nick and Darlene chatted amiably,

I kept my eyes on the choir. When they went on alert it usually signaled that the minister was about to appear. Forewarned, I was ready for action.

"I need to use the ladies' room," I whispered, already moving into the aisle. "It's downstairs next to the Sunday school rooms," I added for Nick's benefit. "If I don't make it back before the service begins, I'll just slip into a pew at the rear so I don't disturb anyone."

I did make use of the facilities.

Then I kept going into what we'd call an ell in Maine — the short section of the building between the church and the church hall. The organist had just begun to play the first hymn when I slipped outside through a back door and headed for my car.

Less than ten minutes later, I parked in front of Sunny Feldman's house.

Chapter 33

"I'd like to talk to you," I said when Sunny
opened her front door.

She didn't look pleased to see me, but she
invited me in and led the way to the library
where she'd been working.

I'd been to Sunny's house a couple of
times before. It was luxurious without being
pretentious. There were no gold toilets, but
she had collected a lovely assortment of
antiques and there were several paintings by
well-known artists gracing the walls of the
library between sets of floor-to-ceiling book-
cases.

One was a portrait of Sunny herself in her
mid-twenties. It showed her as an attractive
young woman, petite and full of laughter,
dark brown eyes all but snapping with good
humor and intelligence. She hadn't been as
plump in her youth as she was now. On the
other hand, her nose was noticeably larger.
I wasn't sure having it fixed was an improve-

ment. As the possessor of a good-sized schnoz myself, I'm of the opinion that such features lend character to a person's face.

Belatedly, I noticed the dozens of black-and-white photographs scattered across the mission-style table at the center of the room. I'd apparently interrupted Sunny in the midst of sorting them.

"Are these for the book?" I asked.

Giving an opinion on which illustrations to include with the text wasn't part of my job, but I was interested in seeing her selections. Before she could answer, I stepped close enough to recognize some pretty famous faces.

Sunny's collection included both candid shots and studio portraits. Several of the latter were autographed, most of them to Sunny's father, Abe Feldman, founder and guiding light of the resort. He'd single-handedly attracted the best comics, the finest singers, and an A-list selection of Hollywood stars to his hotel, if only for a weekend. A slogan I'd heard when I was just a kid came to mind. Without thinking, I repeated it aloud.

"Grossinger's has Eddie Fisher, Brown's has Jerry Lewis, but Feldman's has Trevor Champlain."

Trevor Champlain had attained legendary

status not only through his films but also because he died young in a terrible plane crash. There were several snapshots of him. In one he had his arm draped over Sunny's shoulders.

A strangled sound from behind had me swinging around to stare at her in alarm. "Are you okay?"

She waved off my concern. "It's nothing. What you said just took me by surprise."

"Are you planning to include an anecdote about Champlain in your book?"

"No, I am not." Taking a tighter grip on her cane, she glared at me. "What do you want, Mikki? You didn't just drop in to chat about the good old days."

"No, I didn't, but you'll notice that I *did* wait until after the twenty-seventh to bother you."

Frowning, she gestured for me to precede her out of the library, steering me into the living room instead. Two large cats, one black with white splotches and the other white and yellow with a magnificent striped tail, were already in residence, comfortably sprawled on the sofa. Sunny scooped up the one with the tail and waved me toward the empty cushion.

"Have a seat. Just shove Milo Fuzzypants out of the way if you need more room."

Milo opened one suspicious yellow eye when I transferred him to my lap instead. He weighed at least twice what Calpurnia did, but when I began to stroke his long, soft fur he responded in the same way she would have, with a rumbling purr.

"What's the other one's name?" I asked when Sunny and the second cat were settled in the comfortable-looking armchair opposite me.

"This is Kira, but you didn't come here to talk about my cats. What's the problem?"

Suddenly uncertain how to phrase my question, I hesitated before speaking. *The goal,* I reminded myself, *is to eliminate Sunny as a suspect.* I needed to resolve the discrepancy between what she'd told me and what she'd done.

"You were at the library a couple of days ago." I tensed when I heard my words emerge as an accusation.

Sunny's hand tightened on the head of her cane. For one totally irrational second, I thought she intended to strike me with it. Then I shifted my gaze to her face and realized I hadn't made her angry. To judge by her chagrined expression, she was embarrassed.

"That's right. I was there. And yes, I was looking for stories to back up my memories, just as you've been urging me to. The prohibition against doing any work during the first two days of Passover gave me time to think. I came to the conclusion you were right to push me to verify the facts."

Struck by the first part of what she'd just said, I stopped petting the cat. Milo head-butted my hand to remind me of my obligations.

"*Two* days?" I asked, resuming the rhythmic movement. "You didn't have to avoid work for the entire eight?"

Sunny leaned forward to peer into my face. Whatever she saw there caused her lips to twitch with amusement. "You don't know much about Passover, do you?"

"Not a lot," I admitted. "I don't know much about any Jewish traditions, although I did attend Frank Uberman's bar mitzvah."

"I really doubt that you did." Her voice was dry, but her eyes twinkled. "What you probably went to was the party his parents threw for him afterward."

To mix a metaphor, now that I'd been taken down another peg, I tried to accept my lumps with good grace. "Truthfully, all I remember is that I was twelve and he was thirteen and my mother was the one who picked out his birthday present. It was a biography of a baseball player. I've no idea which one or what team he played for."

Sunny said nothing. Kira appeared to have fallen asleep.

"I thought about asking Frank what's involved in celebrating Passover," I blurted.

She laughed out loud.

I shut my mouth with a snap, afraid that if I opened it again, I'd end up inserting my foot. I wasn't sure what Sunny was thinking, but the last thing I wanted was to inadvertently insult her or her religion.

"That would have been an interesting discussion," she said, still chuckling. "Frank Uberman traded in God for golf a long time ago."

I let out the breath I'd been holding. Clearly, Sunny knew Frank better than I'd realized.

"So where *did* you get your information?" she asked.

"If you mean *mis*information, I looked online under 'Passover traditions' and found a site that describes all the preparations that need to be made. That certainly explained why you told me you'd be right out straight for a few days beforehand. You had to eliminate any traces of chametz, right?"

She corrected my pronunciation but agreed. "Intensive housecleaning. All non-kosher food had to go, and the utensils I use year-round had to be locked away. The refrigerator and cabinets had to be scrubbed so nothing containing grain could contaminate kosher-for-Passover foods. Every crumb of bread had to be eradicated. Even chocolate and fermented drinks are forbidden because of the presence of grain." She shrugged. "There's a lot more to it than that, but you get the drift."

"But the website also said that all eight days of Passover were to be observed as if each one was the Sabbath. There was even a day-by-day calendar and —"

"And you decided one size fits all? Oh, Mikki, that's rich!"

"Hey, at least I tried to find out what it was all about."

"So you did. If it helps, I don't know much about your religion, either. What are you? Methodist? Lutheran? There are plenty of churches to choose from in Lenape Hollow."

"I think of myself as a lapsed Presbyterian, which is why I skipped church services this morning to talk to you."

"Yes. About my trip to the library." Her smile faded as she put two and two together. "You thought I tried to mislead you when I told you I'd be unavailable until after Passover, didn't you? And if I lied about that, then maybe I lied about my connection to Greg Onslow."

I winced. "I did wonder. Is it so surprising that I'd think you were avoiding me because I have a habit of asking nosy questions? And then, what really made me curious was hearing from Giselle that you met with her husband at their house a short time before he was murdered. So tell me, Sunny, why did you *really* want to visit the demolition site?"

"I thought you believed I was motivated by nostalgia."

"You denied it."

She shrugged. "I don't like to admit to sentimentality, but I did want one last look at my family's resort while some of the buildings were still standing." She chucked Kira under the chin and received a sleepy nuzzle in return.

"I guess I can understand that. Was that what your meeting with Onslow was about? Did he turn down your request to tour the property? I can see him doing that just to be spiteful."

Sunny's hands, the bulging veins and crisscrossing creases offering ample proof of her age, rested motionless on the cat's back. Her cane, discarded, was on the floor beside her chair. She took a long time to answer, and when she did, she spoke slowly, hesitating often, as if her memories were painful . . . or she was making things up as she went along.

"When I first heard Greg Onslow had bought the property, I had a moment's regret for selling it in the first place. I still don't know what he had in mind for the land, but given his lack of taste on other projects, I wasn't optimistic."

"Did you offer to buy it back?"

She shook her head. "I pretended to be a potential investor in the hope of discovering what he intended, but I backed out when he refused to divulge his plans. He was a very secretive man."

"He was a very dishonest one."

"Yes, he was." Her agreement was heartfelt. "I was upset about what might become of the property, but I didn't regret walking away. The reason I sold the resort in the first place hasn't changed in all the years since." She looked up and met my eyes. "Resort hotels were failing left and right. I'd have been a fool to try to cling to the past, especially when I was the last of the Feldmans and have no direct heirs."

We sat without speaking for a few minutes. The only sounds in the room were the ticking of a grandfather clock and the purring of the two cats.

"You don't have children, do you?" Sunny asked abruptly.

"No." Automatically, I added, "By choice."

"Do you regret that decision?"

"No."

"We have that in common then. I don't have any regrets, either, not about deciding to remain childless and not about choosing to remain single. I'm perfectly content to live with Kira and Milo Fuzzypants."

I nodded. "Cats are a lot less trouble than children."

"Or husbands," Sunny said with a wry twist to her lips. "I was a bit ahead of my time in that I wasn't looking for one. Fortunately, my mother, who was the heart and soul of Feldman's during its heyday, believed women could and should think for themselves." She chuckled. "She wouldn't have been quite so liberal-minded if she'd known what I got up to with some of the guests, but I have no regrets about any of my love affairs, either."

Her words reminded me of the photographs I'd seen scattered across the table in her library, and of the way she'd reacted to the mention of one particular name. I spoke without thinking. "Not even the one with Trevor Champlain?"

293

The look of sorrow and loss that filled Sunny's eyes made me feel lower than a worm for resurrecting her pain. I started to apologize, but she cut me off with a slashing gesture.

"I lied to you."

"About?" Belatedly, it occurred to me that if she'd been lying when she'd denied killing Greg Onslow, I could be in big trouble. No one knew where I'd gone after I disappeared from the church.

"About why I went to Onslow's house. He contacted me. After all these years, a worker found a box of letters I carelessly left behind in the house I once lived in at the resort. He turned it over to his boss and Onslow opened it and read them."

"Letters to you from Trevor Champlain?" I guessed.

She nodded. "He was such a sweet man, not a snob like some of those Hollywood types."

"Love letters?"

"Not exactly, but they contained information he never wanted to become public knowledge. You have to remember that this was the nineteen fifties." She paused. "Did you know that Trevor Champlain wasn't his real name? He was born Myron Yablonsky."

That didn't surprise me in the least. In

those days, actors were encouraged to disguise their ethnicity and assume marquee-worthy monikers. Rock Hudson used to be Roy Scherer. Tony Curtis was born Bernard Herschel Schwartz. John Wayne's real first name was Marion. And Michael Landon, who once made my pre-teen heart sing as Little Joe on *Bonanza*, started life as Eugene Orowitz.

"That wasn't his only secret. Trevor was bi."

It took me a few seconds to process this second revelation. Coming out as gay or bisexual in the 1950s would have been the kiss of death to an actor's livelihood. Trevor Champlain had been wise to keep mum about his sexual orientation.

"That would have been quite a bomb-shell."

"And it's one I do not intend to explode even now. I paid Onslow a hefty sum to return those letters and swear never to speak of them to anyone else."

"And you trusted him to keep his word?"

"I suppose you think that gave me a mo-tive to kill him."

"I think that when he believed you were trying to sabotage the demolition project, he might have threatened to publicize Trevor's secret in retaliation."

Gently pushing Kira off her lap, Sunny reached for her cane. "I'd have hated it if Onslow had outed Trevor, but in today's world I don't suppose the story would raise many eyebrows. It would have been difficult for me to write, but I'd have added another chapter to my book to show people the kind, generous man I knew."

"And now?"

"Now I will continue to keep Trevor's private life private."

"Because Onslow was conveniently murdered."

She shrugged. "I didn't kill him. I don't even know why he accused me of wanting to shut down work at Feldman's."

"That was Ronnie's doing." I remembered what Ann had told me. "She elaborated on the stories you shared with her in an attempt to get Onslow to release some of the property for a museum."

"Why am I not surprised?"

Sunny rested her head against the back of her chair, a pose that made her fluffy white hair puff out like a halo around her plump face. The impression of sweet innocence lasted only a fraction of a second. There was nothing angelic about the tension that pervaded the rest of her body or the way her lips went flat.

"With friends like Ronnie North," she snarled, "who needs enemies?"

"I've been saying the same thing for half a century."

Although Sunny remained on my list of suspects, she wasn't anywhere near the top. She'd had a reason to silence Onslow, but I believed her when she denied killing him. I also believed she'd find a way to pay Ronnie back for the trouble she'd caused.

Contemplating my old enemy's fate at Sunny's hands reminded me of where Ronnie was at that moment. If I wanted to return before the church service ended, I had to get moving.

CHAPTER 34

I made it back with seconds to spare. People were already beginning to trickle out as I trotted around the corner from the parking lot. I decided to wait on the pillar-lined porch, as if I'd gone out to get a breath of fresh air just before the minister made his way down the aisle for his ritual farewells. I walked faster. If I'd been a few years younger, I'd have taken the steps two at a time.

Now all I had to worry about was whether Nick had looked around for me during the service and noticed my absence. For the past two weeks, worshipers had filled nearly every pew, but some of those folks wouldn't show up again until Christmas. On this first Sunday after Easter, First Presbyterian had been sparsely attended.

I breathed a sigh of relief when I spotted Darlene and she winked at me.

Nick seemed in a good mood as the three

of us walked to the parking lot. My car was in the same spot it had been an hour and a half earlier. As far as I could tell, my nephew didn't suspect a thing.

"What did you think of Pastor Cameron?" I asked during the drive home.

"Not exactly a brilliant speaker, is he?"

"He drones."

"I nearly fell asleep."

"A couple of hundred years ago, they had a solution for that. One of the congregation was assigned to carry a long pole with a feather on the end. If he saw someone drifting off, he thrust the feather under the miscreant's nose and tickled him awake."

"You're making that up."

"I'm not. Here's another true story. When I was in high school, I briefly considered a career as a minister."

He shot me an incredulous look. "I can't see it. The vows and all."

If I hadn't been driving, I'd have smacked him for that. "I said a minister, not a nun. Anyway, I soon traded that ambition for a dream of going on the stage."

"I don't see acting as a career for you, either."

"Which is probably why I ended up as a teacher, but there's a common thread to all three."

"Captive audience?"

Since I'd just pulled into my driveway and killed the engine, I did smack him this time. "Imparting *wisdom.* Knowledge. Entertainment, on a good day." I grinned at him. "But yes, captive audience, too."

"So, are you turning religious again, now that you're older?"

If I'd thought he meant "in your old age" I'd have hit him again, but he sounded sincere.

"Maybe. It's hard to avoid thinking about faith and the afterlife when people you love die off on a regular basis." I tried to keep my tone light, but I don't think he was fooled. He knows how much I miss his uncle.

I might have said more, but by then we'd climbed the steps to the porch. Nick put a hand on my arm and directed my attention to the grouping of wicker furniture around the coffee table.

Ellen Blume sat on the sofa, her hands clasped together in her lap and her shoulders tense. She stood when we approached, her wary gaze fixed on Nick.

"You remember my nephew, Nick Carpenter," I said. "Don't scowl, Nick. I can see that Ellen is in uniform, but I'm pretty sure she's here as a friend."

"I am." No one could doubt her earnestness. "I really need to talk to you." Although she didn't add the qualifier, "in private," it was obvious she didn't feel she could speak freely in front of anyone else.

"Why don't you go on inside, Nick." I handed over my keys. "I'm sure you remember how to turn off the security alarm."

With obvious reluctance, he did as I asked. I gestured for Ellen to sit down again and settled in beside her. If we kept our voices low, Nick wouldn't be able to overhear what she had to say, not even if he lingered close to the door. Despite the easy banter between us in the car, I had no doubt that he was still in protector mode.

"There's something you need to know," Ellen said in a rush. "Earlier today, Detective Brightwell took your cousin to the county jail in Monticello for questioning."

I felt my heart stutter and had to swallow several times before I could ask the obvious question. "Is he under arrest?"

"I don't think so. Not yet. But if Brightwell is talking to Luke *there,* it's serious."

A closer look at her face told me two things. One was that Luke was now a prime suspect in Onslow's murder, and as such was in need of a lawyer. If she'd take him on, Ashley Mills was about to acquire another client. The second thing was that Ellen Blume, a young woman who, to the best of my knowledge, had never so much as exchanged two words with my cousin, was taking a very personal interest in his fate.

"Ellen, is there something else you'd like to tell me?"

The look of anguish on her pale face spoke volumes. She worried her lower lip, hesitating until I placed one hand over hers. Then an astonishing confession burst out of her.

"It's my fault they suspect him. I should have kept my big mouth shut."

"What are you talking about?"

"I had to be honest, didn't I?"

"Of course you did."

Too agitated to remain seated, she pulled free of my loose grip and stood up. Staring out at the street, turned away from me so that I had trouble seeing her expression, she spoke in a choked voice.

"Luke and I spent some . . . time together a few months ago. Detective Hazlett knew. It wasn't any big secret, but when he started asking me questions, I shouldn't have said anything. It was all speculation. Except it turned out it wasn't."

The bitterness inherent in her last statement provided me with the final clue I needed to piece together what she was talking about. "Oh, I see," I said. "You told the police Luke and Giselle were still seeing each other."

"I'm so sorry," she whispered.

"It's not your fault." I rose to stand beside her, wrapping a comforting arm around her waist. "They'd have found out eventually. Besides, you could hardly refuse to tell them what you knew. Even though it's my cousin we're talking about, I wouldn't want you to risk your job in a misguided attempt to protect him."

"I feel so guilty."

"Does Detective Brightwell really believe Luke could have killed Onslow to win Giselle?" If Ellen's guilt meant she was willing to share police business, I had no qualms about taking advantage of it.

"No one's come right out and said so, but I'm pretty sure that's the conclusion he's come to." Looking thoroughly miserable, she stepped away from me, but I heard the conviction in her voice when she added, "He's wrong!"

"Yes, he is. Thank you for coming here to tell me what's going on."

"I . . . I have to get to work." She was on the verge of tears, trying desperately not to break down in front of me.

"Go on, then, and try not to worry. I'll look out for Luke's interests."

I took a few minutes to compose myself before I went inside. I found Nick in the kitchen putting sandwiches together for our lunch.

"What was that all about?" he asked.

There was no reason not to tell him. "My cousin has been taken to the county jail. Brightwell found out that Luke is romantically involved with Greg Onslow's widow. I need to make a phone call and then I'm going to the police station."

"Not alone, you're not. I'll just put these things in the fridge and —"

"Nick, I don't need a bodyguard. No one's going to arrest me."

"Well that's a relief." His words were tinged with sarcasm.

"No archvillain is likely to take potshots at me, either. I'm just going to have a little chat with Detective Hazlett."

"I thought the lead detective's name was Brightwell."

"Different detective. Different department." I sighed. "Don't pretend you don't know who Jonathan Hazlett is. That chatty lawyer you found for me told you all about the other murder investigations I was involved in. She mentioned him by name. We aren't exactly bosom buddies, but I think Detective Hazlett will tell me more than Brightwell would."

"Stay out of it, Aunt Mikki. If they've arrested Luke, they must have found solid evidence against him."

"Are you saying you think he killed Greg Onslow? Because if you believe that, you are greatly mistaken."

"You just told me Brightwell arrested him."

Going around and around with Nick was giving me a headache. I put my hand over my eyes and took a couple of deep breaths. I needed to stay in control of my emotions. I wanted to make peace with my nephew, and it was even more important that I remain calm when I spoke to Hazlett. Statements made by hysterical females tend to be ignored.

"If you want to help," I told Nick, "you can phone Ms. Mills and ask her if she'll represent Luke instead of me. If she won't, or if that's some sort of conflict of interest, then please ask her for a recommendation. Get the name of another lawyer with experience in criminal law."

"I'm not sure I do want to help," Nick muttered. "If Luke is the one who killed that guy, then he's the one who tried to frame you for the murder."

At that, my temper flared. "Either help or go home. You're not welcome in my house if you don't do anything but get in my way."

When Nick winced, I was immediately sorry, both for shouting at him and for what I'd said, but I didn't take back my ultimatum. It's one thing to go to great lengths to avoid conflict with a family member and quite another to sink without protest into the role of docile female. I did not need a big, strong man to make my decisions for me.

After several more calming breaths, I asked, "Will you make the call?"

"Yes. Okay. But are you sure you don't want me to go with you to the police station?"

"I'll be fine on my own." Better, in fact, than if he came with me. "Eat your sandwich. I'll get myself something at Harriet's after I talk to Detective Hazlett. The café is just across the street from the police station."

Before he could suggest he meet me there, I stalked out of the house.

CHAPTER 35

Police stations tend to be security conscious, but luck was on my side. Ellen Blume had come on duty a few minutes before I arrived. And that, I thought, explained why Nick and I hadn't noticed a police car parked on the street in front of my house. She must have been on her way to work, in uniform but still driving her own vehicle.

Stone-faced, ignoring the curious stares we got from her coworkers, she led me straight through to the back hallway where Detective Hazlett had his office.

"Wait here," she said in a low voice. "He's in a conference, but he'll be available to speak with you shortly."

Ellen abandoned me, unsupervised, and slipped out of the building by way of a side door. A few moments later, through a window, I saw her cruiser pass by as she went out on patrol.

She'd left me standing just outside the

door to Hazlett's office. It wasn't all the way closed. From inside came the deep rumble of Detective Brightwell's distinctive voice. I sidled closer, ears stretched.

"Have you arrested Luke Darbee?" I heard Hazlett ask.

I stopped with my hand pressed over my heart, scarcely daring to breathe as I listened for Brightwell's answer.

"Not yet, but it's only a matter of time. The evidence against him is piling up."

Quite suddenly, my eyes grew moist. I missed a few words while I swiped at them, but the next part of what Brightwell said reached me loud and clear.

"The fingerprints we found in Ms. Lincoln's house suggest he's the one who planted that gun on the premises, and now we know that he had a good reason to want Onslow dead. Killing him cleared the way for Darbee to marry the widow. He admitted he's been in touch with her since her husband turned up dead."

I didn't wait to hear any more. Brightwell's calm assumption of Luke's guilt made my blood boil. I rapped once on the doorframe before striding uninvited into Hazlett's office.

Brightwell took an involuntary step back when I entered, not so much because he was wary of me as because, with three people in the room, the quarters were cramped. I sent him my best "you're out of line" glare before turning my back on him and addressing Detective Hazlett.

"Of course Luke's fingerprints were found in my house. He's my cousin. He visits often. You know that. Why aren't you defending him?"

"These prints were on the outside of the sunroom door," Brightwell interjected, "just where they'd be if he came in through the garage during the half hour when your nephew left it unlocked."

"Oh, for heaven's sake! Luke could have left those prints behind months ago. I've never been one for intensive housecleaning." I considered for a moment, running a slideshow of Luke's visits to the house through my mind. "In fact, I can tell you exactly when and how they got there."

Hazlett invited me to take the guest chair while he resumed his seat behind the desk. Brightwell rested one hip on its front edge, folded his arms in front of his chest, and directed a basilisk stare my way, waiting impatiently for me to explain myself. I tried to ignore both the man and his skepticism. Hazlett was not just easier on the eyes, he was also easier to talk to.

"It was when we had that freak snowstorm last month. When I shop, I usually bring the groceries in through the front door, but in just the hour or so I was out, the weather turned nasty. After I pulled into the garage, I decided to unload everything by way of the sunroom."

"Seems to me it would be quicker to do it that way all the time," Brightwell interrupted. "You'd save yourself some steps."

After I took a deep breath, I managed to answer him in a civil manner. "It would be, except that the stairs inside the garage are narrow and steep and I avoid them if I'm wrestling with heavy packages or grocery bags. I also avoid other unnecessary risks. I don't drive on icy roads and I don't teeter on tippy ladders to reach high shelves. May I go on with my story?"

"By all means." There was a hint of amusement in Brightwell's eyes, but at least he was listening.

"Just as I opened the trunk of my car, and before I closed the garage door, Luke pulled into my driveway. He's a caring individual. He made it a point to check on my well-being all winter long, especially when the weather was bad. His concern was unnecessary, of course, but I appreciated it. He's a very responsible young man. From time to time, even on nice days, he'll phone just to make sure I didn't need anything. Naturally, as soon as he saw that I had groceries to unload, he offered to carry them inside for me. *That's* how his fingerprints came to be on the door between the garage and the sunroom."

The two detectives exchanged a blatantly skeptical look that made me bristle with indignation.

"I'll swear to that on a stack of Bibles if need be. I won't have you railroading my cousin just because you're not clever enough to figure out who the real murderer is."

"Whoa!" Hazlett interrupted. "No one's doubting your word, Ms. Lincoln, but your explanation doesn't rule out the possibility that Luke Darbee is the one who hid that gun in your house."

"His affection for me does that. He'd never take the chance that finding it there would lead to my arrest. Any fool could put two and two together and conclude that whoever had possession of that gun was the same person who killed Greg Onslow."

Hazlett sighed. Brightwell just looked grim.

"It *is* the gun used in the murder, isn't it?"

Neither answered. Of course they didn't.

In their book, I was just a nosy civilian with no right to privileged information. It didn't matter. I was sure I was right. If it hadn't been the murder weapon, there would have been no point in planting it in my house.

After a moment, Hazlett asked, "Who do *you* think tried to frame you?"

The name "Giselle Onslow" popped out of my mouth before I could censor myself. "Giselle acting *alone*," I added in a rush.

"Why would Mrs. Onslow pick on you?" Brightwell asked.

"Maybe because she knows I don't approve of my cousin's interest in her."

"So there *is* something between them."

I narrowed my eyes at him. "*You're* the one who just said Luke admitted he's been in contact with her. You're the one who thinks he killed Onslow because he wants to marry the widow. I know you're wrong about him, but you might want to take a closer look at her. Onslow is the second rich husband she's outlived."

For just an instant, Brightwell's cop-face slipped. I swear he *smirked* at me.

"Oh, I get it," I said. "You're going to try to prove Giselle and Luke were working together. Well, forget it. Luke is completely innocent of everything except poor taste in women. And if you want to talk to him again, you'll have to do so with his lawyer present."

Brightwell's voice was mild. "Oh? He has a lawyer now?"

"Yes, he does. I've hired Ashley Mills to represent him."

If Nick hadn't called her by the time I got home, I would attend to that little matter myself. It was obvious, since Hazlett and Brightwell had deigned to tell me as much as they had, that I was no longer on their list of suspects. I wouldn't need Ms. Mills's services, but it appeared increasingly likely that Luke did.

"Mills is good," Hazlett said.

"So I hear." Brightwell eased himself away from the edge of the desk and around my chair to the door. Opening it and holding it that way, he said, "Thank you for clarifying the issue of the fingerprints, Ms. Lincoln."

At what was so clearly a dismissal, I had no choice but to leave. Quitting while I was ahead was probably my wisest course anyway. Trying to say more in Luke's defense might backfire. As any good editor knows, it's far too easy for words to be twisted, taken out of context, or misinterpreted. The last thing I wanted to do was give the police any more ammunition to use against my cousin.

I left the police station with my head held high. Inside I was still seething. Brightwell had his sights set on proving Luke had killed Greg Onslow, even if there wasn't enough evidence to make an arrest. Worse, he seemed determined to disregard a much more likely suspect in order to focus on poor Luke. I wouldn't have thought Brightwell could be taken in by big blue eyes and a killer body, but he'd given every indication that he thought Giselle was innocent. Maybe he even believed Luke had been stalking her after she dumped him to marry Onslow.

Idiot!

I stopped on the sidewalk in front of the police station, waiting for a truck and two cars to pass before I crossed the street to Harriet's. It was obvious to me that the police were barking up the wrong tree. The heck with tying up a few minor loose ends! Since they'd stopped looking at other suspects, I'd have to take up the slack myself. If I kept asking questions, I felt sure I could find proof that Giselle, acting alone, had killed her husband. And if it turned out she was innocent? Even then, I wouldn't give up. I'd just search farther afield until I discovered the true identity of Greg Onslow's killer.

CHAPTER 36

Figuring out the who, what, where, when, and how required fuel for the brain. A bacon cheeseburger and fries, perhaps augmented by a strawberry shake, sounded about right. At a fast-food place, the fat and calories in those would best be described as "a heart attack waiting to happen," but Ada Patel's cooking produces healthier versions that still taste wonderful.

That's my story and I'm sticking to it.

Just before I went inside Harriet's, I pulled out my cell phone and punched in Darlene's number. I was surprised when there was no answer. I'd assumed she was going straight home after church. I didn't bother leaving a message.

Harriet's isn't large and it was crowded. Most people no longer indulge in a big, home-cooked Sunday dinner. Most people don't attend church on Sunday anymore, either, not that everyone did back in the day. Once upon a time, though, churchgoers had been easy to spot. They'd be decked out in their "Sunday best." In my memories of the 1950s, women not only wore dressy hats, some of them also sported white gloves. Their shoes and handbags invariably matched.

The mystery of Darlene's whereabouts was solved within seconds of entering the café. She and Ronnie, dressed in the present-day version of "Sunday best" — nice slacks and pretty blouses — shared a table. Catching sight of me, Darlene motioned for me to join them.

"From the look of things, you're about finished." Ronnie was polishing off a chef's salad while Darlene had eaten all but the last few bites of a turkey club.

"Feel free to sit elsewhere." Ronnie's voice had an edge to it.

"I'm surprised to find you slumming," I shot back. "Doesn't Ann usually fix something fit for a queen on Sundays — ham, or a turkey, or a fatted calf?" It still amazed me that a feisty woman like Ann Ellerby was willing to put up with her employer's demanding nature.

"Ann is on vacation for a few days," Ronnie informed me in clipped tones.

"Cut it out, you two," Darlene interrupted

as I settled into one of the two empty chairs at their four-person table. "Honestly. You'd think you never got past high school. No, make that *grade* school. We haven't had dessert yet, Mikki. Go ahead and order your lunch and then tell us why you dragged your poor nephew to church. It was painfully obvious he was out of his element. He had no idea of the order of service or how much to put in as an offering."

"I hope he was generous."

"He was so embarrassed at having to fumble for his wallet that he tossed in a ten-dollar bill."

"Good for him."

Ronnie snorted. "The question isn't why she made him go to church, Darlene, it's where *she* went after she dumped him in your pew." As one of the greeters, she'd been in an ideal position to observe everyone else's comings and goings.

"I, uh —"

Darlene chuckled. "If you're about to tell us you sat in the last pew after you returned from the bathroom, so you wouldn't disturb anyone, don't bother. You didn't get back until after the benediction. You were gone more than an hour."

Fortunately, the arrival of our waitress with her order pad at the ready gave me an excuse to put off answering right away. The young woman was Joe Ramirez's daughter, Spring, a student at the local community college. She worked at Harriet's part-time during the school year and full-time in the summer. While she wrote down what I wanted for lunch, and took orders for dessert from Ronnie and Darlene, I considered my options.

I could tell Ronnie that where I'd gone was none of her business, but I'd planned to update Darlene the first chance I got. I'd just tried to reach her by phone to request her assistance in tracking down Onslow's killer. Now that I thought about it, I decided that three heads might be better than two.

As soon as Spring was out of earshot, Ronnie pounced. "Well?"

I shrugged. "I had an errand to run and I didn't want Nick tagging along."

"What errand?" Ronnie demanded.

Darlene answered for me. "I'll bet it had to do with the murder. We've been trying to figure out who had the best reason to want Greg Onslow dead."

Ronnie's disdainful sniff was automatic, but the gleam in her eyes betrayed her interest in the subject.

"Want to help?" I asked.

I got a scowl instead of an answer.

318

Shifting in my chair so that I faced Darlene, I said, "Ronnie was worried about me, you know. Back when Onslow's body first turned up, she went so far as to stop by the house and suggest that I hire myself a lawyer."

"Really," Darlene drawled, pretending I hadn't already told her about Ronnie's impromptu visit. "How kind of her, especially when she must have been on the sheriff's department radar herself."

Ronnie grimaced, looking as if she'd bitten into a piece of sour fruit. "Obviously, I've been cleared of all suspicion. Can either of you say the same?"

"Ladies, please," I said with mock severity. "Let's take it as given that none of us did Onslow in, much as we might have wanted to."

I took a deep breath. It was time to stop sparring and take advantage of the opportunity to pick Ronnie's brain.

"Detective Brightwell has fixed his attention on Luke Darbee because my cousin dated Giselle before her marriage."

"Well obviously *he* didn't do it." Darlene was quick to defend him, even though she didn't know him well.

"How can you be so certain?" Ronnie made a little moue of disapproval. "To give

319

credit where credit is due, Giselle is gorgeous, and there's the added incentive of all that money."

I started to tell them that Luke had plenty of money of his own but caught myself before I blabbed that secret. I held back the information not so much because of my promise to him as because I'd just been struck by a thought. It wasn't a new one, but until that moment I'd failed to recognize how significant it might be.

"*Is* Giselle wealthy?" I asked. "Think about it. How can Mongaup Valley Ventures be solvent? Did Onslow successfully complete even one of his Lenape Hollow projects?"

"In at least one instance, he got out before things fell apart," Darlene reminded me. "The other investors were the ones left holding the bag when his plan to renovate the old tannery building collapsed."

"Asbestos in the walls, as I recall," Ronnie murmured.

I persisted. "What about the other enterprises? He bought up multiple downtown storefronts, including the old movie theater. He promised they'd reopen soon, but that was a couple of years ago. They're still boarded up. I haven't seen the slightest indication that any of the shops are being renovated, let alone rented out. And what about Wonderful World? Has any new construction taken place there?"

Onslow's scheme had involved turning 265 acres of land, formerly the village's recreation area plus the grounds of a long-defunct nineteenth-century hotel, into an amusement park. The idea had not been popular with many Lenape Hollow residents.

"No, thank God." Ronnie kept a close eye on the property since it adjoined her own. "Other than letting the historical society use the site for the pageant last summer, there hasn't been any activity at all." She sent Darlene a scathing look. "Why are you smiling?"

"Because of something I came across the other day online. Onslow was such a lowlife that he couldn't even come up with a bad idea on his own. He stole the entire scheme, including giving the place the nickname 'Orlando of the Northeast,' from a plan proposed way back in 1959. It was called Mystic Mountain when a group of businessmen in the town of Liberty considered building it in their backyard."

"Typical," I said. "But that brings us to the demolition of the hotel buildings. Work stopped when Onslow's body was found and it hasn't been resumed. I'd like to know why not."

"Remember the research we did when we were trying to derail Wonderful World?" Darlene asked. "Onslow's past record painted him as nothing more than a con man. The only reason he got loans early in his career was because his late father was a successful entrepreneur. Maybe the lenders finally wised up. That could be why all his current projects have stalled."

"Maybe, but that doesn't explain why he stuck around. His pattern was always to move to a small town, open an investment business, establish a track record with one or two small successes, and then set up a bigger deal that was doomed to failure. By the time the other investors caught on, he'd bailed out. They lost money. Some even had to declare bankruptcy. Contractors went unpaid. Only Onslow profited."

"The difference is that after he landed in Lenape Hollow, he married my grand-daughter." Ronnie's bitterness was palpable.

"And became the victim of a con himself," I reminded her.

"All the more reason for him to have moved on. Why didn't he?" After a moment, Darlene answered her own question. "I suppose he could have been trying to turn over a new leaf and run an honest business for a change." She didn't sound as if she found the explanation convincing.

Ada Patel, the owner of Harriet's, chose that moment to appear beside our table with a tray. "I heard Mongaup Valley Ventures is about to file for bankruptcy." She deftly offloaded my burger, fries, and milkshake, along with the two servings of pie à la mode my companions had ordered. "You have to be careful what you say in a restaurant," she added. "It's far too easy for perfect strangers to overhear private business. Good thing I'm so discreet."

With a wink, she walked away. I swiveled in my chair and was relieved to see that the crowd was considerably smaller than it had been when I arrived. Even better, no one was seated at any of the tables close to us. Satisfied we had sufficient privacy to continue our discussion, I turned back to Darlene and Ronnie and reached for my burger.

"If Onslow's business was failing, it's no wonder he got so angry with Sunny. The slightest hint of a setback on his newest project could have been fatal to the entire company."

"What a pity." Ronnie's smug smile conveyed her total lack of sympathy.

I let one hand fall into my lap and used the other to jab an accusing finger in her direction. "You let Sunny and me take the blame for rumors *you* started. I wonder if the police know about *that*?"

Darlene kicked me under the table before putting in her two cents. There was just the slightest hint of malice beneath the saccharine in her voice. "Gee, Ronnie, if MVV is in financial trouble, shouldn't you be concerned about those shares you inherited from Tiffany?"

Ronnie laughed. "Hardly. I don't own them anymore."

"You mean the court sided with Onslow?" I couldn't hide my astonishment.

Back when Greg Onslow's first wife died, two wills had surfaced. One left everything to the widower. The other left Tiffany's shares in Mongaup Valley Ventures to her grandmother. Each side claimed the other will was a forgery and countersuits were filed, leaving ownership of the shares in limbo until the courts could decide which will was valid.

"An arbitrator came up with an out-of-court settlement," Ronnie explained. "I guess there's no reason not to talk about it now that Onslow is dead. He agreed to let my version of the will stand on the condition that I sell the shares." Her lips twisted into a small, self-satisfied smile that reminded me of Calpurnia after she's polished off a particularly tasty cat treat. "It's not my fault he assumed he'd be the only one interested in buying them."

"Who owns them now?" I asked.

"Ariadne Toothaker made me an offer I couldn't resist. I didn't come away with as much money as I could have pressured Onslow into paying, but possession of those shares put her in a position to demand she be promoted to vice president. He was fit to be tied when he found out what I'd done."

"It's always nice to see a woman get ahead," Darlene said, sotto voce.

"If the company is failing, she didn't make much of a deal." I picked up my burger and bit into it.

"Maybe she'll be able to turn Mongaup Valley Ventures around and save the company from bankruptcy," Ronnie suggested.

"Even better, maybe one or two of MVV's unfinished projects will finally be completed," Darlene said. "I'm getting tired of seeing those boarded-up storefronts."

Since speculating didn't seem to be getting us anywhere, I concentrated on my lunch. I still thought Giselle was the most likely person to have killed her husband.

CHAPTER 37

I spent that afternoon trying to get in touch with Luke. When my call went to voice mail for the tenth time, I began to suspect he was avoiding me. Either that or he'd lost his phone. I hate to confess it, but I'm afraid I took out my frustration on Nick. Although he apologized nicely when I returned home, he was still *hovering.* After supper I told him I had work to do and locked myself in my office until it was time for bed.

I'd also left unanswered messages for Giselle. The next morning, a Monday, I headed out right after breakfast.

All right, I crept out of the house while Nick was in the bathroom.

Although I wasn't certain I'd find MVV's new CEO on the premises, especially so early in the day, I drove to Mongaup Valley Ventures first. It was worth a shot. If I couldn't locate her there, I'd try her house.

I found her ensconced in her late husband's office. Since there was no secretary in the outer room, I went right on in and closed the door behind me. Plunking myself down in a well-cushioned guest chair upholstered in buttery yellow leather, I waited until she glanced up to smile encouragingly.

The look on her face was one of impatience, quickly followed by annoyance, and then by resignation. "What do you want, Mikki?" She tucked a stray lock of her ebony-colored hair behind her ear and leaned back in her chair.

"I'd like to get my cousin off the hook. The police have questioned him again, this time about his relationship to you."

"I know."

My eyebrows shot up. "I thought you agreed not to be in contact with him while the investigation was ongoing."

"I've kept my word. I had another visit from the police. Detective Brightwell made a point of telling me about his suspicions. He wanted to know if Luke had been lurking around our house while Greg was still alive."

I bit back an expletive. That was just what I'd been afraid of. Brightwell not only believed my cousin killed Onslow so he could step in and sweep the new widow off her feet, he also thought Luke had staked out their home, hoping for an opportunity to remove Giselle's husband from the picture. As a theory, I suppose it made sense, but only to someone who didn't know Luke's character as well as I did.

"Do *you* think he killed your husband?" I asked.

Giselle turned her swivel chair so that she was staring out the window instead of facing me directly. There wasn't much to see. Other buildings of the industrial type backed up against run-down houses that predated the construction of those businesses.

"I don't *want* to think that," she said slowly, "but Luke did suggest that we elope. That way, he said, we couldn't be forced to testify against each other."

I'm pretty sure my jaw dropped. I didn't believe for a moment that Luke had made such a ludicrous suggestion. For one thing, that old wife-can't-testify-against-her-husband rule is not exactly accurate. Maybe spouses can't be forced to, but they *can* volunteer testimony. More to the point, the prohibition only applies to information shared *during* the marriage, not what went on beforehand. One of my clients writes short stories in the mystery genre and I had to look up the details of the law as part of my line edit.

No, that was definitely not Luke's idea! That Giselle would marry him in an attempt to keep him quiet appalled me and made me even more certain she was the one who'd killed her husband.

"I'm considering it," Giselle said. "Running away together."

"Reconsider. Luke doesn't need you to keep mum and marrying you will only make him look guiltier."

She didn't like being snapped at and swung around to glare at me. Hostility radiated from every pore. Any moment now, she'd order me out of her office. If I refused to leave, she'd call security and have me evicted.

For one brief moment, I contemplated trying sweet reason, but I didn't have the patience. It's more my style to ask blunt questions. "Do you love Luke or just his fortune?"

Sometimes shock tactics work.

She answered with uncharacteristic honesty. "I'd never marry a poor man!"

"Especially not now."

"What do you mean by that?"

"I know MVV is on the verge of bankruptcy."

"That's ridiculous."

"Is it?"

I gave her the same summary of Onslow's failed projects that I'd sketched out for Darlene and Ronnie. As I ticked them off one by one, Giselle visibly wilted. By the time I stopped speaking, she sat slumped in her executive chair, shoulders hunched and face pale and forlorn.

I ignored the twinge of pity I felt for her. "Well?"

"Yes, the company is in a precarious position." Her voice was so low I had to strain to hear her. "Gregory kept that information from me."

"That was a mistake. If you'd known you weren't going to inherit a fortune from your husband, he'd probably still be alive."

"Is that what you think? That I killed him for his money?" Her choked voice suggested she was on the verge of tears.

I hardened my heart. "You've been married twice, both times to rich men who died not long after the nuptials and left you everything. Who wouldn't wonder if you eliminated husband number two so you could move on to rich prospect number three? Luke is quite wealthy, you know, even though you didn't believe him the first time he tried to tell you that."

"I was perfectly happy in my marriage to

Gregory."

"That didn't stop you from stringing Luke along."

"He's obsessed with me. You can't blame me for that."

The color had returned to her face and then some. Red flags flew in her cheeks as she leaned toward me across the desk. Placing both hands flat on the surface, she rose from her chair.

"I loved Gregory Onslow. He was a genius at business. If he'd lived, he'd have turned Mongaup Valley Ventures around. It isn't too late for the company to recover even now. Once I buy out Ariadne Toothaker, I'll get things back on track. The current decline is all her fault. She tied Gregory's hands. Every time he wanted to expand, she blocked him. That's why the money dried up."

I took this assessment of blame with a grain of salt. Ms. Toothaker had always struck me as an astute and efficient businesswoman. Besides, I very much doubted she'd try to ruin Onslow's business when she owned so many shares of company stock herself.

"It isn't Ms. Toothaker who's being accused of killing your husband," I said as I got to my feet. "It's my cousin. Luke may have his flaws, but he isn't a murderer and I won't let him take the fall for you. You won't have any secrets left by the time I'm through investigating your past."

"Are you threatening me?"

"I'm *warning* you."

I heard my voice rise and feared I was dangerously close to another of those rare, intemperate displays of anger. Despite that, I didn't lower my volume. Letting rip felt too good.

"There's something rotten about this business," I all but shouted, "and I'm going to find out what it is. Count on it."

With that I threw open the door and stalked out, head held high and fire in my eyes. In the outer office Ariadne Toothaker, consternation writ large upon her face, had to step hastily aside to avoid being bowled over. I didn't stop to apologize. I didn't even slow down.

CHAPTER 38

Once clear of the building, I calmed down, but I was far from ready to face the nephew I'd abandoned and explain why I'd given him the slip. Instead of starting the engine after I got into my car, I called the house on my cell phone and left a message on the answering machine. Nick was probably right there listening, but before he could pick up, I concluded with a cheery "be back soon" and disconnected.

I understood exactly why Giselle had upset me so much. I was overprotective of Luke . . . just as Nick was overprotective of me, a conclusion that would give me food for thought when I was in the mood for deep contemplation. This was not the time for it.

Since I didn't want to go home in this mood, I opted for a leisurely drive, just the thing to soothe my jangled nerves. *Enjoy the scenery,* I told myself. *Get a sense of per-*

spective.

As I left the parking lot at Mongaup Valley Ventures and drove toward the village proper — strictly speaking, MVV is in Lenape Falls, not Lenape Hollow — I had a clear line of sight to the tops of the remaining buildings at Feldman's Catskill Resort Hotel. Even on a cloudy day like this one, Greg Onslow must have been struck by the impressiveness of that view every time he drove home from work. No doubt it had led to grandiose plans for the property.

In this particular April, late in the month as it was, the foothills of the Catskills weren't yet lush with spring colors, although they were greening nicely from all the rain. Fruit trees, especially the apples, hadn't yet bloomed, nor had most varieties of flowering shrubs.

I couldn't name them. I've never been good at identifying plants or trees, other than the obvious ones. I can recognize forsythia and lilacs because we had those growing at our place in Maine, and I can tell a maple from other trees by the shape of its leaves. When it comes to the rest, I stick with "what a pretty tree/bush/flower."

My grandfather used to have what he called "snowball bushes" at his house. I suspect they were hydrangeas, but I've never troubled to find out. Thinking about Grampa Greenleigh had me turning left onto Elm Street when I reached the village and heading for Cooper Street, where the house he built back in the early 1900s still stands. I didn't stop. I'd driven past it before and had been pleased to see that someone had spruced the place up with a fresh coat of paint. The steps leading up the double terrace were in good repair, and the steep driveway to one side had been recently paved.

The property stood in stark contrast to the rest of the street. The roadway itself was narrow and full of potholes, as were many of Lenape Hollow's streets. The boarded-up shops on South Main Street weren't the only buildings in need of a facelift. Many of the village's houses were also in a sad state of disrepair.

"Stop depressing yourself," I muttered as I passed what had once been one of the town's two hospitals.

The building had been turned into apartments. There was no landscaping, just a bleak, industrial-looking parking lot. One optimistic soul had put out a window box, but as yet nothing had sprouted.

I tried and failed to find a bright side to

the blight as I continued on, making a wide circle that would eventually take me back home. After a bit, I passed the high school, which had been brand-new when I was a student there but had now begun to show its age. Heading down the steep hill I'd had to walk up every day to get to classes, I passed the turn onto Wedemeyer Terrace and kept going.

Another half hour, I promised myself. It wouldn't do to go back to the house too soon and take out my frustration on Nick.

At the intersection with North Main, I hung a left. I considered stopping at Darlene's house, but drove past instead and kept going until I reached the village limits at the boundary of Lenape Hollow and the hamlet of Muthig Corners. At the far side of a rotary, North Main Street emerges as Park Road.

I made a face. I've never seen the advantage of rotaries over ordinary crossroads. To my mind, they just provide more opportunities for drivers to cut in front of each other at the last moment. Clearly, the highway department doesn't agree with me. They'd installed the twin to this one on the south side of the village, the other point at which Main Street intersects with the Quickway.

Since I had no particular destination in

mind, and had had my fill of narrow, bumpy, poorly maintained streets and back roads, I entered the four-lane highway and headed west. By the time I reached the next exit, I was forced to admit the truth: Zipping along in my bright green Ford Taurus had failed to relax me. Worse, it had not prompted me to come up with any brilliant ideas for solving Greg Onslow's murder.

Rather than waste an entire day driving aimlessly, I turned around and started back toward Lenape Hollow. It was time to go home and have a serious discussion with my nephew.

An overpass crosses the Quickway right before the Park Road and North Main Street exit. I was just about to drive under the bridge when something slammed into my windshield. The impact startled me into hitting the brakes too hard. The car began to fishtail.

As I struggled to regain control, deep cracks spread across the glass in front of me, making me fear that it was about to shatter. I flung my left arm up to protect my face and tried to steer the Taurus one-handed toward a safe spot at the side of the road.

The car lurched and bumped its way across the breakdown lane. I was breathing hard. My right hand was glued to the wheel and my right leg ached from pressing my foot so hard against the brake pedal. Eons seemed to pass before the brakes finally caught. I jolted forward, then back as the vehicle came to an abrupt halt.

Amazingly, the airbags didn't inflate.

For a moment, I just sat where I was, stunned. My breath soughed in and out and my heart raced. I couldn't take my eyes off the spiderweb of cracks in the windshield. If the glass had shattered, I'd have been badly cut. If the car had flipped over, ditto.

Neither of those things happened, I told myself. *You aren't hurt, just shaken.*

After a bit, I shut off the engine and unfastened my seat belt. Opening the door was the next challenge. I'd passed under the bridge before going off the road. The Taurus had come to rest on the shoulder with its passenger side hanging over the edge of a ditch. The driver's side tilted upward at an angle that forced me to keep shoving the door away from me while I jumped from the seat to the ground. I landed awkwardly, but at least I didn't turn an ankle or otherwise injure myself.

Wobbling a bit on unsteady legs, I turned to inspect the damage. My windshield appeared to be the only major casualty.

When I looked up at the bridge, an explanation for what had happened came immediately to mind. Many places have a long history of kids throwing rocks off overpasses. Sometimes those rocks hit a car. The culprits would be long gone. They probably hightailed it out of there the moment they saw me swerve toward the side of the road.

Since I'd had the good sense to drag my tote bag after me when I exited the car, I fished out my cell phone and called 911. It only took me two tries to hit the right numbers. Telling the dispatcher where I was and what had happened had a calming effect on my nerves. I assured her I didn't need an ambulance or the fire department, just the police.

"I'm not sure if I'm within the village limits or not," I added.

"Don't you worry," she said in a soothing voice. "The Lenape Hollow police and the county sheriff's deputies help each other out with traffic accidents all the time. Whatever unit is closest will be there before you know it."

Once I'd been assured that help was on the way, I started to wonder how I was going to get home. I couldn't drive the Taurus until I had the windshield replaced, and I had no idea how long that would take. Since

I'd moved to Lenape Hollow, my car had needed only routine maintenance. I was still trying to decide whether or not to phone Nick when Ellen Blume's cruiser pulled in behind my car.

She gave a low whistle when she saw the damage to the windshield. "Are you okay?" Her sharp-eyed gaze swept over me from head to toe.

"I'm fine."

We both turned to look at the bridge.

"Kids?" I asked.

"Probably. This isn't the first time some idiot teenager has tossed something from up there. It's been a few years since the last incident, though."

"Did you catch the culprit that time?"

"I think so, but it was before I went to work for the PD." She sighed. "Chances are, if underage kids were to blame, they got off with nothing more than a warning. Just a prank, right?"

"I know the score. I taught young teens for decades. In general, they have poor judgment and worse impulse control. They think the most absurd things are funny and tend to react to being caught doing something they shouldn't by running away."

"Either that or they deny everything." She produced a fair imitation of a boy whose

340

voice was changing: "I didn't do nothing! It must have been some other kid who looks like me."

"Let's hope seeing me go off the road put enough of a scare into them that they won't try something this idiotic again."

After she'd inspected the damage to my car more closely, Ellen called for a tow truck. Leaving me to wait for it, she drove up to the overpass, stopped the cruiser, and got out to check the railings on both sides. She returned a few minutes later.

"I couldn't find anything to indicate who was there. We'll ask around, but unless someone saw who threw that rock and can give us an ID, there isn't much hope of an arrest." She glanced at the Taurus, looking as grim as I'd ever seen her. "The damage could have been a lot worse, to the car *and* to you."

CHAPTER 39

Ellen gave me a lift home. As I climbed the porch steps to face my scowling nephew, I felt a reluctant sympathy for the youthful miscreants who'd caused my accident. Although I hadn't done anything wrong, I experienced the strongest urge to run away rather than face the music.

I didn't do nothing, I thought. But, of course, I had.

Nick hadn't yet noticed that my car was missing from the driveway. He was upset with me for sneaking out of the house. Telling him I'd gone to Mongaup Valley Ventures to pay a visit to Giselle didn't do anything to improve his mood.

"What if she's the murderer?"

"She would hardly attack me in her place of business," I shot back.

Thinking to convince him I could look out for myself, I related as much of my conversation with her as I could recall. The effort backfired rather spectacularly, since it made him question my sanity. That was perhaps not the best moment to confess that I'd been in a car accident after I left MVV, but he'd have had to hear about it some-time. He looked like he was about to go ballistic even before I finished filling in the details. Once I'd supplied them, he exploded.

"You could have been killed!"

"Stop shouting at me!" I yelled back. "I'm not a child and you're not my father."

He opened his mouth to say more, but before our quarrel could escalate further, I held up a hand, palm out.

"Enough! I have work to do. We'll talk about this later, when we've both had time to cool down."

With that, I went upstairs and shut myself in my office. Again. I didn't like myself for retreating and hiding out, but sometimes the best choice *is* to run away and "live to fight another day."

I'd told Nick the truth. I had manuscripts to edit. Unfortunately, I couldn't concentrate. Between my trip to MVV and nearly wrecking my car, never mind the close brush with death, I'd had an exhausting morning. After I tried unsuccessfully to reach Luke by phone, I settled into the recliner I'd wisely included in the furnishings for my office and took a nap.

When I woke up, I felt more like myself. Instead of editing, I made a list of all the questions I had about Giselle Onslow. Then I tried again to get hold of Luke. He still wasn't answering his phone.

The supply of snacks I store in a desk drawer kept hunger at bay, and I have an office coffeepot. I didn't need to go downstairs again until early evening and only did so then because I heard the doorbell ring. I reached the foyer just as Nick stepped back to let Luke in.

My nephew had a sour expression on his face, but my cousin didn't spare him so much as a glance. He engulfed me in a bear hug.

"Are you okay?" he asked when he stepped back. His hands remained on my shoulders, resting lightly there while he looked me up and down, making his own assessment of my well-being. "Ellen said you were in an accident on the Quickway."

"I'm fine." I broke free, irritated that he wouldn't take me at my word. "The only casualty was the Taurus. What is it with young men these days? I appreciate that you and Nick are concerned about me, but it isn't as if I'm fragile or prone to fits of the vapors."

Luke's hands shot into the air in a gesture of surrender. "Shall I go away again?"

"Don't you dare." Taking his arm, I dragged him into the living room. "Sit down. We need to talk."

Nick followed after us, taking one of the chairs after Luke and I settled ourselves on the loveseat. Calpurnia, no doubt sensing the tension in the air, was wise enough to avoid the foolish humans. She was nowhere in sight.

"I'm just glad you're okay," Luke said. "You could have been badly hurt, even killed."

"But I wasn't, so there's no reason to make a fuss. Some budding juvenile delinquent decided it would be fun to toss a rock off a bridge and I happened to be in the wrong place at the wrong time. End of story."

"I'm not so sure about that," Nick muttered.

Luke shifted position to send a questioning look in his direction. "Meaning?"

"What if it wasn't a kid? Or an accident?"

"I don't follow you."

"Think about it, Luke. Ever since the murder, Auntie here has been sticking her nose in where it doesn't belong. It's quite a

345

coincidence that her car should be the only one hit by a rock on that stretch of road in over five years." At my startled look, Nick nodded. "Oh, yes. I talked to the police, and I also did some hard thinking while you were holed up in your office. The person who threw that rock could have been trying to put you out of commission, maybe permanently, to stop you from asking questions."

"That's ridiculous. Don't listen to him," I said to Luke. "He's paranoid."

"And you're naïve. If you care about your cousin, Darbee, you'll help me talk some sense into her."

His appeal had an immediate effect on Luke. "What if he's right, Mikki? I know how resourceful you are, but if you had been injured, stranded by the side of the road, your car disabled and no one to help you —"

I fought an urge to roll my eyes. "There is absolutely no point in dwelling on what *might* have happened. I wasn't hurt and the police were there within minutes after I reported the accident."

"You should have called me," Nick said.

"Or me," said Luke.

That did it!

"Luke Darbee, I have been calling you and

calling you and all I ever get is your voice mail."

He had the grace to look embarrassed. "I turned off my phone. I had some thinking to do."

"Yes. I expect you did after Detective Brightwell questioned you. Again. He'd like to arrest you, which is why I found you a lawyer." I glanced at Nick.

His reluctant nod confirmed that he had called Ms. Mills, as I'd asked him to, and had arranged for Luke to have representation.

Luke was shaking his head. "I don't need —"

"Stop right there. You should have asked for a lawyer the moment Brightwell showed up at your door. He's convinced you killed Greg Onslow so you'd have Giselle all to yourself, and it isn't going to help matters any if she tells him you two talked about eloping."

The shocked expression on Luke's face was more convincing than his sputtered protests.

"You *weren't* planning to elope?"

"No! I asked Giselle to marry me, but I never suggested that we run away together, especially not now. I know how bad that would look to the police. Besides, when I

get married, I want the whole nine yards —
church wedding, big reception, and a honey-
moon in Hawaii."

"Hawaii?" I echoed, momentarily distracted. With an effort, I regained my focus
and took both his hands in mine. "I know
you didn't kill Greg Onslow, but I'm not at
all sure Giselle is innocent."

He tried to pull away, but I refused to
loosen my grip.

"Just listen, okay? I know you didn't
murder Onslow with Giselle, or kill him in
order to free her to marry you, but what if
she set you up to take the fall for a crime
she committed?"

"There has to be another explanation." A
spark of desperation lurked beneath his
anger on her behalf. "Lots of people hated
Greg Onslow. One of them —"

Nick interrupted, his voice quiet but carrying. "Could she have planted the gun?"

Luke stared at him. "What gun?"

"The gun used in the murder." Nick
looked at me. "Right?"

I nodded.

"Someone got into this house and hid it
where the police would find it," Nick said.
"Then they called in an anonymous tip.
That person could have been your girl-
friend."

"She'd never do something like that."

In the next instant, the two men were on their feet, squaring off like prizefighters.

"Stop it, both of you!" I thrust myself between them, one hand flat against each chest. When I shoved, Luke stumbled back a step. Nick didn't budge, but his stubborn jaw unclenched a fraction of an inch.

"That's better. Now sit back down and we'll discuss this like rational adults."

"I don't think so. I need to talk to Giselle."

Luke's body language — hands curled into fists at his sides and shoulders tense — should have discouraged further argument, but I couldn't keep my mouth shut.

"That's the last thing you should do."

"She's probably the one who caused the accident, too," Nick said. "Ask Aunt Mikki where she was this morning. She went straight into the lion's den, the headquarters of her prime suspect, and all but accused Giselle of murder to her face."

Nick went on to repeat everything I'd told him about that encounter, but instead of fueling Luke's anger, hearing what Giselle had said about getting married so they couldn't testify against each other had him closing in on himself. He went very still and said nothing.

Switching gears, Nick added, "Your cousin

needs a keeper, Luke. Her infernal meddling has to stop before she ends up seriously hurt or dead."

"I'm standing right here!" I snapped out the words, my voice cold. "If I need a guard dog, I'll call the police . . . or the local animal shelter."

"Fat lot of good the cops will do." Nick glared at Luke. "That policewoman was more concerned with protecting him than with looking out for you."

Luke looked up and blinked in confusion. "What's he talking about?"

"He means Ellen Blume. She's gone out of her way a couple of times to try to help you."

"If she hadn't shown up here, you'd never —"

"Yes, I would have. Give it up, Nick. I'm not going to stop trying to find out the truth, but that's on me. Nobody else bears any responsibility for my actions." I glanced at Luke, taking in his frown. "I gather you and Ellen dated at some point?"

"We went out a couple of times. She's good company and we have some stuff in common, but it wasn't anything serious."

"Because you were still carrying a torch for Giselle." I couldn't repress a sigh. He still was.

"Giselle didn't kill her husband."

"You can't *know* that." He had a blind spot a mile wide where she was concerned.

"Maybe I can't *prove* it, but I'm as sure of her innocence as you are of mine."

We were at an impasse. I couldn't think of anything to say that would convince either Luke or Nick that they were wrong and I was right.

I didn't try.

Luke left a few minutes later. After that, Nick and I said scrupulously polite good-nights to each other and retired to our respective rooms.

CHAPTER 40

The next morning, after a strained half hour sitting across the breakfast table from Nick, I once again retreated to my office. This time Calpurnia accompanied me.

"You couldn't stand being glowered at, either, huh?"

She replied by giving me the hairy eyeball.

More than ever, Nick reminded me of his uncle. Once James formed an opinion, he held on to it, right or wrong. Eventually, a steady application of common sense could convince him to change his mind, but arguing with him never did any good. It just made him dig in his heels.

We'd had forty-five good years together. His occasional pigheadedness had balanced my tendency toward impulsiveness. I couldn't stay mad at Nick when I knew James would have reacted to my situation in exactly the same way.

On the other hand, I'd been on my own

for nearly two years. I was no longer accountable to anyone. I was free to make my own decisions, right or wrong, and I wasn't about to give up my independence.

While Calpurnia sought the best spot for a nap, I plunked myself down in my desk chair, determined to get some work done. No matter what was going on in my personal life, I had an obligation to my clients. I started by printing out a copy of the chapter Sunny had just sent me as an attachment.

Yes, it's quicker to edit online using track changes and different colors, but I prefer to do the first pass on paper with that old-fashioned writing tool, the red pencil. Putting corrections into the electronic copy at a later time doesn't take all that long, and it gives me the opportunity to think through the reasons I made them. It never hurts an editor to self-edit.

I made a start, putting in the copyediting symbol for "delete and close up" and fixing a spelling error, before my mind started to wander. I'd gone to bed early the night before but I hadn't slept well. Both wakeful and dreaming, I'd been haunted by the possibility that we'd never find out who killed Greg Onslow.

As Luke had reminded me, it had been

obvious from the beginning that a great many people had reason to hate him. If Giselle was as innocent as my cousin claimed, which one of the others had let that hatred fester until it pushed him, or her, into murder?

Abandoning Sunny's manuscript, I dug out a lined tablet and a felt-tip pen with the idea of making a list of suspects and motives. I'd compiled a similar list already, but I hoped that by starting over I could gain some perspective. I moved to the recliner and held the pad on my lap, pen poised. Before I could write anything down, Calpurnia hopped onto the arm of the chair.

"Do you want to help?" I asked her.

She bunted her head against the hand holding the pen. I took that for a yes.

"Okay. First suspect — me. Why? Because during that very public quarrel I had with Onslow, I uttered words that some might regard as a threat." I tapped the pen against my name, leaving a series of little black dots on the paper. "Well, we know I didn't do it, and I'm pretty sure the police don't think I did, either."

I crossed out my name, skipped down a line, and wrote in Luke's.

"Plenty of motives there," I told the cat. "Anger over being fired. Jealousy because

Onslow married Giselle. What else? Greed? Lust? Brightwell thinks the murder was an evil scheme designed to end with Luke married to the merry widow."

I could understand why the detective was taking such a hard look at my cousin, but I didn't believe for a moment that Luke was guilty. I started to draw a line through his name, too. I stopped myself only because there seemed no point in making a list if I didn't give serious consideration to everyone on it.

"Who else?"

Calpurnia yawned.

"Okay. Yes. Ronnie." I added her name. "She had a long-standing quarrel with Onslow over his plans to develop the land adjoining hers, and she wanted part of the Feldman property to be set aside for a museum. I suppose she could have thought that would be more likely to happen if she dealt with someone other than Onslow."

I shook my head. Nope. It didn't compute. I couldn't picture her planting the murder weapon in my house, either. We had long been — what? Enemies? Rivals? But the real animosity between us had been during high school, more than five decades ago. She couldn't possibly hold a grudge that long. Could she?

When I had to consider that the killer had not only shot Onslow but had also crept into my house, hidden the murder weapon, and called in an anonymous tip to tell the police where to find it, identifying that person became much more complicated. I had to wonder if framing me had been part of the plan all along, or just a spur-of-the-moment impulse.

"Never underestimate the dumb luck factor," I told Calpurnia.

She made no reply. I was pretty sure she'd fallen asleep.

I went back to my list making, adding Frank and Darlene because Onslow's investment scheme *had* cost them a lot of money. Pam Ingram's name went down next. She'd had a love/hate relationship with the victim, especially after he ended their affair and married Giselle. If revenge was a dish best served cold, she had to be considered a suspect.

I wondered if she'd ever talked to the police. If she hadn't, much as I hated to rat out someone I liked, I'd have to tell them what I knew about her.

"Sunny," I murmured as I added her name. "To keep Trevor Champlain's secret."

I was still shaking my head over that development. I doubted it gave her enough of a motive to kill Onslow, but you never know. Humans are incredibly complicated creatures.

Who else? After a moment's consideration, I wrote Jenni Farquhar's name on the next line. Did she, like Pam, see herself as seduced and abandoned, even though she claimed she hadn't had an affair with Onslow? She'd once hoped to catch a rich husband and had been disappointed.

I caught myself doodling a little heart beside her name. I almost put a line through it. Getting away with murder requires both luck and cunning. If Jenni killed Onslow, I felt certain she'd have given herself away by now.

I started to write Giselle's name, then hesitated. She was still at the top of my mental list of suspects, for all the obvious reasons, but I meant to put her at the bottom of this one. The whole point of the exercise was to consider everyone else who might have had a reason to want Onslow dead.

Instead I wrote "Ariadne Toothaker" on the next line. Her motive: total control of Mongaup Valley Ventures. She'd been promoted to vice president after buying Ronnie's shares in the company. Maybe she'd expected to be able to convince Giselle to sell her the rest of the business once On-slow was out of the way. Giselle had put the kibosh on that plan. From what I'd observed, the widow was in charge of MVV and Ariadne would soon be out on her ear.

Who else? I asked again. One more possibility, albeit a remote one, popped into my mind: Ellen Blume. Like Frank and Darlene, Ellen's mother had lost a lot of money on one of Onslow's schemes. Ellen's feelings for Luke argued against her having committed any act that would make it easier for him to take up with Giselle again, but maybe her intent had been to frame the widow for the crime.

I shook my head, marveling at the flights of fancy of which my imagination was capable. Even if Ellen had killed Onslow, why would she have planted the murder weapon in my house? If I was going to believe that she had, then I might as well accuse her of throwing that rock from the overpass, too.

The smile half formed on my lips faded. For the first time, I gave serious consideration to Nick's theory. Was it really any less likely than the whole gun-in-the-hassock business?

Nonsense.

Coincidence.

With enough force to tear the paper, I crossed out Ellen's name. Calpurnia awoke and sent me a questioning look.

"The next thing you know," I told her, "I'm going to convince myself that one of the neighbors' kids shot Greg Onslow, just because he'd be the least likely suspect."

In capital letters, pressing down to make them darker, I wrote "Giselle Onslow."

"If Nick should *happen* to be right," I told the cat, "Giselle *could* have tailed me when I left the parking lot at MVV and seen me head west on the Quickway. She could have waited on the overpass until she saw me coming back and tried to take me out." I sighed. "Next time I buy a car, Cal, I must remember to choose something less conspicuous."

My bright green Ford Taurus didn't stand out as much as Luke's Jeep with the dragons painted on the sides, but it was distinctive enough to have made an excellent target.

A knock at the office door made me jump. I had just time enough to hide the tablet under the chair before Nick stuck his head in.

"Can we declare a truce?" he asked. "I made lunch."

"Will you promise to stop being such a nag?"

"Sure, if you'll promise to be more careful. All I want is for you to be safe."

"Said the witch to Rapunzel just before she locked her in the tower."

I was teasing him, but Nick's expression was alarmingly serious.

"Don't tempt me," he muttered. "Come on. The soup's getting cold."

CHAPTER 41

By late afternoon the next day, everything seemed to be back on an even keel. My car had been returned, complete with a spanking new windshield. Nick and I had talked without accusations, exasperation, or explosions. He was still planning to stay until the end of the week, but he acknowledged that I'd had years of experience looking after myself and didn't need either a bodyguard or a keeper. He apologized for saying, in the heat of argument, that I did.

In return, I assured him I had no intention of going near Mongaup Valley Ventures or seeing Giselle Onslow again. I couldn't think why I'd want to do either, especially after Darlene called to say she'd finally tracked down the elusive Mr. Wyncoop, Giselle's first husband. Now that she had Giselle's maiden name and place of birth, both of which had been on their marriage license, she was hot on the online trail of

361

more information.

A short time later, I had a long phone conversation with Ashley Mills, currently Luke's lawyer rather than mine. That left me feeling even more optimistic. With his permission, she shared the opinion she'd given him, that she didn't think he was in imminent danger of arrest. According to her, the case against him was all circumstantial and unlikely to convince a jury. Unless some new evidence turned up — and since he was innocent, there couldn't *be* any — Luke didn't have anything to worry about.

My upbeat mood didn't last long. I knew how worrisome it was to have accusations hanging over one's head, whether or not there was any truth to them. There might not be enough proof for an arrest, let alone a conviction, but that wouldn't stop gossip. Rumor and innuendo would haunt everyone whose name surfaced as a suspect in the case.

I tried to convince myself that the police would eventually get to the truth, arrest the real murderer, and free Luke from suspicion. I wasn't very successful. It had already been nearly three weeks since Onslow's murder.

Once again, I looked to work to distract me. Sunny had sent me yet another new chapter to edit.

"Do you mind if I abandon you again?" I asked Nick after the supper dishes had been washed, dried, and put away.

"Go ahead." He sent me a sheepish grin. "I have to admit I'm enjoying your On Demand feature. Julie has us on a strict budget. We get basic cable and nothing more."

"Knock yourself out," I told him.

I'm not into binge watching myself . . . except for the occasional *Firefly* marathon, or catching two or three episodes of *Midsomer Murders* back to back.

It was just starting to get dark when something in Sunny's manuscript made me think about my last visit to Mongaup Valley Ventures. She was reminiscing about the good old days when security precautions at a vacation resort were limited to having someone on call to take complaints. She clearly didn't approve of alarms on doors or cameras in every corner of the public rooms.

"Cameras," I repeated in a whisper.

MVV in the twenty-first century hadn't appeared to have any more security than Feldman's in the mid-twentieth. As a visitor, I hadn't had to sign in or out, and I assumed employees weren't required to either, but surely there had been surveillance cameras discreetly positioned in the lobby and other public spaces. They seem to be everywhere these days, so ubiquitous that no one notices them anymore.

I set the printout of Sunny's pages aside and drummed my knuckles on the surface of the desk. I hadn't left the parking lot at Mongaup Valley Ventures immediately. I had no idea how long I sat in my car. I'd been agitated after my meeting with Giselle and had needed time to calm down. That's why I'd decided to drive around for a bit before going home. There had definitely been time for someone to come out of the building, spot my Taurus, wait for me to leave, and then follow me in the hope of finding an opportunity to do me harm.

"You're getting paranoid," I muttered.

Calpurnia padded into the room and sent me a questioning look.

"*And* I'm talking to myself. That's never a good sign."

Talking to the cat wasn't much better, but discussing this particular subject with Nick was out of the question. Talk about opening up a can of worms!

I stood and began to pace.

If there *were* security cameras at MVV, at least one of them had to be trained on the entrance to the building. There might even be one inside the lobby, pointed at the door. The footage would be time-stamped. If it showed Giselle leaving the building just a few minutes after I did, it wouldn't prove that she followed me, but it would certainly be suggestive.

There was an easy way to find out. All I had to do was convince Jenni Farquhar to do me a favor. Truthfully, I didn't think much of my chances, but I made the call anyway.

Jenni was at home and bored. Her boyfriend had the night shift at MVV.

I did a silent hand pump and mouthed "Yes!" when she told me what a bummer it was that she couldn't spend more time with him after she got off work.

"Can you visit him on the job?" I asked.

"Well, yeah, I could, if I had a way to get there. We've only got the one car and my folks have gone to Middletown to the movies."

I remembered that she lived with her parents in Hurleyville. That was about fifteen miles from MVV, definitely too far to walk.

"What if I pick you up?"

"Really?"

"Sure." I glanced at the clock. It was a little past eight o'clock. "Why not?"

It wasn't until she'd given me directions to her house and I'd disconnected that I remembered why not. I'd promised Nick I wouldn't go near MVV again.

If I listened hard, I could hear a steady murmur of sound — the television in the dining room directly below my office. My nephew was still engrossed in whatever marathon had captured his interest, but that didn't mean he wouldn't hear me if I tried to sneak out the front door.

I couldn't face another argument, especially when explaining where I was going would necessitate admitting that he might have been right when he'd suggested someone was trying to kill me.

My gaze fell on the door to my little balcony, one of the three exits from the house that was not connected to my security system. I could go out that way without being seen or heard.

I told myself that what Nick didn't know wouldn't hurt him. He'd turned in by ten every night he'd been staying with me. By the time I returned, he'd undoubtedly have gone to bed and I could let myself in through the front door.

I tucked my keys into the pocket of my jeans, turned out the lights, and opened the office door halfway, so that when Nick came up it would appear that I'd finished work and gone to bed. I didn't have a coat in the office, so I shrugged into a heavy sweater instead.

"I'm going to test the fire escape," I told Calpurnia as I headed out onto my covered balcony.

If I'd had an umbrella upstairs, I'd have taken it along. It was the first of May, but the evening was chilly and overcast, and I could swear I smelled rain in the air.

There was a short delay while I captured the cat, put her back inside, and shut the balcony door before she could escape a second time. Feeling incredibly daring, I swung my legs over the railing and hopped down onto the roof of the garage. I froze at the sound of my feet hitting metal and moved more carefully after that.

The waning crescent moon would have been of little help even if it hadn't been so cloudy. I had to rely on the streetlight on the other side of Wedemeyer Terrace to see where I was going. Although the slope of the roof was gentle, I kept my arms out to my sides for balance as I descended to its lowest point. Once there, I hesitated.

That seven feet or so down to my neighbors' lawn seemed a lot higher when seen from above. Why, I wondered, had a mature woman in her seventh decade thought this was a good idea? The part of me that still thinks an eighteen-year-old inhabits that body answered the question: *It will be an adventure.* More important, it could establish Giselle Onslow's guilt once and for all.

No more waffling! I backed up a couple of steps, got a running start, and jumped.

Cindy Fry's grassy lawn wasn't nearly as soft as I'd hoped it would be. Damp and squishy, yes, but also hard. I landed with my knees bent and went into a roll. It felt as if I made contact with every pebble and rock in the county before I came to a stop. For a minute or so, I didn't move. While I caught my breath, I evaluated my condition. I didn't appear to have bruised, twisted, or broken anything. Slowly, I sat up and brushed myself off.

I shifted so that my legs dangled over the property line before hopping down to the narrow path that runs alongside my garage. The Taurus awaited me in the driveway — my getaway car. Not a creature stirred as I crept to the driver's side, unlocked the door, and slipped inside. Moments later, feeling just the slightest bit giddy, I was on my way to Hurleyville to pick up Jenni Farquhar.

CHAPTER 42

Everything went as smoothly as I could have wished. The damp spots on my jeans and the condition of my sweater could be passed off as casualties of the weather. It was raining by the time Jenni and I arrived at Mongaup Valley Ventures. Once there, she had no difficulty convincing her boyfriend to let me view the security camera footage from two days earlier.

"It was first thing in the morning," I told him when we were settled in the windowless room used as an office by watchmen working for MVV. A bank of screens took up one wall, showing various locations both within the building and without. "It wasn't any later than nine when I left."

"No problem." He didn't seem at all curious about why I wanted to watch myself leaving the premises or why I'd been at MVV that day.

Brian Keller looked a lot like his brother

Bob, except that Brian sported a jaunty little mustache. From the expression on his face, he was totally smitten with Jenni. *Ah, young love.* I had to clear my throat to get his mind back to the business at hand. He'd have had a hard time punching in the necessary commands if he'd kept one arm wrapped around Jenni's waist.

Aside from being able to do word processing and the most basic of online searches, I am not particularly computer literate. Even my cell phone is old-school — it doesn't do much besides make phone calls and take pictures. I've never bothered to learn how to text. That meant I had no idea what Brian did at his keyboard to access the correct day and time, but it wasn't long before I recognized myself on the monitor. I hadn't expected the quality of the picture to be quite so good. I could see the angry glint in my eyes as I stalked out of the building.

"There," I said. "Can you run it back a little and then slow it down?"

"Ooh," Jenni exclaimed as I appeared on the screen for the second time. "You look pissed!"

"I was a little upset," I said mildly, and made a mental note to find out if an increase in the tendency to lose one's temper is a warning sign of dementia or some other ailment seniors are prone to.

Brian sat at the console while Jenni and I leaned over his shoulders. A small box in the lower corner of the screen showed the time. Seconds, then minutes passed. I tensed as I saw the door begin to open, but it wasn't Giselle who stepped through it.

Instead, two people emerged from the building and walked in the direction of the parking lot. One was Ariadne Toothaker. The other was the new head of personnel, whose name eluded me. They appeared to be deep in a discussion about something or other. I didn't remember noticing either of them while I'd been sitting in my car. I'd been too absorbed in my own thoughts.

The video from the security camera aimed at the exterior of the main entrance — double glass doors with the company name emblazoned on them in gilt letters — continued to play, but no one else appeared. I gave it a full fifteen minutes to be sure, since I wasn't certain how long it had been before I drove away.

"That's enough," I said at last.

Brian stopped the playback, but his curiosity had finally been piqued. "What were you looking for?"

"I wanted to see if anyone followed me when I left the building."

Although I'd originally thought Nick's theory was farfetched, it had been worth pursuing, if only to rule out the possibility. I straightened, prepared to thank the young man for his time and leave, but Jenni had other ideas.

"What about the footage from the camera that covers the back door?" she asked.

"No one goes out that way except the boss," Brian objected.

Jenni sent an unexpectedly perceptive glance my way. "Maybe that's who she's interested in."

Obligingly, he located the day and time I'd specified. Another entrance, this one unmarked and very plain, appeared on the monitor. For fifteen excruciatingly slow minutes we watched absolutely nothing happen. No one went in or came out.

"Are there cameras aimed at the parking lot?" I asked.

In for a penny, in for a pound, as the old saying goes.

I started to ask him to cue up those tapes but stopped before I embarrassed myself. I wasn't up-to-date on the newest terminology, but I had a sneaking suspicion that *tapes* had vanished from geek vocabulary a good long while ago. Brian was young enough that he might never have used the word at all.

He anticipated my request. "Here you go. Since the parking lot is so big, there are three of them to show different areas."

I spotted my Ford Taurus without any trouble. That bright green color stood out. The footage — another archaic word? — also showed me getting into the car, but the angle was wrong to see what I was doing once I was behind the wheel. According to the time on the "tape," eleven minutes and thirty-five seconds passed before I backed out of the parking space and drove away.

In the security feed for other parts of the lot, several cars came and went during that same period. Ariadne and the personnel director got into separate vehicles, both of which left before I did. There was no sign of Giselle.

That's that, then, I thought. *The rock that hit my windshield was a fluke with no connection whatsoever to Greg Onslow's murder.*

At Jenni's request, I left her at MVV with Brian and headed home. It wasn't until I pulled into my driveway that I realized I had a problem. The downstairs lights were still on. Although it was after ten, Nick had not yet gone to bed.

I crept silently up onto the porch to peer through the picture window. The pocket doors between the living room and the dining room stood open. I could see the glow of a reading lamp and a series of flickering images from the TV.

Decisions, decisions. I could let myself in through the front door, but unlike his dear old auntie, Nick had excellent hearing. Even if the glass-paneled door between the foyer and the hall was closed, he'd probably hear the click of my key turning in the lock. If, by some chance, he didn't, I still wouldn't be home free. I wouldn't dare turn on the overhead light in the foyer. I'd have to fumble at the security panel in the dark, trying to punch in the code to keep the alarm from going off, and then I'd have to reset the blasted thing, also in the dark. The faint greenish glow illuminating the keypad didn't give off enough light to guarantee I wouldn't hit any wrong numbers. Assuming I managed that without mishap, I'd still have to get back upstairs without being heard.

If, for whatever reason, Nick came to investigate, he'd know by the way I was dressed that I'd gone out. By this time of night, I was usually in a nightgown, robe, and slippers. To make matters worse, it was still drizzling. I wasn't soaking wet, but neither had I been able to stay completely dry during my outing.

I sat down on the wicker sofa to think. What a ridiculous situation! Here I was, a mature woman in her seventies, so reluctant to provoke a quarrel that I was willing to wait on the porch until Nick finally turned in for the night rather than risk getting caught sneaking into my own house. For all I knew, it could be hours yet before he went to bed. I was tired. It was chilly sitting there in just a sweater. And I was ready to pack it in.

The solution I came up with was no more preposterous than anything else I'd done that evening. I left the porch, ducking raindrops to follow the path alongside the garage until I could peer around the back corner. From that vantage point, I should have been able to look into the house through the dining room windows. As I'd hoped, Nick had drawn the curtains. I couldn't see in. More important, Nick couldn't see out.

It only remained for me to make my way to my next-door neighbors' storage shed and borrow their extension ladder. Once again luck was on my side. When I looked that way, I spotted Cindy Fry in her kitchen. She was getting herself a glass of water at the sink beneath the window and *those* curtains were open.

She looked surprised when she came to her back door in response to my knock, but she didn't balk at granting my rather peculiar request. She accepted my word for it that I'd tell her the whole story at another time.

Ten minutes later, protected by a rain slicker with a hood, she braced the ladder for me while I scrambled up it and climbed onto the slippery metal roof. I stayed on hands and knees until I reached the balcony and eased myself over the railing. I waved to let Cindy know I was okay.

Once I was inside with the door closed, I leaned against it, breathing hard. Then I shot a wary look toward the hallway. There was no sign of Nick. He was still downstairs, ensconced in front of the television. Even Calpurnia wasn't around to bear witness to my unconventional return. I found her in the next room, asleep on my bed. She barely opened her eyes when I shoved her aside to make room for me.

Chapter 43

I was up early the next day. I'd just refilled Calpurnia's food and water bowls and made myself a cup of coffee when the phone rang. I didn't recognize the number and there was no name showing on the caller ID. Most of the time I let such calls go to my answering machine, but once in a while I take a chance and pick up. If it turns out to be a robocall or some other unwelcome solicitation, I can always slam the receiver down in disgust.

In this case, the caller was Ariadne Toothaker. She identified herself and asked if I could meet her a little later that morning.

"What's this about?" I asked, giving a little finger wave to a groggy-looking Nick as he joined me in the kitchen.

"I don't like to say over the phone."

"And I don't like to interrupt my day for no reason." That sounded impossibly rude, but I was still half asleep. Even at the best of times, I lack patience with people who beat around the bush.

After a little silence at the other end of the line, Ariadne spoke in a rush. "I've come across some information about Giselle Onslow. Incriminating information."

My hand tightened on the phone. All of a sudden, I was wide awake. "What have you found?"

"I don't like to say —"

"— over the phone. I get that, but I don't understand why you're telling me. You should go to the police."

"No! You don't understand. The company is in enough trouble without its vice president being the one to turn in the CEO."

I wasn't sure I followed her logic, but I couldn't ignore the panic I heard in her voice. "What do you think I can do?"

"Just meet me. Listen to what I have to say. You're right. This information should go to that detective, but if you take it to him, the impact on Mongaup Valley Ventures won't be as bad."

Nick was staring at me, a look of consternation on his face. I swung around so that my back was to him. "There may be no way to keep you out of it," I warned Ariadne. "Detective Brightwell will want to know my source."

Her muffled sob struck me as totally out of character and made me think she was truly frightened of Giselle. Did she fear Onslow's widow would kill her to keep her silent?

"Where do you want to meet?" I asked.

"At the demolition site in an hour. There's a road that branches off to the left shortly after you crest the hill at the entrance to Feldman's. Drive down that and I'll be waiting."

I held the phone away from my face and stared at it. How stupid did she think I was? Until that moment, I hadn't really suspected Ariadne Toothaker of anything more than being overly ambitious. Now I had to wonder.

"Mikki?"

"I'm here. I'm . . . thinking." And I was — so fast that my brain was in danger of turning into a dreidel.

"Please," she begged. "You're the only one I can trust."

Help me, Obi-Wan, I thought.

Who can resist a plea like that? Besides, she'd aroused my curiosity.

"All right," I said. "I'll meet you there in an hour."

"You have to come alone. I won't talk to you if there's anyone with you." She lowered her voice to a whisper that sounded downright paranoid. "*Anyone* could be a spy for Giselle."

"Yes, anyone could," I agreed, wondering if Ariadne knew what Jenni Farquhar had been up to after her demotion to payroll clerk.

The click when she abruptly disconnected sounded impossibly loud. Deep in thought, I replaced the receiver on its hook and turned to face my nephew. He handed me the hearing aid I'd taken out and the coffee mug I'd abandoned on the counter when I answered the phone and held his questions until I'd inserted the first and taken a long swallow of the second.

"Who was that?"

"Ariadne Toothaker." I explained who she was and gave him a capsule version of the conversation.

His expression grim, he sent me a jaded look. "I'm going to assume you have better sense than to go out there alone."

"It isn't as if it's the dead of night and I'm some Gothic heroine. See." I indicated the fresh pair of jeans and the clean sweatshirt I wore. "No long white dress. No candle. No investigating the cellar or the attic because I heard a strange noise."

"Of course not. Only a visit to a deserted

work site to meet someone who, if she's on the level, ought to have gone straight to the police."

"It's broad daylight and I'm sure there will be workmen around. Security guards at the least."

His eyes narrowed. "Okay, Aunt Mikki. What am I missing? I know you're not stupid enough to walk into a trap."

"What a vote of confidence! If I tell you, you have to promise me you'll stay here." *Out of harm's way,* I added silently.

"No promises until I've heard what you plan to do. *Everything* you plan to do."

"It's possible Ariadne is telling the truth," I said. "If she is, I don't want to scare her off. With the future of MVV at stake, she could panic and destroy whatever evidence she's uncovered rather than risk the company."

"And if this is a setup?"

"Giselle and Ariadne working together?" That seemed unlikely, but anything was possible. "Don't worry. I haven't completely lost my senses."

I held up one finger in the universal gesture for "wait a moment" and reached for the phone.

CHAPTER 44

A little over an hour later, I drove slowly along a rutted, overgrown road between two abandoned resort buildings. It dipped downward before coming to an end at another, slightly smaller structure, one in worse disrepair than any I'd seen. A bulldozer was parked nearby, but I saw no sign of another car. I turned off the engine, took a deep breath, and got out. For a miracle, it wasn't raining, although showers were once more in the forecast.

Ariadne waited for me in the doorway. "We can talk inside." She disappeared into the interior, leaving me to follow her.

Like a lamb to slaughter, I thought, but I went where she led.

The roof over our heads was glass, most of it broken. Almost as much vegetation grew inside the building as out, up to and including a stunted tree rising up out of the center of what appeared to be one large room.

"What is this place?"

"The pool house, and that's an Olympic-size pool." She moved closer to it, stopping only a few inches from the rim.

I scanned the area for exits and located two doors besides the one we'd used to enter. Those three weren't the only way to get in. A section of the back wall was missing, leaving a space big enough for someone to walk through. The rest of that wall and the other three were covered with graffiti. A strong stench of decay, with an overlay of mold and mildew, tickled my nose and made me feel slightly queasy.

"Charming," I said. "Is this the best location you could come up with for a clandestine meeting?"

"It'll do." She shifted the messenger bag slung over her shoulder. "Do you want to see what I have for you or not?"

Wondering if it was possible she was on the level, I walked toward her, but not too quickly. I had to move cautiously, not only because I was wary of Ariadne, but also to avoid tripping over cracks in the floor and the occasional vine. I came to a halt when I reached the edge of the pool, careful to keep a distance of several feet between us. On the phone, she'd urged me to listen to what she had to say. Now, it seemed, she had something to show me.

Pale sunlight filtered through the broken glass to cast eerie shadows on Ariadne Toothaker's face. Her smile looked . . . off. I knew I had been right to be suspicious even before she reached into the messenger bag and pulled out a gun.

"I don't like guns," I said, somewhat inanely.

"Too bad." She gestured with it, indicating I should move closer to the end of the pool where a rusted and wobbly looking ladder was still attached.

Reluctantly, I obeyed.

"Climb down."

Along with weeds and that tree, cracked concrete and what appeared to be years of accumulated garbage covered the bottom. A few fast-food bags were still recognizable. I had a feeling local teens didn't find this place nearly as disgusting as I did. Boys looking for a private place to drink, or maybe one where they could make out with willing girlfriends, aren't all that fussy.

"I don't think so," I said.

"Would you rather I shot you where you stand?"

I'd always wondered why characters in fiction, faced with the same choice, didn't just call the villain's bluff. After all, what murderer wants the cops to find a bullet that can be traced? Now I had an answer. Killers don't think logically. Ariadne's hand might be steady, but there was nothing rational about the look in her eyes.

It struck me that any action that prolonged my time on this earth would be both wise and good. I obediently lowered one foot over the rim of the pool and started down the rickety ladder. I froze when it swayed alarmingly. Afraid I was going to fall if I so much as moved a muscle, I gripped the rusty metal so tightly that it bit into my palms.

"Hurry up," Ariadne snapped.

"Hey, give me a break here. I'm old and slow."

Although I don't consider myself "elderly," I wasn't just stalling for time. The previous night's activities, in particular that jump from the roof to the lawn, had left me stiff and sore. All the walking I'd done, all my time on the stationary bike and doing various stretches and strengthening exercises, had failed to prepare me for such a hard landing.

Clambering up a ladder to return to the house had been a piece of cake compared to going down this one. I was only halfway to the bottom when one of the rungs sagged under my weight. Before it could break, I let myself drop the rest of the way, barely keeping my balance when I landed on the uneven bottom of the pool.

When I looked up, Ariadne had the light behind her. She appeared as little more than a silhouette, but I could tell she still had the gun pointed my way. As I watched, she replaced it in the messenger bag and bent down to pick up a large chunk of debris. I ducked when she threw it at me. She missed, but not by much.

"Hey!" I objected.

"Stand still or I *will* shoot you."

"You know, you'd have had an easier time of it if you'd just hit me over the head with a rock *before* I climbed into the pool. Of course, then you'd have had to push me over the edge. Is that what you did to Greg Onslow?"

Ariadne tossed a chunk of flooring at me. It clipped my arm on its way past. Pain radiated from my shoulder to my wrist but I kept talking. I doubted I could move fast enough to avoid a bullet, but with rocks the odds were better. If I played for time, I might also find out why she'd suddenly decided she had to get rid of me.

"What's the plan?" I shouted up at her. "Bury me with debris? How will you explain my being here when my body is found?"

"It won't be," Ariadne said. "We resume demolition this afternoon, starting with this building."

"You were hoping that's what would happen with your boss's remains. You miscalculated then. What makes you think you'll be any more successful this time?"

Her shoulders lifted in a shrug. "It won't matter if you *are* found. Your own curiosity will be blamed for your death. You came out here to snoop and part of the building collapsed on top of you."

I jumped out of the way of a third chunk of debris. "The least you can do is tell me *why* I have to die. Do you really think I'd have come here alone if I'd had any inkling that you killed Onslow?"

"You'd have figured it out soon enough. I know your reputation."

She threw. I leapt sideways, but it cost me. I twisted something in my back in my rush to move out of the line of fire.

"You were getting too close." Ariadne was panting as she stooped to pick up another hunk of concrete. "I'm minimizing my risk. That's just good business."

I'd been close to figuring things out? That was news to me.

"You should never have asked to see that

security footage." Using both arms, she held the next projectile clutched against her chest and stepped closer to the rim of the pool.

I shaded my eyes in an attempt to see her face as she continued talking.

"It's a real pity you didn't caution your little helpers to keep their mouths shut. I went in to the office early this morning and found Brian Keller and Jenni Farquhar in a compromising position. With Brian's job on the line, they couldn't confess fast enough. They told me all about your visit to MVV last night."

She heaved her missile. I skipped backward to avoid being struck, tripped on a root, windmilled my arms, and righted myself just in time to see her start to fumble in her messenger bag. It appeared she'd run out of patience. If I didn't think of something fast, she was going to shoot me.

"If they told you everything, then you know I was looking for proof *Giselle* followed me, and that I didn't find any."

"You saw *me* leaving the building."

I stared up at her, dumbfounded. "Are you saying *you* followed me? That *you* tossed that rock at my car from the overpass?"

What was it with this woman and throwing things?

I still couldn't see her expression, but her body language told me she was fed up with answering questions.

"You aren't as smart as I gave you credit for, are you?" I heard the sneer in her voice. "Too bad. You know too much now."

In my opinion, I didn't know nearly enough, but at any moment she was going to make good on her threat to kill me. There was no more time to goad her into "the obligatory spilling of the beans," as I'd once heard it called in relation to the penultimate chapter of a mystery novel.

Hoping I hadn't been wrong to put my faith in a hastily conceived plan to spring Ariadne's trap without getting caught in it, I took a deep breath and screamed.

My lung power is prodigious. I'd had years of practice pitching my voice loud enough to be heard above the babble of junior high students.

Ariadne was so startled that she backed up a step. The gun in her hand wobbled in such an alarming fashion that I looked around for something to duck behind. The only possibility in sight, the stunted tree growing up through the concrete, wasn't big enough to protect me from a bullet.

By the time I glanced up again, Ariadne held the gun in both hands and was taking aim. Until he reached around her in an attempt to grab the weapon, she was unaware that Nick had crept up behind her.

He caught her off guard, but she reacted before he could disarm her, jamming an elbow into his midsection. He lost his hold, giving her the chance to put some distance between them. As I watched in horror, she leveled the gun again, this time at my nephew. Still bent over and gasping for breath, he was oblivious to his danger.

Ariadne had forgotten all about me. My movements fueled by adrenaline and panic, I staggered over to the ladder and scrambled up and out of the pool. Terrified that I was about to witness Nick's death, desperate to save him, I launched myself at Ariadne.

I suppose I had some idea of taking her down with a flying tackle. At eighteen, I might have managed it. At seventy, I landed ignominiously on the concrete skirting, a foot short of my goal. The impact bruised my cheek and rattled every bone in my body.

Ariadne barely spared me a glance. She kept the gun trained on Nick, who now stood with his hands raised.

"Stand over there next to your aunt," she ordered.

"Sorry," he whispered as he hauled me to my feet.

"So am I."

Nick was *not* the one I'd expected to bolt out of cover in response to my scream. I swayed a bit, hoping to get Ariadne to focus on me. Out of the corner of my eye, I caught a flicker of movement.

Better late than never.

"It's going to be tricky explaining two bodies," I said in a conversational tone of voice.

Ariadne smirked. "No one can prove I killed Greg Onslow and no one will ever connect me with your murders, either. The only mistake I made is in not shooting you to begin with."

I expected Ellen Blume to materialize behind Ariadne, much as Nick had, except that she'd have a gun of her own. I was half right. She did sneak up on the other woman, but when she got close enough for it to be effective, she used her Taser.

Ariadne went rigid and dropped like a stone, letting go of her weapon on the way down. Ellen used her foot to kick it farther away from the writhing form. The piece of police equipment she used next was her radio.

We didn't have long to wait for the cavalry to arrive, but in those few minutes, I once again came very close to losing my temper.

"Nick Carpenter, what on earth did you think you were *doing*?"

"I wasn't about to sit back and let her shoot you!"

"Don't you ever watch action movies? Trying to take the gun away from the bad guy never works out well. They struggle. The weapon ends up between them. Then the gun goes off and someone gets killed or horribly wounded. That could have been you." I punched him on the upper arm with enough force to make him wince.

He rubbed the spot and muttered, "That face plant you took wasn't exactly a stellar move, either."

Until that moment, I'd been too pumped up to assess the damages. I reached up to touch my cheek and winced. My fingers came away caked with blood and grit. My face throbbed. In fact, I ached all over, although I didn't think I'd done any serious damage to myself. Unwanted, tears welled up in my eyes. We'd had a close call. Both of us.

"You promised you'd stay at the house," I whispered.

"So did you, but strangely enough, you managed to visit Mongaup Valley Ventures last night."

I opened my mouth and closed it again.

There was no point in trying to deny what he'd overheard. It was probably fortunate that the sound of rapidly approaching sirens interrupted us just then.

Ellen had already snapped handcuffs on Ariadne Toothaker. When she started to come around, Ellen read her her rights.

"You can't arrest me." Ariadne's speech was slurred and her eyes were out of focus, but her defiance was unimpaired. "I'm an important person in this town."

"Think again." Ellen took hold of her arm to help her to her feet.

Ariadne staggered, still fighting off the effects of being tased.

"You just admitted to killing Greg Onslow in front of three witnesses," I said, "all three of whom will also testify to the fact that you were about to shoot two more people."

Ariadne fell silent, a sulky look on her face.

Nick and I made eye contact. We spoke in unison. "I was just trying to protect you."

His lips twitched. I felt my earlier anger dissipate as a chuckle fought its way to the surface. By the time Detective Brightwell strode into the pool house, Nick and I were grinning at each other like a couple of fools.

CHAPTER 45

"I made two calls after I got off the phone with Ariadne," I told Luke that evening. "One was to Jenni, to find out if her boyfriend had talked to his boss. The second was to Ellen, to ask her to back me up."

"I thought she was making a mountain out of a molehill," Ellen confessed, helping herself to another handful of popcorn.

The four of us — Luke, Ellen, Nick, and I — sat in a cozy circle in my living room. I was on the loveseat next to my nephew with Calpurnia on my lap. The other two had settled into two separate chairs.

"Aunt Mikki was suspicious," Nick said. "So was I."

"Cautious," I corrected him. "But as things turned out, it's a good thing I was. There was something that just didn't ring true about Ariadne's sudden desire for a secret meeting. I took the precaution of asking Ellen to arrive early at the location

Ariadne chose. She was to eavesdrop and interfere if things got dicey. If Ariadne did know something that proved Giselle was guilty, I'd have insisted she give Ellen a statement then and there."

"The pool house seemed like a curious spot to meet," Ellen said. "I parked my cruiser out of sight. I was well hidden behind some rotting deck chairs before anyone else showed up. I could see and hear what was going on, but I promised Mikki I'd hold off revealing my presence for as long as possible."

"You could have moved in a *little* sooner," Nick complained.

"*You* weren't supposed to be there at all." For Luke's benefit, I added, "I wanted Nick to stay here. I don't know why I expected him to cooperate. Stubborn man!"

Nick took up the story. "I knew where Aunt Mikki was going, so I left a few minutes after she did. When I got there, she was already inside. I scouted around, found where a section of the back wall was missing, and positioned myself just outside so I could keep an eye on things."

"He crept inside while Ariadne was distracted." I took a long swallow of cold beer, hoping it would not only ease my aches and pains but also make me more forgiving when it came to my nephew's highhanded behavior.

"Distracted?" Nick snorted. "Is that what you call it? She was trying to kill you."

"And she might easily have shot you, too. Honestly, Nick, it about gave me a heart attack when she turned that gun on you."

Nick sent a fulminating glare in Ellen's direction.

"Hey, don't blame me," she protested. "I saved your bacon."

"So," Luke said, "Ariadne admitted to murdering Greg Onslow, but did she tell you why?"

"No, worst luck. I suppose it was because she wanted to take over Mongaup Valley Ventures."

Ellen cleared her throat. "I've been keeping my ear to the ground at the PD and, as it happens, Detective Brightwell was already building a case against Ms. Toothaker. I don't know all the details, but he started to focus on her when the computer guru on his team discovered that she was the one who posted that video of your fight with Onslow."

I put my glass down on the end table with a thump. "Wait a minute. Are you telling me she intended to frame me for his murder from the very beginning?"

"Brightwell thinks she's been planning to kill her boss for some time. When his quarrel with you provided her with a potential scapegoat, she was ready to act. She knew the security guards' schedule at the demolition site and lured Onslow there with a phone call. His cell is still missing, probably destroyed, but phone company records show someone contacted him just after midnight. The call came from a burner phone. If Ariadne told him there was trouble at Feldman's and that they both needed to get over there pronto, he'd have gone."

"He didn't drive himself," I said thoughtfully. "His car wasn't there."

"Maybe she picked him up," Luke suggested. "The Onslow house is between Ariadne's apartment and the site."

"He wasn't supposed to be found." I repressed a shudder.

"No, but you were her backup plan in case he was." Ellen saluted me by lifting her glass.

"She must have been watching the house," Nick mused. "Waiting for a chance to plant the murder weapon. I should never have gone out and left the garage unlocked."

"Stop kicking yourself," I chided him. "You didn't know anyone could get in that way."

Nick took a long pull on his Sam Adams, looking disgruntled.

"She was taking quite a risk." I helped myself to more popcorn. "She probably wouldn't have thought to plant that gun here if Giselle hadn't hired me to do that editing job for MVV. That brought me and my questions a little too close for comfort."

Luke grinned. "She was right to worry."

I did a quick mental calculation. "It was three days after I talked to her there that Brightwell got his anonymous tip. I suppose she could have had me under surveillance the whole time, but it seems more likely it was pure dumb luck that she drove by the house just as Nick was leaving."

"Why did she follow you after your second visit to MVV?" Ellen asked.

"I'm still having a hard time making sense of that. It was *Giselle* I threatened." Thinking back, I couldn't recall my exact words, but I supposed it was possible Ariadne overheard part of what I said to Giselle and feared I intended to dig into *her* past. "I don't even understand why Ariadne wanted Onslow dead. It was Giselle who ended up with control of the company. That's why I never considered Ariadne a serious suspect."

"I think it has to do with her father," Ellen said.

My hand stilled on Calpurnia's back as I remembered something Darlene had unearthed. "Her father," I said slowly, "lived in Danvers, Idaho. He died shortly before Onslow pulled up stakes and moved his con game from there to Lenape Hollow."

"Not exactly," Ellen said. "Ariadne's father committed suicide."

"Was he an investor in one of Onslow's scams?"

"That seems likely. And if his daughter was aware of that —"

"She went to work for Mongaup Valley Ventures intending to take Onslow down. Talk about playing the long game!"

"She might have gotten away with it if she hadn't picked the wrong scapegoat," Nick mused. "You'd have figured everything out eventually."

"I'm not so sure about that. I didn't really have any doubts about Ariadne until she phoned here and asked me to meet her. I was convinced Giselle had killed her husband. She was the most obvious suspect." I frowned. "Why on earth didn't Ariadne try to frame her?" I answered my own question before anyone else could say the words. "Oh, my God! I wasn't the backup plan. I was the backup for the backup. Plan A — the body is never found. Plan B — the police arrest Giselle, Plan C — shift blame onto me."

"Plan C would never have worked," Ellen said. "The gun that killed Onslow was one of several owned by Mongaup Valley Ventures for use by their security guards. There was no way you could have gotten your hands on it."

"I wonder if she had a Plan D — plant the second gun on Giselle?" I shivered. "Maybe she meant to get rid of Brian Keller and Jenni Farquhar, too. They might have told someone I'd seen footage of Ariadne leaving Mongaup Valley Ventures a few minutes after I did."

"Unless she confesses, we'll never know for certain what she was thinking," Ellen said, "but she'll be convicted of killing Onslow and trying to kill you and your nephew, and everyone who was under a cloud of suspicion can breathe easier now that their innocence has been established."

She was watching Luke as she spoke.

"Right. Innocent." His expression grim, he studied his hands as if they were the most fascinating appendages in the universe. "Giselle didn't murder her husband but, trust me, she's no innocent. How could I not have seen it? Ariadne wasn't the only one playing a long game."

His anguish tore at my heart. As soon as he'd heard Ariadne had been arrested, he'd paid a visit to Giselle. It had not gone well, but I didn't know why.

"What happened when you talked to her?" I asked

"I caught her popping the cork on a bottle of champagne, but it wasn't to celebrate the fact that we were in the clear. Oh, no. She was over the moon because now Ariadne will have to sell her shares in MVV to pay for a lawyer. That's all Giselle really wanted. Money and power, not love. Never love."

Ellen had been comfortably curled up in one of my easy chairs. She moved to the arm of the other, perching there to slide one arm around Luke's slumped shoulders. "I'm so sorry," she whispered.

Disillusionment hurts, but love can heal. Exchanging a look with Nick, I stood up, taking my drink with me. He grabbed the bowl of popcorn and followed me out of the living room.

"I'll be heading home tomorrow," he said when we were seated facing each other across the dinette table. "If there's one thing I've learned from all this, it's that you are perfectly capable of taking care of yourself."

"It's been good spending time with you, even if things were a bit . . . fraught here and there."

He laughed. "I'm glad I came, but if Mom ever again decides you need someone to look after you, she's going to have to send my sister."

A RANDOM SELECTION FROM "THE WRITE RIGHT WRIGHT'S LANGUAGE AND GRAMMAR TIPS" BY MIKKI LINCOLN

Watch out for split infinitives. They're everywhere. I blame *Star Trek* for confusing the issue. A split infinitive is when the writer places a word between *to* and the base form of a verb, as in "to boldly go where no man has gone before." To be correct, that famous line should have been "to go boldly."

Use *this* and *these* when referring to objects within reach and *that* and *those* when referring to objects out of reach.

Were is used instead of *was* in the line "If I were a rich man" in *Fiddler on the Roof* because the character is expressing a wish. *Were* is also appropriate if the speaker has doubts or is guessing. Otherwise, use was.

One of the most famous examples of a dangling modifier is in the form of a joke told by Groucho Marx: "One morning I shot an elephant in my pajamas. How he got in my pajamas, I'll never know." Anytime a misplaced pronoun phrase leaves the subject of a sentence unclear (is it Marx or the elephant in the pajamas?), the sentence should be rewritten for clarity. Another example found in numerous places, with slight variations, reads: "Having been tossed high in the air, the dog caught the ball." One hopes it was the ball that was tossed, not the dog.

Have you ever heard of a modal? No, I haven't misspelled *model*. Modals are *would, could, should, must, might,* and *may.* None of them should ever be combined with the word *of.* Don't say or write "should of known" when it should be "should have known."

The words *cement* and *concrete* are not interchangeable. Cement is an ingredient used to make concrete.

Comparisons have some complicated rules. Using *smaller* and *larger* to compare two items and *smallest* and *largest* for more than two is simple enough, but did you know you're supposed to use *more* or *less* to compare two things if the modifier has three syllables or more? To compare three or more things with a modifier of three syllables or more, or when an adverb ends in -ly, use *most* or *least*.

Many people confuse and misuse the words *ironic* and *sarcastic.* Both are forms of expression used to convey meaning in an oblique manner, most often using words to express the *opposite* of their literal meaning. An ironic response to someone saying "Why bother exercising? You could have a heart attack while you're out jogging." might be "Oh, that's a cheery thought!" Whether that's irony or sarcasm depends in part on the speaker's intent. It is sarcasm if the intent is to taunt or ridicule. Irony is a more subtle form of mockery. However, when Luke says "How's that for irony? The one time I willingly admit to being heir to a fortune and she thinks I'm making it up!" he is misusing the term. Her reaction may have been annoying, but it was not ironic.

For National Grammar Day, March 4, many newspapers ran stories related to that topic. The *South Florida Reporter,* for example, published a list of fun facts. Here are a few of my favorites:

"Go!" is the shortest grammatically correct

sentence in English.

The most common adjective in English is *good.*

The word *good* has the most synonyms of any other word in the English language — 380.

"The quick brown fox jumps over the lazy dog." is a pangram, a sentence that contains every letter in the language.

The word *swims* is an ambigram. It looks the same when it's turned upside down.

And finally, a word on the difference between swearing and using foul language. They are not the same thing. Swearing is taking the name of God in vain, unless you're being sworn into office or swearing "to tell the truth, the whole truth, and nothing but" at a hearing or a trial. To be swearing or cussing, the curse words have to have a religious component. If the objectionable words are crude sexual references or scatological in nature, they fall into the broader category of foul language.

ACKNOWLEDGMENTS

Lenape Hollow is fiction, and so is Feldman's Catskill Resort Hotel, but I will admit to being inspired by then-and-now photographs of real Sullivan County places. Similarly, characters in this novel should not be confused with real people. The only exception is Mikki, to whom I have given some of my personal experiences and feelings, but even those have been altered to suit the story and her personality, which is decidedly different from mine.

I am grateful to high school friends, especially Sharon Zamansky Kushner, for jogging my memory and for answering some of the innumerable questions that come up during the writing process. My thanks, too, to those who post on the "People Who Come From Liberty, NY" Facebook page, especially Harriet Stephanie Forshay, who lets us know what each day's weather is like in the old hometown.

Special thanks go to Kate Willett and Sandy Sechrest, who generously bid for the opportunity to name Sunny Feldman's cats at the Malice Domestic charity auction in 2019.

ABOUT THE AUTHOR

Kaitlyn Dunnett grew up in the Borscht Belt of New York State, otherwise known as the Sullivan County Catskills, the area she writes about in the Deadly Edits mysteries. These days, Kaitlyn lives in the mountains of western Maine with her husband and cats and can be reached through her website at www.kaitlyndunnett.com.

The employees of Thorndike Press hope you have enjoyed this Large Print book. All our Thorndike, Wheeler, and Kennebec Large Print titles are designed for easy reading, and all our books are made to last. Other Thorndike Press Large Print books are available at your library, through selected bookstores, or directly from us.

For information about titles, please call:
  (800) 223-1244

or visit our website at:
  gale.com/thorndike

To share your comments, please write:
  Publisher
  Thorndike Press
  10 Water St., Suite 310
  Waterville, ME 04901